THE SELFLESS ACT OF BREATHING

JJ BOLA

dialogue
books

DIALOGUE BOOKS

First published in Great Britain in 2021 by Dialogue Books
This paperback edition published in 2022 by Dialogue Books

10 9 8 7 6 5 4 3 2 1

A CIP catalogue record for this book
is available from the British Library.

ISBN 978-0-349-70206-3

Typeset in Berling by M Rules
Printed and bound in Great Britain by
Clays Ltd, Elcograf S.p.A.

Papers used by Dialogue Books are from well-managed forests
and other responsible sources.

Dialogue Books
An imprint of
Little, Brown Book Group
Carmelite House
50 Victoria Embankment
London EC4Y 0DZ

An Hachette UK Company
www.hachette.co.uk

www.littlebrown.co.uk

JJ Bola is a writer, poet, educator and UNHCR Ambassador, born in Kinshasa, Democratic Republic of Congo, and raised in London. He has written three poetry collections – *Elevate (2012)*, *Daughter of the Sun (2014)*, and *WORD (2015)* – published in a definitive collection, *Refuge (2018)*. He was one of Spread the Word's Flight Associates in 2017, and a Birkbeck University MA Graduate in Creative Writing.

His debut novel, *No Place to Call Home*, was published in the UK in 2017, and in 2018 in North America – then later translated into French as *Nulle Part Où Poser Sa Tête* in 2022. His second novel, *The Selfless Act of Breathing*, was published in the UK in 2021, and in the U.S/North America in 2022, with translations also into Brazilian-Portuguese, German, French, Italian, Japanese and more. *The Selfless Act of Breathing* has also been acquired by BRON Studios for film adaption.

JJ also wrote the non-fiction book, *Mask Off: Masculinity Redefined*, published in the UK in 2019. This has also been translated into other languages, including German, Italian, Brazilian-Portuguese, Spanish, and Finnish.

JJ Bola is based in London, but often travels across the UK, and internationally, for workshops, lectures, and talks. He is passionate about empowering people to transform their lives. And loves basketball, and carrot cake. He works in mental health and is currently writing his third novel.

Windsor and Maidenhead

95800000216230

'Heartfelt and searing ... Devastating and insightful ... Readers will be swept up in the sheer beauty of Bola's writing'

The i

'Arresting ... Important and emotive ... Powerfully raw'

Guardian

'A spark of hope'

Observer

'It's uncompromising stuff, but injections of precipitous drama –a car-jacking in LA; a doomed love affair in New York – together with unexpected flights of lyricism keep things moving. An emotive, brave novel that ultimately holds out the prospect of salvation, without sacrificing any of its power'

Daily Mail

'Bola's insightful, intimate and lyrical work has been entrancing readers ... Reminiscent of Paul Beatty and Ralph Ellison'

The Bookseller

'In this wonderfully tender novel about masculinity and mental health, about being lost and finding yourself again, Bola's vulnerable delicate writing conveys so much truth and heart about how we are now, how closed we are, how much goes unsaid and the quiet pain in our hearts'

Nikesh Shukla

'This book is a bold work with a broad scope, bravely tackling masculinity, hopelessness and despair with force and directness'

Okechukwu Nzelu

'A beautiful, absorbing read. By turns searing and quietly devastating'

Irenosen Okojie

'I knew from the opening, that this book was going to break my heart. *The Selfless Act of Breathing* left me breathless. It is beautifully tender'

Yvonne Battle-Felton

'*The Selfless Act of Breathing* feels existential and urgent as a millennial *Mrs. Dalloway* for a Black man who must straddle two worlds, two cultures, and two timelines, deciding where – and if – he wants to live. With prose as intimate as a private diary, as lush as spoken-word poetry, JJ Bola has artfully rendered this portrait of depression at once achingly empathetic and remarkably insightful'

Afia Atakora

'Narrated with haunting lyricism, *The Selfless Act of Breathing* is an intimate journey through the darkest of human impulses to the gleaming flickers of love and radical hope'

Susan Abulhawa

'In a world that makes it difficult for many of us to articulate our suffering, *The Selfless Act of Breathing* is a necessary invitation to scream when we feel like screaming, cry when we feel like crying, and prioritize our own often-neglected needs for love. JJ Bola crafted a soul-shifting novel that will let millions know it's okay to not be okay, and that the one of the most rewarding, and healing, places we can travel is into ourselves. The unwavering courage and care that Bola demonstrates with this work is to be revered'

Mateo Askaripour

Also by JJ Bola

No Place to Call Home: Love, Loss, Belonging!
Mask Off: Masculinity Redefined

POETRY

Elevate
Daughter of the Sun
Word
Refuge

To those who have let go, and to those still holding on

Part I

Memento Mori

Chapter 1

London Heathrow Airport Terminal 2; 9 a.m.

I quit my job, I am taking my life savings – $9,021 – and when it runs out, I am going to kill myself. The flight is in one hour. He left with more than enough time to get there, yet somehow it was lost; hesitation, fear, anxiety. Bodies pass him in every direction. He stands still, looks up to the board to find the check-in. He sees a young, blonde-haired mother carrying her child. Behind them is a tall man, eyes closed, earphones in, hair tied in locs, carrying a backpack and a guitar, wearing harem pants, looking as though he is going on an adventure to find himself. Two pilots and a quartet of flight attendants glide through in coordinated steps, emanating a glow as if the path beneath them is lit up, followed by two lovers with matching stonewash jeans delicately in each other's arms.

He rushes over to the queue. 9.15 a.m. He reaches the front and passes his burgundy-red passport to the lady at the counter. This passport, a thing hoped for, a blessing, a prayer, can save a life, can make a life; can take a life, too.

This passport, split between red and blue, between land and sea, between hope and despair. *This passport, without it I have no place to call—*

'Good morning, sir,' she says and flashes her per-hour smile. He mumbles a greeting, tapping his fingers on the desk.

'What is your destination, sir?'

'San Francisco.'

She types into the keyboard with a blank expression. She calls her colleague, who has already checked in three customers in this time. They both stare at the screen diligently.

'What's going on?' he says, with palpable frustration.

'I'm sorry, sir,' the other colleague says, her heavily made-up face – contoured nose, lips painted a burgundy wine – distracting him, 'we can't seem to find your booking.'

'That's wrong! I booked the flight myself. My name is definitely there. Michael Kabongo. I can't miss this flight. Look again,' he calls out, raising his voice and flailing his arms, pointing; drawing attention. They look up at him, ignoring his outburst, then at each other.

'I do apologise, sir, you're at the wrong check-in. You need to go to . . .'

His heart thuds as her voice fades out. He watches the direction she points in. He snatches his passport back. 9.20 a.m. His lungs tighten and breath shortens as he runs through the crowd. He feels too hot for this brisk autumn morning. His skin boils under his coat; his scarf suffocates him. He starts to sweat. He is at the back of a long S-shaped queue. 9.22 a.m. He bobs up and down on his toes with the same kind of urgency as a child bursting to pee. He mumbles under his breath, prompting others to look at him with suspicion.

Someone at the front of the queue is loud, meandering, making conversation, being friendly, wasting time.

'Hurry up please, old man,' Michael shouts out. The others do that judgemental thing where they pretend not to have seen you. *I can't go back. I can't miss this flight.*

'Is there anyone in this queue for the AO1K23 flight to San Francisco International Airport?' A man's voice floats through the air.

Michael lunges forward, and so does a woman waiting a few places behind him in the queue; her face the same picture of relief as his. They are brought to the front. The man with brown hair behind the check-in counter takes his passport and types into the computer.

'Any luggage to check in?'

He places his backpack on the scale.

'Travelling light?' the man says, smiling, which Michael does not respond to.

'You're all checked in, sir. But you have to be fast. The plane will be boarding very soon. Please make your way across to airport security as fast as you can.'

Michael is running again. He arrives at security and sees a swarm of people waiting as if queuing to enter a football stadium. He paces up and down, trying to find a way to the front. He sees a customer assistant letting people through, two at a time.

'Please,' he implores, 'my flight is at ten o'clock. I have to go through now!' She looks at his boarding pass and quickly lets him through. 9.35 a.m. The gate closes fifteen minutes before the flight. *I have ten minutes left.* His legs tighten, shaking, hands cramping up. He drops his passport and boarding pass on the floor, fumbles trying to pick them up. He rapidly takes off his jacket and scarf, belt, satchel, everything out of his pockets and throws them on to a tray.

9.39 a.m. Michael goes through the metal detector and the alarm bleeps. The security officer approaches him, looks down at his feet, and tells him to take off his boots and go back. He returns and tries to untangle the laces of his boots, which are strapped up to the ankle, twisted and curled like vines around a tree. He undoes them and rushes through the metal detectors. The security officer waves him on. He grabs his possessions and runs once again, running, always running. Gate 13. 9.43.

9.44. Michael is running through duty free, each step a stomp heavy enough to leave its footprint through the floor. 9.45. He sees Gate 13 up ahead in the distance. 9.46. He arrives at the gate. There is no one there. He falls on to his knees, panting. What a fucking waste. Maybe none of this was meant to be.

In-between a mouthful of expletives, a woman appears from behind the desk like a guardian angel and quiets his ranting.

'Boarding pass, sir?'

Michael hands her his boarding pass and clutches his chest.

'Just in time, sir. Please take a breath and make your way through.'

'Thank you,' he replies repeatedly, overflowing with gratitude.

Michael walks through the plane door and is met with the smiling faces of the flight attendants. He smiles back at them. It is meant to be. He walks past the business-class flyers, who don't look up at him, and into the economy area to his seat by the window. He sits beside a man whose belly is struggling against the seatbelt and a woman who has already medicated herself halfway to sleep. He collapses on to the seat, and feels a calmness settle within him, the sun hanging on a distant horizon. This is the beginning of the end.

Chapter 2

Grace Heart Academy, London; 10.45 a.m.

'Settle down, settle down.' The class quietened; a few excited voices still lingered.

'There are fifteen minutes left. If you haven't completed your work, you'll spend your lunch with me, organising my stamp collection.' The Year 11 class groaned.

As the autumn sun beamed down from above, I watched the students lower their heads and scribble into their books. All except for one: Duwayne. This was to be expected. On the best of days, he was in class, sat on a chair staring out of the window. With luck, he may answer a question. On the worst days, the whole school was put on notice, sometimes even the police. Duwayne sat at the back of the classroom, in the corner, sideways on the chair, head leant back on the wall, eyes drifting to the world outside.

'Time to pack up.' They shuffled, packing their books into their bags. The beeping bell rang. Some fast ones tried to sprint out of the door, but I shouted, 'The bell doesn't dismiss you, I do!', stopping them. Then I added 'You may go', and the students spilled out of the class, happy and cheering. Duwayne lagged behind, last to leave.

'See you later, Duwayne.' He nodded, not at me, but at least he nodded. I grabbed my phone from my jacket hung over my chair and texted Sandra.

> Work-wife, where are you?

> I'm on duty, in the football playground. I haven't eaten today . . . Sandra replied.

> Is that your way of asking me for lunch?

> My work-husband would already know the answer to that question.

'A tuna sandwich? Really? That's all you brought me?' she said when I joined her in the school playground.

'Tuna and sweetcorn, actually,' I replied, to the background sound of roaring children. 'With mayo,' I added. She snatched it out of my hands.

'Nothing . . . with some spices?'

'Look where we are. What kind of spices are you expecting from this place?'

'Umm, you're supposed to cook for me and bring it in.' She placed her open palm out as if to ask why I had not done so today, or ever. 'You know, like a dutiful work-husband does,' she continued.

'That's your boyfriend's job . . .'

'Oh, really?' she huffed.

'And anyway, I think you've got it the wrong way around.' I gave her a stretched, thin-lipped smile. 'I'm not sure this work-marriage thing is working out. I should divorce you. Take half your money ...'

'You won't get anything anyway cos I'm broke, babyyyyy—'

'Afternoon, sir.' A chirpy voice broke into our conversation. It moved towards us from behind. I knew who it was. We both did. We both dreaded it, too.

'I bet you she tells us to move apart,' Sandra quickly whispered.

'Afternoon, Mrs Sundermeyer,' we both replied; one voice in bass, the other in tenor, harmonising. Mrs Sundermeyer was the head teacher. She powered around the school in a power suit, after powering up the greasy ladder and powering through the glass ceiling. On casual dress days, she always wore her 'Who Run the World? Girls!' T-shirt, and never hesitated to remind everyone that her husband was 'at home looking after the kids'.

'How's it looking out there?' Mrs Sundermeyer asked, a question she already knew the answer to. She only asked questions she already knew the answer to.

'All good,' Sandra replied, along with a few nods to fill the void of what else she did not know to say. I nodded along too.

'Brilliant,' Mrs Sundermeyer said, in the high-pitch tone her voice went into whenever she expressed contentment. She leant in closer and said, 'Would you mind moving to separate parts of the playground, just so the children know there is staff presence? Thank you.'

'Of course,' Sandra said and looked at me with glaring eyes

that said *I told you so* as she walked to the opposite side of the playground. The bell rang.

'Our focus has to be on attainment; we are working to transform the lives of these young people. Giving them the life skills that will allow them to take control of their future ...' Mrs Sundermeyer spoke from the podium at the staff meeting after school. Her voice faded into the background as I looked around the room and watched everyone nod enthusiastically and take notes.

'We have the potential to be the best school in the borough, even the city. We are on our way to being an outstanding school and with your passion and hard work, we will make it happen.' She had a ministerial quality about her, a hybrid of teacher, preacher and politician. I sat, unconvinced, and wondered if there was something that they were hearing that I wasn't; something that I had not heard a thousand times before. Nonetheless, I remained hopeful that I was doing the right thing; that I was making a change, although it felt less and less so. Beside me was Mr Barnes, with the top button of his shirt undone and his tie loosened, leaning forwards, as if being pulled by some undeniable force. Mr Barnes. I always called him Mr Barnes, never by his first name. There's a fine line between colleague and friend, and no one really knows when, where and how that line is crossed. I preferred to keep the line clear and visible, so if in any case it started to wear and appear thin, I would redraw it: Mr Barnes. When I would call him, he invariably replied, 'That's who I am, and that's where I'm from.' The same line he used on his students. Nonetheless, I liked him, sort of. I admired his boldness, his ability to be himself, regardless of how mind-numbingly dull that may be.

I returned to my classroom after the meeting, watching the looming grey clouds pass. Light rain fell from the broken sky, forming streaks down the body of the glass window. London must be the only city in the world that can give you all the seasons in one day. So depressing. The wind blew the branches left and right, swaying them side to side as if in praise of an unseen god. I played classical music to match my mood and continued marking. I felt a pair of hands on my shoulders, which startled me, but slightly eased a tension I did not realise I had.

'Oh, it's you.'

'Six thirty, and you're still here. Didn't you see me come in?' replied Sandra.

'No.'

'You looked lost in your own world. What are you listening to?' She took the headphones from my head and put them on. Her face squeezed into itself, narrowing in a confused expression.

'It's Frédéric Chopin.'

'You're so weird. Can't you listen to regular music, like regular people?'

'Chopin – Prelude in C-Minor Opus 28, Number 20 is regular music . . . it's a certified banger.'

'Ugh. How long are you staying for?'

'I'm ready to go when you are.'

It was calm and quiet, peaceful throughout the whole school. It felt as though the school had fallen asleep and was now dreaming quiet dreams of tomorrows, laid on its side, hands tucked under its cheek, with its legs curled into its chest. Waiting at the reception were the pub regulars: the teachers who would religiously venture to the local for drinks only to complain about a hangover the next day. If nothing else, it gave them something to talk about during the awkward staffroom kitchen encounter where they waited for the long beep of the microwave.

Cameron, the PE teacher who wore shorts everywhere, even to the job interview here, was the first one to spot us as we walked into the reception. I looked at Sandra and could see her holding in a silent scream. We walked towards them, wishing to somehow shrink and disappear.

'Where are you two off to, then?' Cameron asked suggestively. Everything was suggestive to him.

'Home,' I replied. Cameron raised his eyebrows. 'I'm going to my home,' I added, erasing any insinuation.

'See you guys later.'

'He's so annoying,' Sandra whispered to me, as we walked off.

The setting sun brought a chill wind into the bones. Lampposts stretched above, like giant wilting flowers, casting a dull light that barely showed the path ahead. In a shared silence, we walked through the small park, with faded grass, red-brick arches and metallic benches where the street wanderers, the homeless and those seeking company gathered and emptied cans deep into the abyss of their bodies. We walked past the alleyway where phantom figures with hoods up stood; past tower block after tower block, each a trap for a thousand broken dreams; past the bars that kept them in; past the pub where the staring, chain-smoking man dared you to enter; past the chicken shop, next to the chicken shop, across the road from the chicken shop; past the artisanal café, with a menu of avocado and pumpkin-spiced somethings; past the Bible-wielding preacher man on the corner searching for souls to be saved; past the bus stop where a congregation of tired bodies waited for their gods to take them home, where stood a man, who, every day, between 3.30 p.m. and 7.30 p.m., shouted, 'The best of luck! The best of luck!', to everyone and no one at the same time; past the traffic lights at the junction, where cars rarely waited for the green light; to the mouth of the tube station, that quietly whispered a lullaby or a song, calling us home.

'So, it's Friday night, where are you going? Out on the town?' Sandra asked. She looked up at me, her eyes widening, pupils dilating, as if seeing some bright light she wanted to take in.

'I'm going home,' I replied, knowing this was not the invitation she'd been hoping for.

'Fine. Have a good weekend, then,' she said disappointedly, retreating into herself.

The tension between us grew thick, like smoke from a forest fire. I hugged her and left.

Chapter 3

Peckriver Estate, London; 8.15 p.m.

I took a deep breath and opened the door. It was quiet and dark, save for the light of the moon shining through the corridor window. I walked straight into my room and fell on to the bed, letting my body crash down like a bag of bricks from above. I felt my shoulders stiffen and tighten as if two giant clamps had been clasped over them. I lay watching the ceiling, drifting halfway between daydreams and sleep, between lullaby and song, between now and a time to come.

'I'm so tired,' I groaned. I closed my eyes and, in the darkness, saw little floating droplets of light scattered around the room, a constellation of fireflies; Orion's Belt, and Cassiopeia, gleaming. A voice shook my body and echoed through the entire room, calling my name.

'Yes, Mami,' I grumbled. She knocked and entered.

'Tu dors?' she whispered. I remained silent, nodded my reply, then feigned going back to sleep as if to convince her. She froze for a moment, then backed out of the room. I slowly got up and sat on the chair by the desk in the corner.

I left the lights off and used the moonlight to guide me. I felt lead-heavy, sinking in a stagnant, odorous pool. The screen of my phone lit up bright on the desk in the all-encompassing darkness.

> What you doing tonight? We're going out.
> Getting the drinks in. Come.
>
> Hey, what you up to?
>
> Fine. Don't reply then. Leave me on read . . .
>
> Are you okay? I haven't heard from you.
>
> Bro, I need your help, man.

The messages came like a deluge. I could feel myself sinking deeper and deeper after each one; drowning. I picked up my phone and switched it off, then reached for the pack of K Cider I had bought on my way home. Just one. Then one more. I sat in the comfort of the darkness, and felt it smother me; a possessive lover.

I arrived late, but at least I went. There were some new faces at the door that greeted me eagerly, as though I was a wayward stranger. I sat in the back row of chairs behind the pews. Pastor Baptiste stood at the altar, looking up into the clouds as if there was no ceiling. The band played: a Phil Collins-esque drummer in an isolated booth, a keyboardist playing with a side-to-side Stevie Wonder sway, the lead electric guitarist with watered-down Jimi Hendrix riffs, and the acoustic guitarist strumming passionately like Ray LaMontagne. They were accompanying the young choir led by a Sister Deloris, at least that's what I called her as her real name always evaded me. Her rendition of 'Oh Happy Day' was uncanny, at the least, and at the most could have been a rehearsal for Part 3 of the *Sister Act* movie. I noticed Mami in the front row, stretching her hands in praise, clapping in rhythm to the songs. Pastor Baptiste slowly picked up the microphone. He spoke softly and slowly, but with a self-assured bass in his voice.

'Today, we will read from Romans, chapter ten: verses nine and ten. We shall begin reading in the name of the Father, and of the Son, and of the Holy Ghost: "If you declare with your mouth, 'Jesus is Lord', and believe in your heart that God raised him from the dead, you will be saved. For it is with your heart that you believe and are justified, and it is with your mouth that you profess your faith and are saved."

Pastor Baptiste finished reading and closed the Bible. The congregation waited. I watched as the room was swept with stillness, a stillness I found myself outside of.

'Family, let me tell you about the time that I was saved by the Lord … Those of you who know me will know that I was a troubled man. I was led astray and lived a life in service of ego and greed and basic desires. My path to faith was not without its struggles, family, but the Lord's work is never without struggle.'

'Amen,' a solitary voice called out, followed by others.

'But it is promised: those who work for the Lord in the now will be abundantly rewarded in the hereafter.'

'Amen!' the entire congregation chorused.

Pastor Baptiste continued: 'It was a cold autumn evening, maybe even night. All I remember was that the darkness had long fallen, and the wind was howling like a wild animal. I was sat in a cold alleyway leaning against a lamp-post in absolute agony and despair. Sex, drink, drugs, debt, violence – you name it, I did it all. At that moment, I heard a voice, something clear and distinct, cutting through the noise like diamond on glass. I couldn't tell you what it said, but I heard it and I felt it. I knew I could not go on this way, or else I would die.

'Family, many times in our lives, we know better, but we don't do better. And it takes until we are at our most desperate for us to be rescued. But just know that the Lord will never abandon you; his light watches over you wherever you are, and wherever you shall go.'

Rapturous applause filled the air, accompanied by enthusiastic whoops and cheers; a bright sun beamed through stained-glass windows, coloured light fell upon the congregation.

I waited outside while people slowly spilled into the side room, where they would chat, or more so gossip, over tea and biscuits. I pretended to be on my phone to avoid eye contact and unwanted conversation, but there's only so much social media you can pretend to scroll before you have to look up; the nerves start to kick in when your battery reaches red and you realise you will have to socialise sooner or later.

Mami didn't know I was coming. I wanted to surprise her, make her feel it was my own will. She had been attending this church for a few years, after a few years of church-hopping. Finding a good church is like finding the right sports team to support: you have to believe that the players want to be there as much as you do. That isn't what she told me, but I figured it made about as much sense as any other reason I had been given – the choir, the music, the preaching – or any reason I would use – the food. I was glad she had finally found a place, a place that she had settled into quite comfortably in the informal role of church councillor. She was there for everybody, whether on the phone or in person. And this was reflected in the way people flocked to her.

Mami stood by the entrance with a few people ready to leave. During their conversation, I went up and tapped her on her shoulder. She turned and gasped. Her reaction startled me; had I not come to church for that long? I wondered. I forgot how long she had been asking me whether I was coming to church. I always found a creative way to say no without saying no. She would refuse to speak to me for the entire week, looking at me as if I wasn't her only son; as if she had another back-up to replace me, one who wouldn't disappoint her. Perhaps it was her way of showing she cared.

She yelped excitedly, causing some of the other church members to look around. 'This is my son.' I was met with stares of intrigue from some of the women and head-nods of affirmation from some of the men. Mami pulled me by the hand and took me back through the church, all the way to Pastor Baptiste, who was surrounded by a group of people indulging in his presence, drinking him up as though horses at a stream.

'Pastor, I'd like you to meet my son.'

'Hi, I think we've met before,' I said, remembering the last time Mami dragged me to meet him in the same fashion.

'Praise be, brother. Pleasure to meet you.'

'Interesting story you told earlier.'

'I am merely the mouthpiece, it is He,' he looked upwards, 'who tells the story.'

I, too, looked up, not sure what I was expected to see.

I said goodbye to Mami; we hugged and parted ways. I looked back, watching her and Pastor Baptiste walk away, his hand softly cupping hers. I left knowing that, at least, I had bought some time. Knowing I would not be asked if I was going to church, if I had been saying my prayers, if I was worried about going to hell or saving my soul; things that did not concern me. Walking through the high street full of people, I pulled out my phone.

'Yo, it's me. I've finished, shall I come through?'

Chapter 4

San Francisco International Airport, California; 1.15 p.m.

The water is a bright clear blue below a skyline reaching up like stretched fingers. The sun bounces off the surface, reflecting little sparkles of gold. Tiny cars back up on to each other along a small grey-silver bridge, and just beyond, the bright red bridge towers behind like an attention-seeking sibling. *So many have met their fate there, The Bridge, but mine will be elsewhere; same fate, different journey.* The plane descends on to the runway and gently lands as an autumn leaf to the ground.

'Welcome to San Francisco International Airport,' a voice announces. There is quiet relief in Michael's heart, for he knows why he has arrived. He puts on his long black winter coat and scarf and mounts his backpack. He walks towards the exit and a flurry of accents, like every TV show he has ever watched, switch on at the same time and rush to him. *I feel as though I'm walking through someone else's life, and yet, it is somehow my own.* He steps out and feels a wave of heat pounce on him; sweat trails down his forehead.

'Taxi!' Michael shouts and motions a taxi towards him. He throws his backpack into the back seat and unravels.

'Where to, my man?' the taxi driver asks, looking at him in the rear-view mirror. His Californian accent is strong, almost exaggerated in tone – as if he learned it elsewhere before he arrived here.

'One second, I've just got to look for the address,' Michael says, and the driver's facial expression relaxes.

'Where you from?' the driver asks.

Michael scrambles through his backpack, searching for his notebook.

'London.'

I'm not from anywhere.

'London!' The driver repeats.

Michael finds the notebook, rips out the page where the address is written and hands it to him.

'Yes.'

'Allo, guvna.' The driver chuckles to himself. 'Have you had tea with the Queen?' he asks, and Michael laughs along with him; a forced laugh.

I'd heard about this phenomenon, this fascination, of Americans and their asking British tourists if they'd had tea with the Queen. I wonder where this drinking of tea with the Queen would have taken place. At Buckingham Palace? A place I had not visited since our family trip, and thought it was a museum rather than someone's home. A café? Probably in Kensington, independent – where they display their twelve types of cheese behind a glass panel. Definitely not a chain; being conscientious of her status, I would spare her of having to say 'the Queen', when asked for her name to write on the side of her cup, and then having to hear 'the Queen'

*called out when her order is ready; 'One was so embarrassed,' I
imagine her saying, and I would reply, 'You're the Queen, you
can't be embarrassed', as we guffaw and sip our chai something
somethings. Or a caff; an actual cafe but without the French accent
and before people went there with laptops and headphones in so
they can 'write'. An actual cafe, somewhere in Finsbury Park,
with builders in high-vis jackets, tabloid newspapers spread out
in front of them, hard hats placed on the floor beside them, and
tan-coloured steel-toecap boots, who'd say, 'Alright, Your Maj,' to
her as we walk in. And who would, most likely, ignore me.*

'No, I haven't had tea with the Queen,' Michael answers.
The driver laughs.

They pass through the city; building after building, each
neatly lined up, row after row, like Lego blocks. It is bright;
perhaps there is a different kind of sun that shines here.
Everything looks crisp and sharpened; filtered. Michael
listens to the taxi driver talk incessantly, responding just
enough, with 'yeah' in agreement, or 'really?' in surprise, to
keep the conversation going.

'Here it is.' The driver pulls up to the kerb and stops the
meter. 'That'll be forty dollars.'

Michael unravels the Monopoly-looking money from his
jeans pocket and hands it over. The driver wishes him well
and says, 'Don't get too wild while you're here ... or do!',
which only he laughs out loud to.

I'm here.

He sends the text while waiting conspicuously in front of a
door in-between two shops.

'Hi!' A voice emerges. He turns to see a woman standing before him. She looks exactly how she sounds: energetic, enthusiastic, excited about life, as if there is something to live for that he does not know about.

She sticks out her free hand and says her name, but Michael doesn't bother to remember it. What's the point of remembering new names? What's the point of remembering anything at all? Her other hand holds both a large plastic cup from a chain café (with the French accent *aigu*) and a set of dangling keys. He shakes her hand.

'Follow me.'

She leads, he follows, his one step to her every three. They enter an apartment building. She has bright streaks of blonde in her ginger-brown hair and wears stonewash blue jeans, ripped and faded. They talk about the weather, how he didn't realise it would be so warm. She tells him about the drought in California, and how it would be great if it rained. He tells her that it rains all the time in London, and she suggests they should swap the weather for a day, to which, he extends and suggests even a week, which, after deliberation they both decide is unfeasible, the main reason being that both populations of said cities would quickly start to complain.

'So, this is it.' They walk into the apartment. It is spacious, open plan, artistic – paintings of figures with stretched limbs – and creative – sunflowers in recycled glass jars.

'And these are your keys.' She throws them up in the air, trusting his reflexes, and he instinctively reaches out and catches them. 'Feel free to make yourself comfortable however you wish. I may have to occasionally pop by and pick up a few things, but I'll always call you beforehand to make sure it's convenient.'

Michael walks out of the flat in a T-shirt. The bright sun strikes his eyes, leaving his vision jaded. He feels its warmth: small surges of electricity coursing through his skin. His breath is even, balanced, calm. *This is the sum of being alive – to be anywhere but where I have been before; to be present, fixed in the here and now.*

He steps out to cross the road, looking to the right, and a car honks, twice, loud, whooshing closely by him. He raises his hands in frustration; exclamation – You almost killed me, you prick – then realises that he was looking the wrong way. Even crossing the road loses its natural automaticity, but where one thing is lost another is gained. The other side of the street looks too far away to cross over; he thinks how these wide three-lane roads would only be found on motorways back home. Back home. He hears this, and it echoes home, home, home.

Michael enters the store and is greeted by the per-hour smiling faces of the workers. 'Hello, sir, welcome to Target,' one says, in an enthusiastic, high-pitched, singing voice. He looks down and sees a petite, 5-foot-1 at best, woman, with dark hair tinged red. He feels as though he has seen her face before, or would have, in a music video or a magazine; posing in glamorous haute couture clothing, not in the khaki chinos and dull red T-shirt uniform she is currently wearing. He imagines her working somewhere else than here, living someone else's life.

'Hi,' Michael replies, breathless. She keeps her smile as he walks past to the electronics section with cinema-size TV screens, flashing bright colours of happy faces holding up one product after another, after another, to the clothes section, with camouflage pants and boot-cut jeans and T-shirts, in various shapes and sizes, from small all the way up to the multiple-X Ls.

He is exhausted; his feet feel like he has been walking on burning sand. Pangs of pain thrust through his lower back. He wants to sit down. He looks around. There is only the floor. He picks up a box of chocolate chip cookies, green tea, bananas, and a few other things.

'Hi, sir, how are you today?' the cashier says enthusiastically.

'I'm good, thanks,' Michael replies and places his items on the counter. She has olive skin, high cheekbones; her rounded face softens and relaxes. The scanner beeps.

'Is that all?' she asks, leaning towards him, looking at his mouth.

'I'm not trying to splash and spend all my money at once.' He laughs nervously.

'That's fine,' she says, her look now becoming a stare. 'I do enjoy a cup of tea, but I'm more of a coffee person.' Her tone implies that he is supposed to consider this a notable piece of information.

'Some people prefer tea; some people prefer coffee,' he replies. She smiles politely.

'That'll be nineteen dollars.' He reaches for the twenty dollars in his back pocket and gives it to her. She returns the change to him: a crisp one-dollar bill, which he places in his wallet.

'Have a nice day,' she says. He offers her a smile in reply.

He puts the items in a bag and walks towards the exit. Two security guards, dressed in all black – jet-black shiny boots, black socks, black combat chinos with the chunky side pockets – look at him sternly, with suspicion. He recalls walking into the local supermarket with Sandra after work, wearing his white chequered shirt, polka-dot red knitted tie, pleated trousers and wingtip brogue shoes, and the security guard following him aisle to aisle, which, whilst not in the least entertaining, he found bemusing. He had chuckled to himself and when the security guard had realised that he had been noticed, he'd walked in a different direction. He still remembers Sandra's response: *You're overthinking it.* He remembers Sandra. This is the first time, since leaving, he's thought of her in any kind of way. Sometimes it is easier to forget than to heal. The burden weighs heavy on his mind, so he blocks her out, closing curtains to the world outside his mind.

Michael walks slowly, hesitantly, and, after a few paces, exits the store. He looks back at the security guards. They are still looking, staring; it seems some things are universal.

$8,806

Chapter 5

Embarcadero, San Francisco, California; 12.50 p.m.

San Francisco is a city of things: of buildings and monuments, each one different from the next. Of things: big green trees interspersed with tall lamp-posts. Of things: hills and flats, and hills and flats. Of things: art, bright, colourful expressions along the floors, the walls, and impossible-to-reach places. Of things: poetry and music, food and drink, joy and sorrow. Of things: an unravelling of people, a million stories told.

1 p.m. Michael walks surrounded by people as if on a mission they are not too sure of. White shirts, bland ties, grey trousers and black loafers, rinse and repeat, each person as nondescript as the next. He has a deep feeling of *sonder*, that each person's life is as complex as his own. In the near distance, he sees a tall building, a hybrid of a rocket and a pyramid, needle-point sharp at the top, aligned in a row with the other buildings. There looks to be something special about it – like it is keeping a secret, like the building is him.

He breaks off from the crowd going back to their offices

and takes the next left. He looks up and sees the road continue up, and up, and up, levelling off flat in-between, and
then up and up, and on and on, as if whoever built the streets
decided to take planned breaks along the way. He takes it as
a challenge to himself to reach the top. He begins to walk,
one steady step after another.

The sky looks in a confused mood, clear bright blue
mixed with gloomy grey clouds, sunshine flirting with rain.
Everything leads towards it, the sky, all the way up; the
parked cars, the trees, the lamp-posts. He walks, moving
closer to the top, past the alluring smells of local restaurants,
past a building on the corner, teal-coloured, a row of small
trees, opposite a big tree on the other side, past a large parked
truck in front of the labourers, whose mouths he watches,
imagining what would come out of them, and whether they
say the same things here as they do back home, in front of
buildings with climbing rails and ladders on the outside. A
motorbike whizzes by. He feels its vibration through the air.
On the ground, in the middle of the street, he sees a circu-
lar sewer entrance and imagines the Teenage Mutant Ninja
Turtles bursting out of there to save the day: the 'Heroes in
a half shell, Turtle Power!' theme song plays in his head. He
walks past a couple, an older man and woman, in matching
khaki chinos and faded leather bumbags, taking pictures
with their loud, protruding cameras, 'tourists', he scoffs,
then remembers he is one too . . . sort of. The pavement, next
to the pristine plain white shoe of the older man, has 'Jack
Kerouac' engraved in faded gold, with an inscription written
above; verses of poetry ring in his head. He looks up and
emblazoned above in a banner of black and yellow is 'City

Lights Books' next to a blue-green landscape wall painting. He walks into the bookshop.

'A bookshop is the garden of your mind where the flowers are not plucked, but grown: if you love something, do not yank it from the ground and yield it unto your possession; instead, water it, give it light, step back, and watch it grow.'

Michael reads the signage as he walks past the counter and is met by the smiles of the booksellers. He smiles back and looks around at the blossoming flowers on the shelves. He takes in the smell; it is old, but not of something ageing, more so something that has lived, something experienced, something steeped in the history of being, something etched deep in the memory of the world. He walks to a door in the back, past a thick, square, wooden-framed mirror hung up on the wall. For the first time in a long time, Michael sees himself: eyes, ears, nose, mouth. He sees his face: one half his mother, the other half an empty memory. Papa. He walks up the narrow sand-brown steps in-between white walls and notices, on one of the steps, 'poetry room' written in black, and he softens.

In the garden, the 'poetry room', is the fountain, from where water flows pure and true; it always gives, taking shape and form however it must, nourishing all, with sustenance and life. Michael imagines what it must have been like to be living in another time: Ginsberg; *I can't stand my own mind*, tearing worlds down with their words, and building new worlds back up again. He imagines the unknown audiences who filled rooms, and gave their ears, but more so, gave their hearts.

Around the room are photographs of solemn faces peering down like ancient gods. Written on pieces of plain white paper are little idioms, commandments on stone tablets: 'sit here and read', 'educate yourself', 'read here 14 hours a day'.

2.30 p.m. He walks down to the basement full of books. Every room a discovery of a new world, a new dimension. Here, there are places to rest. In the garden, this is the porch. He feels his feet throb as if they are expanding out of his deep-brown leather boots and sits on the nearest chair. Surrounded by various books, from Native-American history to World War II, he sees a book on Buddhism, bright red, glowing, from the bottom shelf, as if it had been awaiting his arrival. He opens it on a random page.

Breathe. Everything is you. Everything is coming to you. There is nothing that you do not know; that you have not always known. You are not the body, you are not the mind, you are nothing, and everything, eternal and current, distant and near. Release yourself of attachment, of possessions, of all things that bind you, and bring yourself to freedom.

5 p.m. Hours have passed. Time itself has become timeless, as if it did not exist; as if it were an esoteric, magical thing, a Paul Lewin painting of an ancestor bringing gifts in a dream.

Michael leaves the bookstore with two new books. To the left, he sees a flurry of books suspended in mid-air like a flock of birds in flight along the electric wires above. Behind it, painted on the wall above a restaurant, a melancholic man solemnly plays the piano buried deep in his solitude. San Francisco is a city of things.

He goes higher and higher up a hill. It falls quiet. There are few people here, few enough for warm greetings to be exchanged: a smile, a wave, a hello. He continues up and the hill gets steeper, dramatically steep, so much so that the cars parked diagonally look like they are going to succumb to gravity and roll all the way down at any given moment. He briefly watches a man struggle to park. He walks up a flight of concrete steps. He passes a metallic gate covered by a leafy shrub, through which there is a dimly lit lamp that looks as though it leads to an enchanted place. He walks up on to a platform. He rests, looking out, back down into the distance.

The sky is luminous as the sun sets; it appears punctuated with brushstrokes of sparkling gold, flaming orange and burgundy. Michael sees the tall rocket building, its needle tip kissing the sky, the water in the distance reflecting the song of the sunset, and a bridge splitting the frame horizontally. The streets go down, all the way down, until they fade out of sight, and he wonders how it would feel to go downhill on an open set of wheels. He closes his eyes. He feels the rush, the adrenalin, the freedom; the breeze rushing towards him as he screams into the open air. Freedom. Freedom. Free.

Back in the flat, Michael sits on the sofa in solitude, staring out of the window, into the ever-fading darkness save the glow of the moon. He eats the Chinese takeaway he bought on the way home, and listens to the raspy wallow *en misère* of a bearded man with a guitar, on repeat until all is lost; until the music fades, until the world turns, and the sun rises once again. *I feel a sense of calm unlike anything I've ever felt before. An acceptance of everything; a feeling bound towards peace.*

$8,586

Chapter 6

Colindale, North London; 6.15 p.m.

I knocked on the door. It was quiet on this cul-de-sac, under the shadows of bare autumn trees outstretched like haunting figures. Cars passed infrequently with a lone whoosh. I looked left to right; not a single light flickered, not a single soul shifted.

'Yooooooooooooooo!' Jalil said from behind the door. He swung it open and held his arms wide apart.

'Yooooooooooooooo!' I replied, with equal enthusiasm; the length of the 'o' in the greeting indicated how excited we were to see each other. We hugged and held it a little longer than we usually would. Jalil had just returned from a long trip to Afghanistan to visit family. His trips would often extend to volunteering with a local orphanage, school, crisis centre, humanitarian aid centre, or exploring the wilderness, with no contact to the outside world, to find himself.

'Come in, man. Come in,' he insisted, as I entered and took off my shoes. He lived in a two-storey house, with a garden and a garage. He was an only child. His mother, an Englishwoman, had passed before he entered secondary school, and his father, having waited until Jalil graduated from university and could take care of himself, had returned to his home village to remarry, open a small school and start a new family, leaving Jalil in the house by himself. He wore a long, flowing thobe over his peach-olive-skinned and 6-foot-plus frame, with size 13 feet protruding from beneath.

'I got back last week,' Jalil answered as we walked into the kitchen.

'How was it?'

'You know how it is.' He looked at me with solemnness and serenity. 'Really puts everything in perspective,' he added, the music of his voice shifting from major key to minor.

'Anyway, what are you saying?' he asked enthusiastically as the kettle boiled. He served green tea for both of us. He was the kind of person who, when they asked this question, of how you are, they meant it. They really wanted you to say how things really were, the bad and the good, the ugly and the beautiful. This did not make the question any easier to answer, at least not for me. Because what was I supposed to say? Good? Great? Even though I felt as though things were falling apart.

'All good,' I answered, not sure whether I was trying to convince him or myself.

He looked at me curiously, with investigative eyes. I looked away.

'Just work and the usual grind,' I added. I wanted to tell him about this growing feeling of isolation, despair, hopelessness; I was a burden to the world, to everyone around me. There was an engulfing greyness creeping in from the corners of my being to the core. I couldn't tell if this was imagination or reality, but I knew it was there.

Jalil and I entered the living room – where he sleeps, eats and reads – which he refers to as 'the Cave – Plato's, not Batman's'; flexing the remnants of his philosophy, politics and economics degree from Oxford like a man in front of a mirror at the gym, and sometimes, 'the Cave, the Prophet's, of course, peace be upon him', which cave depending on whether he was wearing the thobe or not. He slumped on to the wide sofa-bed, sending the laptop jumping up and down, and I slumped on to the beanbag in the middle of the floor. Looking around, the room could be described as a vintage collectors' museum: VHS tapes, cassettes, games console with the cartridges, a record player in the corner, shelves of classic books in their original hardbacks, and a pair of Air Jordans and various pieces of art.

'Where did you get that from?' I asked, pointing my cup of tea towards the painting of a floating planet in front of a backdrop of constellations and shooting stars, and a spaceship whizzing by.

'It's mine.'

'I know that, I'm asking where you got it from.'

'No, it's mine as in I painted it.'

'What?' I got up for a closer inspection.

'It's so detailed. When did you do this?'

'A little while ago, I've been taking an art class.'

'No way. Wow. You kept that one a secret.'

He shrugged in response, picked up the laptop and flipped it open. His fingers scattered rapidly across the keyboard, followed by one loud tap; scattered across, tap; repeated rhythmically, as if adding a full stop to a long sentence each time.

'Bro, I'm getting old.'

I chuckled at his random existential outburst. 'What do you mean?'

'I had to sign up to this dating site. Look.' He flashed the laptop briefly at me, but not long enough for me to really look.

'It's a website for single Muslims looking for marriage.'

'Marriage? Are you trying to turn a hijabi into a housewife?'

'Ha, yeah, something like that. It's time for me to get serious. I'm nearly thirty.'

'Are you sure that's the only reason?'

'Well, that and the fact that Baba keeps stressing me out. He says if I don't find someone soon, he's going to set me up with some girl from the village.'

'That might not be a bad thing. What if she's fine?'

'He showed me pictures . . . ' I looked at him for a reaction. He waited for me to say something.

'Beauty is in the eye of the beholder.'

'Well, I don't wanna be holding no one in those pictures,' he replied and laughed an uneasy kind of laugh, a shortness of breath.

'Surely you saw some beautiful village girls while you were back?'

'Bro, I couldn't stop seeing them.'

'I'm sure.'

'No, I mean, they were all beautiful; it's a different kind of beauty. Your eyes just adjust; you look through a different lens. Non-Eurocentric beauty ideals . . . decolonise, innit?'

'So why didn't you say hello, go and speak to some?'

'It doesn't work like that.' Jalil laughed at my naivety. 'It's not like I can just go and say, "Hey, baby, how you doing?" There's tradition and culture to follow. I have to speak to my baba and my baba goes and talks to their baba. Imagine your dad being your wingman.'

'Well, you've got to do something. Otherwise your dad is going to keep choosing for you.'

'It's just so hard to get to know someone, though. Dating is impossible. You meet someone, and you have to do all the nice things and go to places neither of you really want to go; if you're lucky, you make a connection, and then they just end up ghosting you.'

'Or you ghosting them. Sounds as if you're scared of commitment ... attachment issues.'

'Okay, relax with the Freudian analysis. I was actually hugged enough as a child. The only thing I'm scared of is committing to the wrong person.' Jalil paused for a moment, as if looking into a future that petrified him.

'That's why I'm creating this profile,' he continued. 'It cuts through the mess. I'm not quite sure what to say, though. Shall I just tell them I ride a motorcycle?'

'That will get you married off in no time.'

'Seriously?' He started to type rapidly.

'No!' I replied, waving my hands. 'I think women look for a bit more substance in a husband than whether or not they have a motor.'

'It's the size of the motor that really matters, though, right?'

'No. Stop. Look, how about I write the profile for you?'

'*What?*' he said, in a panicked, high-pitched voice.

'It makes sense; think about it. We're best friends. I

know you better than anyone else, sometimes better than yourself. Eh?'

'You're never going to let that go, are you?'

'Never ever.'

'Fine, go on, then.' He threw the laptop and I watched it drift through the air and fall comfortably into the space beside me on the beanbag. I opened the laptop and stretched my fingers theatrically. I looked up and saw him staring at me with nervous curiosity and anticipation. Once finished, I closed the laptop and threw it back to him. He eagerly snatched it mid-air.

'"Hi, my name is Jalil, I'm a soon-to-be-30 traveller, adventurer and liver of life. I am passionate about politics and philosophy, learning about different cultures, languages (I can order food in five languages and I know how to laugh in every language), and people. I like to paint and go on long walks. I'm just looking for someone to join me on this long walk of life." That's not bad, bro, well done ... Wait, there's more. "If all of that doesn't interest you, I have a really cool motorbike. Big engine." Ha! What happened to all that "women look for a bit more in a husband"?'

'I'm just trying to widen your chances. You're not working with much.' Jalil pulled a face that resembled a meme. The clock struck midnight.

'I need to go, I have work in the morning,' I said, halfway falling asleep.

As soon as the alarm rang, I knew I was late. I ran straight into the bathroom. I brushed my teeth and had a quick shower. I left, slamming the front door, as if fleeing for my life; shirt flapping in the wind, tie flailing behind me, rucksack bumping up and down on my back. A cheap imitation of Clark Kent out of the phone box as Superman, only without the powers; perhaps Teacher Man could be a superhero? Saving everyone but himself. God, I hate my job.

8 a.m. I texted Sandra. I did not wait for a reply. I flew down the escalators, my feet barely touching the steps. I was temporarily blocked by someone standing on the left – definitely a tourist, an annoying 8-a.m. tourist, an annoying 8-a.m. tourist who should be avoiding the rush hour. I manoeuvred around them. Next train in four mins. 'Aaargh,' I groaned, and everyone around me froze and watched in silence, doing that thing where they pretend not to have heard or seen you. The train arrived and I forced my way on, surrounded by bad breath, sweat patches and waistlines touching too close for comfort.

'SETTLE DOWN!' The class immediately fell silent as I walked into the classroom. Students sitting on the tables went back to their chairs, another slowly lowered his arm in mid-throw, scrunched-up paper ball in hand. There was an expression of relief on the face of the supply teacher whose name I had not bothered to remember.

'Thank you, miss. I'll continue from here.' She smiled. 'Excited Year 8s,' I whispered to her as she gratefully left the classroom.

'You should know better than to mess around when you have a supply teacher. You're better than that. And anyway, I find out everything in the end, don't I? Marlon? Ruby? Jasvinder?'

'Ah, sir, you can't bait out man's government. It's Jazz.'

'I find out everything, don't I ... Jasvinder?' I repeated, locking eyes.

'Sorry, sir,' he replied, mumbling in defeat.

'Now, open your books; we're going to have silent reading for the remainder of the lesson.' The class groaned in unison. 'I said silent!'

> RIP Michael Kabongo.
>> Time of death: 11.35 a.m.
>> Cause of death: unknown – may involve rude, screaming children and stress.
>> Tombstone reads: Herein lies a man who died as he lived: tired.
>
> Ha! That is too funny. Where are you?
>
> I die, and you think it's funny? How insensitive. Where are you??
>
> I don't even know why I'm surprised. I should never have expected more of you. Where are you??!!!
>
> I'm in my grave.
>
> Okay, this whole dead joke is dead now. Where are you?
>
> I'm in class.
>
> Oh, you made it in then.

Yes. I was late. Didn't you get my text?

No.

Well, this is awkward.

Aren't you coming out for break? Come to the staffroom.

Why?

I'm there.

. . .

Fine.

I'm too tired. It'll be a miracle if I leave this chair, let alone go to the staffroom. And I'm on duty today.

You want me to cover you?

Omg, would you?

No.

Wow.

Oh, well! There goes the bell! Good luck!

The shrieks and roars of excited students quickly filled the corridors.

10.50 a.m. The day had barely even started, and I was already prepared for it to end. I wheeled my chair over to the door.

'Er, Year 11, you're supposed to be lining up quietly,' I said, raising my voice above theirs. They slowly shuffled into line.

'Sir, why are you sitting down?' asked Alex all the As.

'I . . . I hurt my leg.'

He looked at me as if to say, 'yeah, right'; so much so that I could almost see the judgement in his eyes. They settled into class.

Is this life?

The class eventually finished. The Year 11 students packed up and went to lunch. The door was left open. I mumbled words of discontent under my breath. I rolled over to close the door. Sandra appeared and started laughing at me. Tempted as I was to close the door in her face, I decided to let her in.

'You didn't reply to my message.'

She placed a sandwich on my desk.

'You brought me food?'

'Well, after how you sounded this morning, and after seeing your last message, I thought you'd need a bit of cheering up.'

'Aw, thank you, work-wife. Tuna and sweetcorn . . . my favourite.'

'With mayo. Yeah, your favourite. How are you feeling?'

'My legs feel like I'm being stabbed with a thousand tiny needles. I haven't got up from this chair since I first sat down in period one. And I refuse to get up for the rest of the day.'

Sandra laughed at another case of my 'dramatic ridiculousness', which I did not – now or ever – consider dramatic or ridiculous. I noticed how gentle her face appeared when she laughed; how her cheekbones lifted, her chin relaxed into itself, dimples dipped and eyes closed, creasing at the corners.

'Wait! Aren't you supposed to be on duty?'

'Ohhhhh . . . ' I groaned and held back the next few words. I always tell the kids swearing is a limitation of vocabulary, but sometimes it's a perfect encapsulation of an emotion, because when you're at work and want to quit, the only fitting words are 'fuck this shit'. That's how I felt right at that moment. I attempted to drag myself out, still on my chair, as Sandra giggled behind me.

'Fifteen minutes have already passed. If I don't go, it's not like anyone is going to notice?'

Sandra lifted her shoulders and shrugged in response. I rolled my chair back behind my desk.

Chapter 7

Grace Heart Academy, London; 2.45 p.m.

The Year 11s were quietly reading. I tried to resist checking the time every two minutes. I watched the hands of the clock above stay in the same position for fifteen minutes, or what felt like fifteen minutes; a stubborn mule refusing to be cajoled. Pangs of hunger struck my stomach, sending rumbles through, and my head began to pound as though it was a punching bag for an amateur boxer with post-break-up repressed aggression. I felt my legs tremble and wondered how much longer I must survive this madness.

At the back of the class Duwayne slouched in his chair, staring out of the window. He had one hand down the trousers of his school uniform, which he wore low, revealing the tracksuit bottoms underneath. Our eyes locked. He was so used to not being looked at, let alone stared at, that he tried to hide being startled. I nodded at his hand, and he lifted it out of his trousers. I wondered where these ridiculous trends came from, and why the students kept following them, but then I remembered how I was as a teenager, and how we would wear our tracksuits low, roll up one trouser leg and leave the other down, and bop around as if we were doing something that set fire to the world.

'Are you all right?' I whispered. Duwayne rocked his head up and down slightly, this time not looking at me but at the floor.

'How much have you read?' I asked, knowing that he had not read at all. The book lay face down on the table. I picked it up, *The Lonely Londoners*. 'Interesting book,' I said and flipped it open.

'Don't care, ain't mine,' he replied as I returned it to the table.

'You should care. You should learn about the *Windrush*, and how our people came to this country.'

Duwayne shrugged.

'Stick around after class; I want to speak to you quickly,' I said. His body stayed still; his soul sank further into the chair.

The bell rang as I walked back to my seat. The students quickly packed away and waited to be dismissed, before spilling out of class into the corridors. 'Come,' I said to Duwayne, who had not moved. He laboriously stood up and approached my desk, dragging his feet, in the latest Nike Air Max shoes that looked expensive and custom made.

'Is everything all right?'

He nodded.

'Did you get any reading done in the end?'

He shook his head.

'Why not? Didn't you enjoy it?'

He shrugged his shoulders.

'Look, you're in Year 11, Duwayne. It's your GCSEs. Your final school exams. I know the year has just started, but you have to pick it up. I don't want to see you fail.'

He shrugged his shoulders.

'You're going to have to speak eventually,' I added in frustration.

'Can I go?' he said, short, sharp, staccato. Fed up, I nodded at him. He stomped out, swinging the door wide open and leaving it dangling. I huffed and opened my email.

From: Admin
Subject: Lunch Duty

Please provide a reason why you failed to show for lunch duty.
    If you fail to provide a satisfactory reason, it will be deducted from your pay.
    Kind Regards,
    Admin

I stared at the email with a fiery intensity. I saw my phone light up on the table: a message from Sandra.

Are you still dead?

I think I have resurrected.

Please don't make any religious jokes.

Come on, I would not do such a
thing . . . by text.

One day, I'm going to snap, and you'll still be
silly enough to wonder why.

I'm surprised you haven't already. Must not be
brave enough. #shookones

I'll ignore that (for now). How do you feel?

I'm already Thursday tired, but it's
only Monday.

Well, better muster up some energy because
we have a staff meeting.

WHAT? No way!

Well, not tonight. Tomorrow. Got you
twice in one day. This is unlike you.
I would have paid good money to see
the look on your face. You're off your
game, son.

Don't son me! So, there's no meeting? Omg.
One day, I'm gonna snap and . . .

and it won't have anything to do with me!

I chuckled and logged back into my computer, on to my
emails. Click. Delete.

*

I walked into the cacophony and searched for a place to sit. Although I tried to ignore him by pretending I had not seen him, I ended up next to Mr Barnes, who waved and pulled out a seat for me to join him.

'Hey, thanks, man. Didn't see you there for a second.'

'I hope you're feeling super this morning,' he replied as I nodded and kept doing so. 'I was wondering ...' And just before he could continue, Mrs Sundermeyer entered and the room fell silent. Her heels click-clacked on the hardwood floor as she walked to the centre.

'Good morning all,' she said, in a firm, self-assured tone, certain of a reply.

'Good morning,' they replied in unison. I remained quiet; my silence consumed by the chorus.

'We're only a few weeks into the year, and it's been a great start so far. We do have to stay motivated, and on top of things, challenging those who do well to excel, encouraging those who need a bit of a push, and nipping any defiance or developing behavioural issues in the bud.' She spoke as if she was on show, as if there were more than just the people in that room watching her. I admired her enthusiasm and passion, but I also loathed it – it made me feel tired; because I would start to question why this enthusiasm and passion was missing in me. Mr Barnes took notes beside me. I watched him for a moment, and then looked away. After a few announcements from other staff, most of whom were trying to assert an authority far beyond their reach, the bell rang, and the teachers dispersed to their classrooms.

I had a free morning, so I walked along the corridors, and watched the excitable children make their way into their classrooms. I felt a sweeping wave of nostalgia; everything reminded me of a time before. It was as though the same school that was failing me was failing these children. Appearing from the stairwell and filling up the corridor was Mr Black. His body widened as he approached, and I looked up, having to adjust my neck to say hello. He stood at 6 foot 6, at least, and was almost as wide as he was tall. He wore an immaculately maintained short-sleeved white shirt, tight around his biceps, and a red tie with dark grey trousers as uniform. I imagined he had an entire wardrobe of the same outfit ready for wear.

'Morning, sir,' Mr Black said, in a sousaphone voice, reverberating off the walls. He was the kind of person you felt safe around, regardless of the situation; if the building suddenly started to crumble, the bricks would fall away from him as if even they were too scared to make contact. We spoke about the NBA Finals of that summer; whether the Warriors would have won if Irving and Love had not got injured, the season to come, the school basketball team and the London Schools Championship he was so determined to win. All of which were subjects I had very little opinion on but made for worthwhile conversation. For a moment, it felt as though we were two guys hanging out after work at a bar. He always struck me as a faithful married man, one who wanted for others what he had for himself – this eternal peace, this happiness. In many ways he reminded me of who I imagined my father to have been; a man I never knew. And oh, how an attack of loneliness falls sudden upon you, triggered by a memory.

Mr Black patted me on my shoulder, a clutch from a giant's

hand, and pulled me out of my descent, back to reality. 'Right, back to work,' he said before walking off.

I returned to my classroom and was sat at my desk responding to emails, listening to classical music – Vivaldi, *The Four Seasons* – when I heard muffled voices coming from the classroom next door. It was a new teacher, Mrs Kaptch ... Mrs Kap, I did not remember, but I know I called her Mrs K for short; at which she smiled and accepted my overfamiliarity. She taught one of the social sciences, I did not care to remember which.

The rumbling voices echoed back and forth, like two barking dogs, like water brought to boil. Mrs K screamed something inaudible, and I leapt from my chair, rushing to the classroom. I opened the door and saw her standing at the front, frozen, hands trembling from panic. In a rapturous chorus, the students roared, 'Fight! Fight! Fight!' They were huddled together forming an octagon ring around the two bodies scuffling on the ground, oohs and aahs echoed to every punch thrown, every kick and every headlock. I manoeuvred over and around the chairs, shouting 'MOVE!' through the group.

'Duwayne! Alex!' I shouted, in shock, as Duwayne held Alex in a headlock; arms long like an octopus around his neck and head, legs wrapped around his torso. Alex began to gasp, losing air. I jumped on to the floor with them, trying to unlock Duwayne's arms from Alex's head, but to no avail. His arms were more securely locked than an expensive bike in a city of thieves. Then, by a sheer invisible force, Alex rolled over on to his stomach, curled up his knees, lifted himself off the ground with Duwayne on his back, and flipped backwards and dropped, flattening Duwayne on the floor. Duwayne's head snapped back with the thud of a bass drum, causing him to immediately release his impenetrable lock and grasp the back of his head and roll away. Alex stood up above him, and before he could think about doing anything else, I flung myself in-between them. A large shadow then appeared above me like a dark cloud, blocking the dull daylight creeping through the windows. Mr Black. He lifted Duwayne off the floor with one hand, like you would a doll or puppet.

'Right, young man. Come with me!' he said and stomped out of the room, Duwayne lagging in his possession. I got to my feet, and with an imitative authority, beckoned Alex to follow me.

'And the rest of you,' I roared, 'need to sit down and shut up! I don't want to hear another sound coming from this room.' They quickly and quietly shuffled, returning to their seats. I surprised even myself with this outburst, but it had succeeded.

'Mrs K, if you need me, I'll be next door.' She looked back at me, blank-faced, as though she had seen an ex-lover, a deceased parent, a failed dream; anything that haunted her.

I held the door to my classroom open for Alex as we walked in. I stared at him. He looked at the floor; shoulders slouched, back hunched over, arms dragging by his side. He sat near the back row by the window and gazed out.

'Alex ... Alex all the As.' He didn't respond, did not flinch, barely even a blink. I logged on to the computer, and began furiously typing, hitting the keyboard so fast that my hands started to cramp.

'I expect better from you.' We sat in a heavy silence until

the bell went. Alex dismissed himself, getting up not a second after the bell, dragging his bag on the floor while he left.

It was the end of the day. I was at my desk once again, feeling as though I had been emptied of all that was in me; energy, passion, enthusiasm spilling on to the floor, as if I had been stabbed and was incessantly bleeding, too tired to cover the wound. It was midweek, and I was struggling to see how I would make the end of it. That is often what we live for: the Fridays, the weekends, a chance to relax and be who you want to be while you're not forced to be who you have to be. But what if you can barely see tomorrow, let alone the end of the week? Then it arrives, this heavy feeling, light but heavy, not there then sudden and all at once. I felt my breath shorten and my chest tighten the more I thought about this: being here, now, on this chair, in this classroom. It was raining outside, and I somehow felt even the texture of the air change; thicker, darker, dim. I breathed. I realised I had zoned out and was now staring at the back of the classroom. Mr Barnes appeared.

'Hello, sir,' he said, popping his head through the door first, before he walked in, as if asking for permission.

'You all right? Come in,' I replied, reluctantly reassuring him that it was okay to enter.

'How was your day?' he asked, meaning well. I wanted to tell him it was bad, really bad; how tired I was, how I'd had to stop a fight before I had even started teaching; how in the last lesson I had sent out so many children from the class, I may as well have been teaching myself; and how I wanted to curl up into a ball and sleep, for a while, a long while.

'It was good,' I replied. 'How was yours?'

'A bit rough.' He let out a deep sigh, and sat on the table in front of me. 'Maybe it was something in the air today.'

I nodded and remained in my realm of silence.

'Thought I'd go for a quick one after work. Want to join me?' he offered, smiling, eyebrows raised, lines appearing on his forehead.

'I'm afraid I can't … It's a late one for me, I've got too much work on.' No matter how many times I said no, he kept on asking, and a part of me admired that, but another part hated it.

'No worries, mate.' He sounded dejected, flattened even, but still hopeful. 'Maybe next time.'

'Are you cycling home?' I asked, trying to make amends for the rejection.

'Yeah,' he replied.

'Be careful. It's started to rain out there.'

Chapter 8

San Francisco, California; 9.39 p.m.

Michael sits staring deeply into the bottom of his glass. His fourth drink. The drink warms his bones and loosens him. Still, he cannot come out of himself enough to talk to anyone. The bartender hands him his bill – $50 – and looks at him with untrusting eyes. The bar is playing loud thumping music, bodies collide in song and dance, and he is sat, in the middle of it, the eye of the storm, the nucleus of a cell, sinking. More people enter and brush past him as though he were a ghost. He thinks about leaving, but it would be more difficult to get out than to sit there and wait. So he sits, quiet, not moving, wondering why he even came. The ways we are seen and not seen, the ways we are invisible in this world; and the ways we long to be seen, and then, eventually, not. We fight to be seen, for the world to know that we are here, only for us to be forgotten, to be invisible once again; the difference is our choosing, whether we are seen or not seen, we give that power back to us. But, in our absence, the world goes on. The world always goes on. *And it will go on without me.*

Michael's thoughts drift. He looks at his phone; staring at the pictures he took earlier standing next to thing after thing after thing. I've never seen an unhappy tourist. If there is such joy in leaving home, why do we ever stay? He is learning to relax into himself more, to be someone that he otherwise would not be.

'Hey, those are some cool pictures.' He looks up from his phone and sees a pair of hazel-green eyes, bouncy golden curls and a bright smile. He gasps at her beauty, his mouth ajar, throat overflowing with desire.

'You must not be from around here ...' She chuckles gently. 'I'm Sara.' She looks at the seat next to him and invites herself. 'What brings you to the Bay?' she asks, gesturing.

'Oh,' he feels rattled, startled, unprepared, 'I'm just here on a trip.'

'Business or pleasure?' she continues, teasingly. He doesn't reply.

'Well, whatever it is, you don't seem too excited about it.'

Michael looks at her, empty of words, or rather, held back lest he give himself away. They continue, and she notices his accent, how his words bend differently to hers and carry a weight. She lightly places her hand on his shoulder and does all the gentle things that people on dates are supposed to do: pay attention, listen, open up and give that person a place to stay; let them know they are safe here.

'This feels like a date ... ?' he says.

'Really?' she replies, laughing nervously like a teenager whose diary has been read aloud. 'Is this your way of asking?' she adds. He laughs now. She takes a napkin from the bar and writes her phone number. He looks at it with caution and inquisitiveness. She plants a kiss on his cheek and then disappears back into the dark room of bumping bodies and basslines. He folds the napkin into his pocket.

Michael rides the BART home: Montgomery, Embarcadero. He looks across at the seat next to him, and there is sat a man who shares his expression: tired, fed up, fatigued, not wanting to be here but he is still here. Michael knows this feeling well. He looks at him and their eyes share the same invisible tears. Not being able to stare into the mirror of each other for too long, they quickly look away. West Oakland, 19th St Oakland, MacArthur.

He gets off and walks towards the shuttle bus that will take him back to the flat. There are a few people standing at the bus stop and he hears, through the music in his earphones, their frustrations in the form of grunts and mild obscenities as they find out the shuttle bus is no longer running. He carries on, walking past as if he never intended to take the bus. He takes a turn to the right and then right again, and he finds himself on an eerily quiet, dimly lit street; shadows of lampposts outstretch like limbs, and the fronts of cars watch like staring faces.

12 a.m. He turns off the music in his earphones and diligently watches the shapes that rise and fall around him. His heart begins to race as he hears footsteps emerge from behind him. The footsteps pound closer and he cannot tell if it is the footsteps or his throbbing heart, but something is uncontrollably beating. He sees a shadow loom and creep up on him. He slows down and clenches his fists, ready for the fear to pass. *It's either you or me.* He sees a young man pull up beside

him, tall as he, dark as he, head down, hair covered in a durag, baggy T-shirt, combat chino shorts and basketball shoes.

'What's up, brother?' the young man greets him.

Why was I scared? Michael asks himself, after responding to the young man's greeting. That was me walking past. He feels his heart slow down from pounding and return to rest. His pace slows, and the young man passes. Michael stops in front of a shop window. A poster catches his eye: a smiling Malcolm X, alongside posters of Marcus Garvey, Harriet Tubman, and many more historical figures in their glory who he has yet to know. They seem much less like posters, and more like paintings; art brought to life. He places his hands on the window and is compelled to go in. The door is locked. There are rows and rows of books: *Nile Valley Contributions to Civilisation, Before the Slave Trade, Civilisation or Barbarism*, and other esoteric artworks and ornaments that hang across the wall, of deities and gods from a time before. He steps back, looks at the signage above the store, and leaves behind the history that lives in his bones.

Walking down 40th Street under a bright clear-blue sky, Michael reaches into the left pocket of his jeans – the same pair he wore the night before. The napkin is still inside. After much contemplation, he pulls his phone out and dials the number. It rings. Just as he's about to hang up, there's an answer.

'Hello?'

'Hi, is that Sara?' he asks nervously.

'Yeah . . . '

'Hey, we met at the bar last night. You gave me your—'

'I know who it is. I remember. And plus, you're the only guy I know with a cute British accent like that.'

He laughs, adding an extra layer of bass to his voice.

'So, I was wondering if we could hang out sometime?'

'Sure, I'd love to,' she replied with an enthusiasm he's not used to. 'What did you have in mind?'

'I was thinking maybe we could get something to eat and catch a show ... '

'That sounds great.'

'In LA?'

'*What?*' she shrieks in reply. 'LA ... as in?'

'Yeah, City of Angels.'

'Los Angeles.'

'Yeah.'

'But I have class ... and work.'

'So, you miss a few days cos you're sick. What's the big deal?'

'Traffic is kind of crazy, and the drive is really long, and I don't have the kind of money to—'

'What drive? There's no traffic in the skies. And don't worry, I'll take care of it.'

She coughs slightly. 'I think you're right. There is something going around.' Another cough. 'I think I may be sick,' she adds.

'That's great! I'll call you again when I get back to my flat and we can sort it all out later.' He hangs up the phone and running jumps into the air, pumping his fist like Michael Jordan after scoring the game-winning shot. The onlookers and passers-by stare in excitement, some whooping and cheering for him: 'Go on, boy!'

'I can't believe we're in LA.'

'Ummmm, shouldn't I be saying that? It's my first time; you already live in California.'

'I know, but I mean I can't believe we're in LA now,' she laughs. Her eyes squint, the corner of her mouth lifts slightly, revealing a row of straight teeth. 'I should be sitting at my desk, answering emails and taking phone calls – "Hello, Bright Insurance, how can I help you today?" – and rejecting advances from my creepy boss.'

'All in a regular day's work?'

'Yeah, if you can bear it.'

'So, you don't hate your job?'

'Not even a little bit.'

'I know the feeling.'

They break the conversation to indulge in their lunchtime meal. It is hot; upbeat pop music plays through the air while the large screen mounted on the wall shows a Lakers game.

'Thank you for coming, though.'

'Shouldn't I say thank you for inviting me? You paid for the flights and that tiny, slightly weird apartment we're staying in . . .'

'Weird, yes, but also eccentric and one of a kind?'

'The shower and kitchen are in the same room.'

'That's still one of a kind. You can save the planet by using your shower water to boil your kettle . . .'

'Ew. No, no, no. You should have just let me book it. I know LA better than you.'

'What happened to "I can't believe we're in LA"?'

'What happened to "I don't really talk much, I prefer to listen"?'

'Touché.'

'I needed this escape; things had gotten me down lately. And I know we're virtually strangers . . . correction . . . we are strangers,' she smiles, 'but I trust you. There's something about you that makes me feel safe. I like that.' She shifts the smile from her mouth to her eyes.

The waiter approaches; a tall, slim man, tanned, dark haired with a thick moustache.

'Are you enjoying your meal?' he asks in a thick, heavy-weighted Mexican accent. They both nod.

'And it also helps,' Sara continues, 'that we got to hang out a few days before and you let me look at all your Facebook friends, pictures and status updates. It surprised me, quite philosophical; you don't seem like the why-are-we-here and what-is-the-meaning-of-all-this type. That's cool.'

I should delete all of my social media.

'Not as cool as this status.' He looks up from his phone and shows her the screen.

'"Touched down in LA-town." Really? Are you sure?'

'Yeah, like Chi-town ... LA-town.'

'Literally, no one calls it that.' She tries to reach for the phone. 'Gimme that. You need to delete it before you embarrass yourself.'

He pulls it away and puts it face-down on the table, wagging his finger.

Michael asks for the bill, and when it arrives, he puts down forty dollars to cover it. They have a brief argument about whether a tip is mandatory or not, which he loses, and leaves five dollars on top, to which she adds another five dollars, saying, 'I'm making you look better. Thanks for lunch.'

Sara reaches out and delicately brushes her smooth palm along his forearm, raising all the small hairs on his skin. She places her hand on top of his. Her touch sends a surge through his body, as if it were being brought back to life.

They're in the rented car, on the road, driving through a part of LA neither of them knows well, or even at all.

'Okay, damn. Mr Formula One, huh?' she remarks about his speed, and they laugh together. She reaches over and places her hand delicately on his, and runs it up his arm, to his hair, which she strokes tenderly. Michael finds it hard to concentrate on the road.

Venice Beach, Hollywood, Walk of Fame, Beverly Hills; they saw it all today, everything short of watching the Lakers at the Staples Center, back seat full of shopping bags, front seat full of desire, yet Michael felt unsatisfied. *I want to see the LA that looks like me, that walks how I walk, and talks how I would talk if I were from this city.*

It is late. The moon appears coyly behind slow-passing clouds. They wind to a halt, stuck in bumper-to-bumper traffic on a bridge – city skyline creeping behind them. A broadcast radio voice interrupts the music with the latest traffic reports.

'Traffic!' Sara says as she slumps into her seat and switches off the radio. 'Well, they do say you haven't been to LA until you've experienced the traffic.'

'Who says that?' Michael asks.

'What do you mean, who says that?'

'I mean, who? You said "they". Who are "they"?'

'Well, "they" aren't actual real people, it's what people say.'

'So "they" aren't real, which means no one actually says it.'

'It's not like they are waiting in a room, thinking of things to say and send out to the world! Damn, Michael.'

'This isn't exactly my idea of cruising,' Sara adds. She groans and hits the seat in frustration. An exit appears ahead, which Michael pulls off into when they reach it.

'Do you even know where you're going?'

'Can't be that hard to find our way home. Moving is better than sitting in traffic . . . they say.'

Sara pulls a wry smile at Michael's smug face. They drive through a long, dimly lit road, with trees leaning over as if they were haunting the streets.

'I can't wait to get home and try on all these clothes we bought. And then, maybe, take them off too.' Sara looks over at Michael and smiles. She looks down at the butterfly tattoo on her wrist.

'Aren't you going to show me the tattoo you got?'

'No.'

'Well, that's rude. It was your idea. I showed you mine.'

They stop at a red light. The engine hums quietly.

'Yours was a butterfly. It doesn't mean anything.'

'It means something to me.'

'Okay, fine. What does it mean, then?'

'When I was a child—'

There's a loud crash on the car from behind. It jolts them forward. Michael, holding the steering wheel, braces the impact. Sara is whipped forward; she holds her neck in anguish. The car screeches to a halt.

'What was that?' Michael feels his heart beat with fear. There is knock on the window, the distinct sound of metal on glass.

Chapter 9

'Get the fuck out the car.' A muffled voice emerges from the other side, face hidden behind a bandana and a hooded jumper. The door opens and Michael is pulled out. Then, from the other side, so is Sara. They are forced on to the sidewalk, sitting. The engine runs. There are two men, boys even, resembling his former students. Michael thinks of them, thinks of Duwayne. A dark sparkle of metal glimmers from one of their waists but Michael cannot tell what it is.

'Gimme everything you got, motherfucker. Hurry up.'

Michael looks at the terror on Sara's face. How tears form at the bottom of her eyes like lakes. He hesitates.

'What are you, deaf?' the young man roars. Michael huffs and then begrudgingly empties his pockets: wallet, phone and cash; the hundred-dollar bills. For fuck sake. The other picks up the items from the floor and counts the cash. They nod at each other. Mission complete. The other runs back to their car and drives off hurriedly, while his partner gets into Michael's car.

'Is that it?' Michael shouts. The man stops, looks at him, then at Sara, and then back at him. Even Sara pulls a face at him for his outburst, but Michael ignores her.

'What you say?'

'You heard me, you little prick. I said is that it?'

'The fuck you talking about?'

'Yeah, what are you talking about? Shut up,' Sara says, no longer crying. She hits Michael on his arm as if to knock some sense into him. The man with the shimmering metal on his waist steps back out of the car. Michael can see what it is now. The man walks around to Michael and pushes him in the face, full force, with the bottom of his foot, knocking him to the ground. Sara holds in a scream.

'Are you crazy?' the guy says.

Michael sits back up from the floor and checks his face for bleeding. He lets out a deep sigh as if he has been inconvenienced, like when someone cuts in front of you in a queue or steps on your shoe in public.

'Listen, I'm just trying to help you out,' Michael says, as though he were giving a lesson. 'By the time you try to use the credit cards, they'll be cancelled. The cash will quickly be spent on bills and that bad haircut of yours. By the way, you call that a fade? And before you know it, you'll be back on the streets, waiting in the dark, at night, to rob another car. It just seems a waste of time to me. You can do better.'

'You trying to be a motivational speaker? On these streets?' He laughs. 'Understand that you lucky to be alive right now. I could kill you,' the guy adds, reaching for his waist.

'So, go on then,' Michael roars. He stands up and stretches out his hands, his body, as if to provide a better target.

'Go on! I don't give a fuck. Put me out of my misery.' Michael huffs impatiently. He strikes fear into the guy's heart, as if it were he who was carrying the weapon.

'You can't kill a man who's already dead,' Michael whispers. 'Look . . . ' he continues as he reaches into his sock, 'here's five hundred dollars, take it and give me back the wallet. You won't be able to use the cards anyway, it's worthless to you. But I need that wallet.'

The man opens the wallet and finds nothing of value inside. 'Nah, you crazy man. There's nothing in here but some chump change.'

There is some noise in the distance, approaching. The man throws the wallet at Michael and grabs the money from his hand. The man runs to the car, gets in and revs it before screeching the tyres and speeding off to his escape, leaving them in the dark cold of the night. Sara stares at Michael in disbelief.

Michael lies down, watching the ceiling. Darkness surrounds him. Hours have passed since they made it home. Yet restlessness creeps under his skin, lingers in his bones, keeps him awake. Sara is sleeping on the couch, in the living room of the flat they rent. She did not say a word to Michael, she barely looked at him. Once they returned, she laid her head down and fell asleep. Michael stared at her for a while, wondering what she was thinking, before going into the bedroom. It is peaceful here. The train tracks echo in the distance and he wonders whether they are coming or going. Sleep escapes him. His thoughts submerge him.

Is there no way out? No way out of the mind? Out of this

prison, this hell, less, this purgatory – this wasteland of nothing-
ness? Where nothing lives, where nothing breathes. And to think,
the only way to escape the mind is to escape the body. And I, of
both body and mind, am no longer shrinking from annihilation.
No longer shrinking from death. I am walking to it, running,
even. I want to walk into the oblivion of my being, the disintegra-
tion of my existence from this world. Like dust, swept up by wind,
into the air, into a tornado, hurricane, storm. Listen to my words.
I want to die, yet I speak not as a man who wants to die, but as
a man who wants to live, and dying is the only way I know how.

Footsteps creak along the wooden floor, alerting Michael to
full attention. His eyes remain fixed, the sight ahead equally
dark whether they are open or closed. The sound moves
closer. The door slowly swings and closes again. All movement is quiet, calm, like a library, or temple. Sara. He feels
her weight shift on to the bed.

There is no hesitation in her movement. He feels the touch
of her skin against his as she lays beside him. Her warmness spreads on to him. He trembles. They lay in silence
for a while.

'Are you sleeping?' she whispers. Michael shakes his head.
She looks up at him, in the darkness, trying to find his face.

'What's going on with you, Michael? What happened
out there?'

Michael let out an exhausted sigh.

'You know, you don't have to do that.'

'Do what?'

'Play hero.'

'I wasn't.'

'So what was that?'

'What?'

'You could have got us killed.'

'I could have got me killed.'

'But why, Michael? Why would you want to do that? It's not a game.'

'Because I want to.'

'You want to ...'

'Yes. I want to die. I don't care about my life, about the world.'

'Oh, Michael,' she said, her voice breaking.

'It'd be better if I was gone.'

She moved closer, holding him tighter than before. As if she could breathe some of her life into him. Michael remained stiff, unmoving.

'I'm only telling you because, truly, I don't know you. And I won't know you after this,' he says.

'But we could ...'

'No. That's not what this is about.'

'So, what is this about?'

'I don't know. I am just trying to live, trying to experience some last moments of my life before ... ' Michael pauses, and lets another fatigued breath escape him.

Sara leans in to kiss him. Her lips touch his cheek, delicate. Her hands begin to stroke him, begin to explore the soft body of his earth. He stops her.

'I can't do this. I haven't been able to do this ... for a while.

'See, I've always kept everyone at a distance, at arm's length, never opening up, never letting them in. Not because I'm scared of emotions, of being hurt or of vulnerability, but because deep down inside I've always known I want to die, and it was a way of saving them from the pain and torment of what they would go through when I do.'

Sara is silent but Michael can tell she is crying. They lie tenderly awake in the darkness, holding each other, as dusk passes to dawn. *I made a mistake. I can't let anyone else get this close to me. I can't let anyone else know. It only increases the hurt, and the pain, and I too often feel theirs as if it were my own. No matter how much I crave intimacy, crave to be touched, and to be held, I'll remain in this world as I tend to leave it: alone.*

Tomorrow, they'll make their return trip, in silence – as if they are mourning. Asking nothing more of each other than the banalities – have you packed, the cab is here, are you hungry, can I have the window seat. They'll go back to the normality of their lives, back to their own relative obscurity. They'll hug and wave goodbye to each other at the airport when they land and go back to the strangers they were before.

$6,621

Chapter 10

Grace Heart Academy School, London; 10.23 a.m.

Have you ever loved, knowing it would end, but giving with your whole heart regardless?

Christelle came to me like a wave of river, the eleventh hour, life giver – she breathed life into me. I knew the moment I saw her face that it was hers my eyes wanted to look at until death or blindness, not fearing whichever came first. Her face was lifted, elevated like something on display. An art exhibit or a sacred shrine. We started, as you do, with messages: me trying to show my witty quips; her matching; neither keeping the other waiting. Then we moved to phone calls. I noticed her accent, how it carried the different parts of the world she had called home. I wanted to know her journey, and whether she had yet arrived, whether I could walk with her. We would speak for hours, often until the only conversation left was quiet breathing.

On our first date we met by the river. I arrived thirty minutes early to steel my nerves. It worked, only until the moment she arrived. My nerves then exploded as though someone had lit fireworks along my veins. We walked invisible among a swarm of people – in our world, newly discovered, there was only us. We went to a bookshop and created a new sanctuary we could both escape into. She loved books in a different way than I; it brought her back into the world but helped me escape. I would watch her eyes light up, sparkling at the corners, when she spoke about her favourite book, *The Little Prince*. I had not read the book, but already loved it, for if it was this book that brought her this light, then this book deserved to be loved. I wanted to be this book; I wanted to bring out this light of hers.

We sat to have dinner, I across from her, staring into the galaxy of her eyes, her across from me, a flower unfolding. We spoke of everything, of art, of culture, music and tradition, of the future, and where we saw ourselves in it. The restaurant transformed from raucous laughter echoing around the other diners to just the two of us floating in the ocean of our quiet. We strolled along the river, lit by the dim lamp-posts, serenaded by the busker playing a song for hearts. Twice our hands touched side by side, first by accident, igniting a spark, second on purpose, intertwining. Time is suspended, everything around us moves in slow motion and we pass at the speed of light. I tell her I want to kiss her. She wonders why I took so long. As our lips touch, the shape of our mouths fitting comfortably into each other's, it sends us hurtling into another dimension. Our bodies are weightless, we float through space.

With her, life was a promise fulfilled. We would spend hours lying in each other's arms, quiet, still in our shared solitude; a world we created and let each other into. I remember when I first saw her cry. It wasn't due to sadness, woe or misery. It was because the words I spoke were the same words that her heart had longed to hear. As we sat in the darkness, under the light of the full moon, she placed her arms around me, and I knew at that moment I had arrived. It was her. She had lifted a tension in my shoulders that had been coiled like springs. Her touch was a weight, a heaviness, leaving my body. It was her. I knew it. Her arms, her hands, her skin, her shallow breathing while she slept, left eye slightly open as if she was looking at me, her 'why'd you take so long to get back to me?'; her 'I just missed you, that's all'; her fears and her wildest dreams, which I would carry on my back like a cross or like wings. So, this is what love is, to be burdened yet weightless, to be bound yet free.

My friends slowly started to find out about us, about my secrecy and unavailability, why my time was no longer my own, and I welcomed it. I found ways to include her name in conversations that did not even involve her; I became the people I despised: the romantics, the over-lovers, the passionate, the obsessives. If love is a field, then romance is the rain that grows the flowers.

I thought about the day I would introduce her to Mami. She would be the first girl I'd introduce to her – the only girl. Mami would say: Bring home a good girl from your country who can move back with you some day. But how do I say to her, my mother, that I have no country? That I am a man without borders, I remember not well enough from where I came nor do I know where I am going. For I am the road, the path, the journey, without place, without home. I belong to nowhere and I belong to everywhere. But somehow, she settled all of that. The feet get tired, and the soul gets weary. She gave me rest. When they met, Mother could sense that about her; she saw the change in me and liked it. It was set, this was our path, our journey; but it did not last.

The essential detail of all tragedies is that you do not see them coming. The tragedy creeps up on you; shadows in the unflinching darkness, the all-consuming night, like death and dying. The very thing that tore us apart was the same thing that brought us together: faith, mine in her, hers in the above. See, I believed in her to the point of worship. Would kneel, palms touching, hands clasped, eyes closed, to a god with her face, praying she would never leave. It felt as though my prayers were being heard, but the day she left came to me like a summer storm. We were having dinner. The esoteric mystery of her presence, the air riddled with magic, was as present as ever. But at the end, she said, in a voice of mundane normality, as if mentioning the weather or asking for the time, that she was leaving me. It was a rapid descent, a clean break that I never saw coming.

I begged, I pleaded; neither pride nor dignity stopped me from falling to my knees. But what good is prayer to a god who does not hear? I thought about how she must have known she was leaving, even before she left; maybe even known whilst we last kissed, held hands or even lay together. In the end, everybody leaves – we even leave ourselves. In a field of forever, she planted seeds of impermanence. The thing about losing love is it makes you feel like you can never love again, like you are not worthy.

Late that night, I arrived home, went into the darkness and lay there, sinking. I wept. I thought about death. I thought about what it would be like not to exist, to die, but without dying; without mourning, without wake, without funeral and procession, without burial and memorial. An act such as this is prepared in the quiet of the heart. To disappear into the ether, erased from earth's eternal memory, any space I previously filled replaced with a void, an emptiness. I wanted it, I longed for it, yearned for it, this absence, like the love I had lost. This feeling I thought had left now returned – in truth, it was always there, dormant and waiting. I realised that this was not the first time I had felt this feeling. It had been a growing thing, since I was a child: dust in the corner of a room, damp in a beautiful house, a thousand tiny spiders crawling all over your naked skin. I died that night, like the many nights that I had died before, that I will die again. I was a soul much more prone to my solitude. Not everyone seeks love, some seek quiet, seek peace. I slowly distanced myself from those around me and returned into the quiet where I had been all along. Where I long to be.

I snapped out of this daydream, eyes refocusing on the class in front of me with their heads down, writing into their books. I wondered how long I was gone for, into this daydream; each time feels longer than the last. A few students tried to pop their heads up but were met with my glaring gaze into the nothing beyond them; they quickly got back to work, Jasvinder in particular. He could not sit still for longer than thirty seconds. He found comfort in being the funniest; you could see his small brain processing as he ransacked his mind for the next punchline in a conversation. I admired his chameleon, shapeshifting abilities; to be both rude-boy and geek

is a refined act of dualism. Of course, he was completely unaware, but more so stuck between the rock of peer-pressure
conformity and the hard place of parental expectations; he
would sag his jeans low but would pull them up long before
he arrived home. I saw Jasvinder with his mother shopping
at the local supermarket. She was a tiny woman who he had
already outgrown enough to make him look older than he
was. He looked at me, blank-faced, trying to hide the surprise in his eyes. Much like his mother, he was dressed in a
traditional garb. I didn't know whether they were coming or
going but Jasvinder made it known that I had seen a side of
him he was not yet ready to show the world. It was as though
a part of who he was had been revealed, his secret identity
discovered, unsure whether it was a super power or a sordid
secret. I smiled and continued with my shopping. Since that
moment, he had not crossed the proverbial line of disruption.
He looked up again, distracted from the work, and I met his
eyes with raised eyebrows. He quickly returned to his book.

The bell rang, and I dismissed the students. I felt a sinking
feeling even though it was the end of the month. I got paid
a little less than usual, my faux rebellion over lunch duties,
initially because of fatigue, had persisted into disaffection,
or, as I would say when Sandra accused me of being lazy,
'efficient energy resource allocation'. It just reminded me
how things had changed. When I first started here, I was
super-enthusiastic, on time for everything. I would sit at the
front of staff meetings, notepad at the ready, ears open like a
flower to the sun. But gradually I wilted, began being a little
bit late, and then a bit more, and then a bit more, not reply-
ing to emails that weren't urgent, not turning up to duty or

meetings. When you fulfil all that is expected of you, there is no reward or acknowledgement, but when you begin to falter, the consequences appear – people only love you as far as you do what they need of you, when you do what you need for yourself, they fade like shadows in the dark.

Staff Meeting – delete.

Drinks – delete.

Football after work – delete.

Line Management – I guess I must read this.

Update your progression targets – delete.

Student Suspension: DHB – I almost deleted this one too, but doubled back and opened it.

This email is to inform you of the five-day suspension of Duwayne Harvey Brown, 11 S, for a period of three days. Please can you send planned work for the student to complete . . .

I huffed a gust of air and felt my shoulders slump. I was not surprised. Disappointed, but not surprised. More disappointed in myself for having expectations, for wanting more for Duwayne than he did for himself. But is this not the stuff of life? I wondered how many people had given up on him because he had not met their expectations. Are we not the sum of those who have never given up on us? I was determined not to let him be just another boy who fails.

Chapter 11

I was woken up by blaring gospel music and folk songs of praise. Mami played the music as if the sound would travel through walls to lost souls and bring them salvation. I heard a loud crash of pots. This was also routine. Mami would stomp around the house, footsteps louder and hastier than usual, cluttering and clanging, slamming doors and cupboards, cleaning frantically, rustling and ruffling, rushing as though time was not on her side. And if I slept in too long, she would switch on the hoover, bringing it louder and louder, close to my bedroom door as if a volcano of dust had just erupted that she had to clean. She switched off the hoover and knocked on my door.

'Lamuka! Lamuka! Lelo mukolo ya yenga.'

'I know what day it is,' I grumbled.

Sundays were no different from any other day, at least not for me, but even standing at 6 foot 1 and 95 kilos (on a good week), I could not muster the courage to say this to my 5-foot-2 mother.

'Olali?'

'No. I'm awake.'

'Kasi, bima te.'

'I'm coming.'

I got out of bed, as ordered, gathered myself and went into the kitchen where Mami was now talking on the phone, reassuring the person on the line that she was listening and that everything was going to be okay. I poured myself a bowl of cereal and went to sit down in the front room to watch TV. She followed me, still on the phone, then paused and asked me if I was coming to church.

'No. I'm not going today. I'm really busy ...' She huffed at my reply. 'With work,' I added, as if to validate my reason.

'Mais, comment chaque fois c'est "I'm busy, I'm busy", hein!' She exploded into a high-pitched tirade, 'Il faut que tu viens! Pastor Baptiste te cherche tout le temps, qu'est-ce que je vais dire?'

'I don't care if the Pastor wants to speak to me.'

'Alors!' she yelled, covering the phone with her hand.

'I'm busy. I'm not coming!' I replied, trying to force out some authority. I really wanted to shout, to roar, as I do to my students, set fear swimming into the blood. But I couldn't, I could barely manage a response.

'You know, sometimes you really are a stupid boy!' Mami said, and slapped me across the back of my head – just hard enough to let me know that she could still do it, spilling the spoon of cereal and milk I was delicately guiding through the air to my open mouth.

Mami continued as normal, back on the phone, rushing around and past me, as if I was invisible. My heart pounded as if it were a boxing bag being hit by two giant fists. I left the front room and walked back towards my room with lead-heavy steps. I opened the door, and slammed it behind me – not too much, but enough for her to know it had been slammed.

After a few moments of blazing gospel music and cacoph-onous sounds around the house, it fell silent, then I heard the front door open and slam shut. I lay on my bed, staring at the ceiling, wondering whether my friends had it the same. Probably not. Most don't still live with their mums. Saving money to move out felt increasingly futile, especially in this city. Maybe, some years down the line, I'll be able to put down a deposit on a shed and move in with someone who also wouldn't mind sleeping standing up. But it wasn't always this way: the pressure, the burden. When Father was around, it felt different, but that was decades ago – though his presence still lingers, in framed photos and conversations. In truth, he didn't leave, but that feels easier to say than he died, because death does things; it brings before us the realisation that there is an end. That it will all one day end. When I say that he left, it makes me feel as though he is still out there in the world, living, being a man, no matter how righteous or flawed. After all, he was a popular man. This is what I was told by others, though Mami does not speak of him much. Others would say, 'Your father was such a tall man, and wide – he was like a bear, but gentle and softly spoken', 'Your father helped me in ways I can never repay', 'I see him every time I look at your face'. Referring to the other half of my face I do not know. I forget that I carry one half of somebody else's face. That, to others, I am not even my own person.

Maybe I should leave this place too, somehow, but I keep worrying about Mami and what would happen if she were left alone. Perhaps, ultimately, all leaving is the same, whether death or absconding. Everybody leaves. And in the end, what is this salvation we seek? What is faith if nothing else but believing that there is someone out there who will never leave us? What does it mean to be saved and who are we being saved from if not ourselves? If not our demons and our fears? All of which are us. Monsters, in us and of us, these faceless figures lurking in the shadows. We hold up mirrors to ourselves and run at the sight of what we see, but the monsters run with us, step by step, for they reside deep inside.

Night fell. I went for a walk. It was cold. The wind blew harshly across my face – a single teardrop trickled down my cheek. I felt as though I could cry, right there, on the street in front of all those people, staggering and stumbling in their lacklustre, carefree world. Such sadness, like the wind, comes from a place I do not know.

I walked through the high street of busy commercial shops, all closed save the pubs and bars beside them, to the canal by a hidden path past the bridge. The wind felt even harsher there, but it was strangely comforting. Sometimes a pain you are used to can comfort you if you have nothing else. After all, it is what you know that keeps you, whether sadness or joy. It reminds you that you still feel.

The canal water looked dull and murky, like a thing that is slowly dying. It had a dim glow from the houses lit up above it. I had been thinking about death and dying more and more. Not the actual physical act, but the act of not existing: of not inhabiting a body, a name, an identity; the act of existing but somewhere in the unseen, somewhere in the forgotten. What would it mean to be a body, sunk at the bottom of the canal? A body, swimming in a dying thing. Just a body, or less than that.

We were often warned not to go there as children. I remember stories from teachers, parents and other children about limbs found floating in the water, and kidnappings and robberies, but as I've got older, it has become a place of solitude, an open sanctuary where I come to seek solace, and meet others doing the same. I looked around and saw lugubrious shadows lurking in the corners – a homeless man and the company he keeps – but they did not scare me, I was more scared of the binge-drunk, high-street wanderers, for our worlds were much closer than we realised. Both temporal and fleeting, both worlds hanging in impermanence, steeped for ever in the now.

I walked back towards the main high street, and up ahead I saw shadows lurking on the bridge, a group in tracksuits, with hoods, standing around, smoke floating above them. I moved towards them, the bridge being the only path for me to get home. I felt my heart start to beat faster. Was this fear? As I got closer, their faces slowly emerged, some visible, some dark, some still hidden. I approached cautiously. All the 'what if' scenarios raced through my mind. What if they've got a knife? If they don't let me pass? If they start a fight? If they rob me? I know this corner. I know it well. I knew what it meant to be there, late at night. It was not a congregation for a sermon, or a gathering of old friends. They sold drugs. The people on this bridge had always sold drugs; it had been this way for years, ever since my childhood on these streets. However, what had changed was who was selling. Every two or three years, there seemed to be a new cycle of people – and I would wonder what happened to the others: prison or death? After school, I used to know them, dress like them, hood up, jeans low, stop and talk, but now these faces are alien to me, and I look alien to them as I try to pass by in my chinos, brogues and trench coat. I live in a different world to them now but still in the same place.

'What you saying, big man?' I heard, as I excused myself, navigating through the group. *Look down. Keep walking. Don't reply. Don't make eye contact.* But I shouldn't be scared. I am from here. I looked up to my right and made eye contact. I saw a face I knew, or at least I thought I knew, the same despondent face that has looked up at me several times from his chair, and then back down, his eyes red and hazed, his mouth blowing smoke. Duwayne. I stared, said nothing, put my head back down and continued walking.

After an excited exchange of yooos to greet each other, we settled down for a cup of fresh mint tea that Jalil had got on another one of his adventure trips. Jalil was on his laptop, furiously tapping away as if writing a last-minute essay due in the morning, and I lay back on a beanbag watching him. I did this more and more. I admired how he could get so passionately lost in his own world, oblivious to all around him.

We watched a video about a philosopher with a French-sounding name, talking about love, the perils of modern dating and why we are destined to settle with the wrong person. Jalil loved watching these videos. Each time he learned something new, he would try to put it into practice; sometimes actually recording the action and the result, doing everything just short of plotting a correlation chart.

'I watched this the other day. It's crazy, isn't it?' he said. His excitement arose at observing my reaction, and I, not caring about the video – just happy to be there – tried to show a matching enthusiasm. Truth is, I did not care for love or who I would be settling down with, and not much else either – it had somehow become this way. But it mattered to him, and he mattered to me, so I continued to feign interest.

'So, how's the dating site?' My question was met with a smirk. 'Have you met anyone?' I added, knowing that smirk meant there was something to be excavated.

'Firstly, it's not a dating site, it's a . . .'

'A what?'

'A platform for marriage aspiration.'

'So, a dating site?'

'I mean—'

'It's okay. You can say dating site, it's pretty much okay now, everyone uses them.'

'Right?' he replied, high-pitched with relief and reassurance. 'I mean, yeah, but it just feels weird.'

'Why?'

'It's okay for other people to use them . . . I just never thought that those other people would be me. Don't laugh, you must know what I mean,' Jalil continued.

'Well, not really.'

'I just never thought that I would need to use a dating site.'

'There, now you've said it, it's not so bad.'

'I guess I always just associated it with some desperate

nerdy guy with glasses, sitting in some dingy room or base-ment, sending a long email to some girl he claims is the love of his life, who he has only seen one picture of.'

'So ... you?'

He looked at me with subtle discontent as I laughed and reassured him it was a joke.

'You watched way too many nineties romantic movies growing up,' I added.

'I did not.'

'You've literally described at least five different movies.'

'True. They were so good, though.' We laughed again, and both felt at ease.

'But we've always used dating sites, though.'

'What do you mean?' he replied inquisitively.

'Those chatrooms back in the day were basically dating sites ... and do you remember MSN? One big dating site.'

'MSN Messenger? No, it wasn't.'

'No? So, are you telling me you used to log on for the scintillating conversation and to be updated on current global affairs?'

I watched Jalil's pupils veer to the corners of his eyes as he fetched a distant memory.

'Exactly.' I interrupted his nostalgia. 'We were horny teen-agers asking girls to switch on their webcams.'

'Simple times.'

'So, who's this girl, then?'

His face went from a smirk to a wide smile.

'Her name's Aminah. She's so beautiful. Shall I show you a pic?'

He reached for his laptop, and I quickly stopped him: 'No,

just tell me about her,' I said. Beauty was always something quite tangible for him, always a picture to be seen or shown.

'Well, her family is from Pakistan, she's moderate, looking for something long term, leading to marriage.' As he spoke, his face lit up as though there were fireflies perched beneath his cheekbones, or a child imagining a future when asked what they want to be when they grow up; anything was possible.

'We've been talking for a couple of weeks and she's so cool. Her voice is so sexy, when we spoke, I proper got a har—'

'Whoa! Okay!'

'What?' he laughed.

'Too much information,' I replied, and he laughed again, and I laughed, and I watched his mouth burst with joy.

Part II

The Absurd

Chapter 12

Oakland, California; 10.04 a.m.

Michael walks up 64th Street. It is a quiet and serene Sunday morning. He is alone, save the cool breeze trailing him. He hears his footsteps crunching the autumn leaves on the ground. His tan-brown boots blend in with the fallen leaves from the parallel trees that lead all the way up. The houses are neatly arranged and painted with colours of different shades: grey to blue, red, all white, and so on. He feels out of place – out of body. He passes house after house that appear alive with memory. Up ahead he sees an older woman approaching – her dog, a cute, black-haired breed of something he cannot name, scuffles in front on a leash. He prepares a smile to greet her.

To his left, Michael notices a house different from the rest. It is dilapidated, worn; its wooden panels faded, paintwork peeling like flaking skin. An overgrown bright green bush spreads on to the sidewalk and up the walls on the outside. It covers the garage door and submerges the car, contrasting against its rusty sky-blue paintwork. There are two windows on the second floor; one is boarded up, the other is cracked, hanging glass in-between the edges, with a black metal fence covering them, adjacent to a set of stairs that lead to a boarded-up front door. *This house is tired, tired of life. This house looks how I feel.*

Michael takes a seat on the front steps. The older woman appears, her dog leading the way with its wagging tail. She is not startled by his presence, though he expects her to be. They exchange greetings. Her excited dog comes to him. 'She likes you,' the older woman says, 'she doesn't like many people.'

'I was just walking by and I noticed the house,' Michael says, pointing. 'Do you know what happened to it?'

'Oh,' she responds, 'there was a terrible fire,' she pauses, 'about two years ago.' The older woman continued, saying the woman who owns the house kept mentioning she would restore it but never did. Michael stands in silence, absorbing the story. The woman pauses, says goodbye and walks off with her dog. He continues up the road, thinking about this house that was once a home. About the memories lingering, alive in each of the rooms; the laughter, the crying, the smells – of cooked food, of perfumes, then of burning, of burning, of burning. Maybe homes are much like people too. That, like homes, we also need to be taken care of as much as we can; and to have something live inside us in order for us to live. But regardless, in the end, we eventually go back to nature, back to death, submerged by the will of the earth. And that, in our most earnest moments, maybe we are all just homes, burning, and love is the water that saves us. And maybe, love is that someone who still sees, in all the burned-down brokenness of our house, the beauty in us – the stories and memories that we hold inside – and restores us and makes us home.

Michael reaches the top of the road and turns left. A church appears, a large cross hanging above its entrance. On the front lawn, planted into the ground, there are several crosses, tens, dozens, painted in a glowing white, with names and dates written on them. As he watches, he hears a voice speak from behind, deep with whiskey-induced hoarseness, ubiquitous in its vibration: 'The crosses are for each person shot dead in the city this year.' Michael looks at the man talking, a man standing tall, wide-shouldered in a leather jacket, black-tinted glasses, thin strands of silky black hair straddling his olive-skinned and stubble-haired face. 'It was put up by the church; they do a lot of great work in the community. They recognise the importance of being remembered. Some here are for grown men, some are for children . . . ' The man points. 'This is my daughter's . . . ' His voice surrenders into submission.

'I'm sorry,' Michael replies after a momentary stunned silence. The man nods at him.

'Such a tragic loss of life. You should come in,' the man says, pointing to the entrance of the church with large, open wooden doors.

Michael hesitates, his words spluttering like a faulty engine. 'I'm not really a church person—'

'Don't worry,' the man interrupts, 'neither am I.' A contagious smile breaks out on his face, which sends them both into a smiling fever.

Michael follows the man into the church. At the bottom of the aisle with parallel pews hangs a burnished Black Jesus on a cross up above, all black and glistening from the light breaking through the stained-glass windows. Michael follows the man as they walk to the left pew, passing by the welcoming faces. On the walls are paintings of saints, but as he looks closer, he realises they are activists and world figures: Martin Luther King, Cesar Chavez, Mother Teresa, reimagined as saints with beaming halos crowned above them. Michael imagines the heaven in which they reside, a heaven of justice, where peace reigns eternal. He notices a plaque inscribed 'memento mori' hanging on the wall as they quietly shuffle into their seats.

The Reverend is addressing the congregation. His accent sounds as though it has crossed continents and skipped oceans, calling many places home. The Reverend's voice has a quality of certainty to it, as though his words come not from his own mouth. Michael listens, not to the words, but to the vibration – a soothing harmony, a meditation, a prayer different to that which he has heard before.

This is the first time he's been to a church since attending Mami's, and he would not go back there even if it was the second coming. Anyway, he could not go back. There is no going back. The line has already been crossed. However, Michael feels different here; he feels as though he can rest, even if only for a little while.

The Reverend says it is time to pray, and in a synchronised motion, everyone closes their eyes, bows their heads and holds hands. Michael feels the soft touch of the woman sat next to him as she reaches for his hand and grasp it firm, tight. The man he entered with also holds his hand; it is warm and delicate, a contrast with the man's hardened appearance. Michael now feels comfortable holding hands with a stranger, some-thing he would never do. The congregation shout their prayers from the peak of their lungs. Lord, I pray for my mother bat-tling cancer; I pray for the homeless and the hungry; I pray for all of those who are stuck in or fleeing conflicts around the world, in Syria, in Congo, Somalia, West Papua, Sudan. Michael closes his eyes and goes within himself.

Inside me there is a man who lives in an abandoned city, and he walks around looking for company; another life, another soul, someone to touch, someone to hold. The city is endless, it has no limits, nothing to differentiate where it would end, or begin. Every day, this man wakes up and walks. He walks until his feet are blackened and burning like charcoal, until his limbs collapse into themselves and he can walk no more. Then he falls and lays there to rest – this man has no home. The next day, he wakes and walks again, and again, and again. But each day, he walks a little less than the day before, each day he gets a little more tired. This man knows it, feels it, that it's only a matter of time until he can walk no more, and his only desire is to lie wherever he finds himself and sleep eternally. He can feel his body succumbing to this will as it grows heavier, as though he is pushing a rock up a mountain, only the mountain is the streets and the rock is his own body. This man wants to sleep, eternally, he knows he cannot walk any further. This man is me. A man with no prayer, no hope, a man with no home.

Michael opens his eyes as he feels the prayers being cast into the air by the congregation submerging him like an ocean wave offering pure ablution, a holy wave washing over him. The Reverend says a final prayer and in unison they say, 'Amen.' The congregation breaks off and start greeting each other, warmly, with affection, and Michael, in the midst of it all, slowly slips away unnoticed, passing inconspicuously along the side pew. On his way out, he once again notices the inscription 'memento mori': 'remember you must die'.

Michael arrives home after wandering for miles. His feet ache. He sits by the table, with a cup of tea warming his hands, and looks out of the window into the bright lights of the city set against the beautiful dark skin of the sky. Mother. Mami is all he can think about. Her words, her strength, the way she just kept on going and going. Something compels him – a push and pull of two forces in his gut – to write to her. She has not heard from him, she would not have. That is the way he wanted it, to slowly disappear. But this feeling is stronger than his will to resist it. So, he reaches for a pen and paper and begins to write.

Mami,

May these words find you rested and free of burden. May the sun never set in your sky, may the birds never stop singing, may the flowers forever bloom, may all the things you find beautiful in the world multiply. Do you remember? When I was a child, we would write each other letters no matter how near or far we were. I would write you poems:

like a bird flying high like a cloud
in the sky like the leaves in a tree
you make me feel free

But the letters stopped. The words were no more. I kept them locked inside. I let them be taken, swept away by anger, by rage. I knew tragedy too young, too soon. What hope is there for a child that is exposed to the cruel face of this world? We were separated, kept apart by borders. I would not ask, 'Where's Mummy?' I asked, 'Is mummy dead?' And the empty looks on the faces of the strangers who raised me said more than their silence. Do you remember? When we saw each other again, I had grown too big for you to pick me up and carry me on your hip like you used to. That day I hugged you and made a promise that I would never leave you. That nothing would ever separate us; not borders, not war, nothing. But promises are like fairy tales, they are made-up stories for children. And I cannot keep promises any more, not when nothing was promised to me.

With love,

Your son, Michael

$6,512

Chapter 13

Grace Heart Academy School, London; 5.30 p.m.

Monday: rain fell with fury from thunderous clouds. The grey gloom hovered above like an inverted shadow walking the sky. I stood at the school reception looking through the long glass-pane windows, waiting for the right moment to leave. I accepted that I would get soaked, and so I left, holding my bag above my head. After a few steps jogging on my toes, I was already drenched, so I slowed to a defeated pace. I heard laughing, not the insidious or malicious kind, but familiar; the laughter of friends regardless of whether it is with you or at you. I turned around and saw Sandra chuckling while suitably dry under a large umbrella. And she had every right to do so: she looked cosy, like rising bread in an oven, and I looked like I had taken a shower in my work clothes. She lifted the umbrella so that I could join her under it. We walked towards the station.

'How was your day?' she said excitedly, still laughing. I didn't reply. I knew she was not asking a question to be answered. While we walked, she kept lowering her arm and my head kept hitting the umbrella.

'We're going to have to change this set-up. Let me carry it.' I took the umbrella from her and held it high enough to cover the both of us. 'See? Much better.' She smiled. We walked on, and she wrapped her arm around me, holding the soft part just above the bone of my hip, and still held the same smile as we now walked with synchronised steps. It was odd, but it felt good. I noticed her smell: a bouquet of flowers, or strawberries. It lifted the gloom.

'How was your day?' I asked.

'Oh, it was good. But I've already got so much marking to do. These kids are going to drive me insane. And I'm pretty sure Mrs Sundermeyer is on my case. You know how she does that thing where she'll randomly go into your class and stand at the back and watch you teach? She did that to me twice! In two days!'

'She's never done that to me. You're right, she might be after you.' Sandra looked at me with an annoyed face that I brushed off with laughter.

We reached the high street and were met by the man with the booming voice who shouted, 'The best of luck! The best of luck! The best of luck!' to everyone who passed him. We arrived at the entrance of the station, and I lowered the umbrella and returned it to Sandra. She smiled a kind of victorious smile of self-congratulation. A car drove past and splashed a large puddle all over me, soaking me from my shirt down to my trousers in murky rainwater. Sandra laughed again – her voice was music – as I stood there, further soaked.

'Ha ha, your luck is bad. Look at the state of you. I love you,' she said, as she continued to laugh.

'What?' I replied.

'What?' she said, still chuckling, as she reached into her bag for tissues that she helped wipe my forehead with.

'I don't think that's going to make much difference.'

'Well, you might as well take the whole thing. For your journey.'

I huffed, and we hugged goodbye. She held on a little longer than usual, and so did I, growing accustomed to her warmth on this cold, wet, autumn evening, wishing for a moment that she would not let go.

Tuesday: there was no rain today, only cloud. And though the grey gloom remains, the light relief from the rain was welcomed as though it were sunshine. I decided to go into Mr Barnes's classroom, and pay him a visit; I could not recall the last time I did, or if I ever did for that matter, but I figured me visiting him would keep him out of my classroom, and, as a good gesture had been passed on to me, I would pass it on to another unsuspecting recipient.

I opened the door, hesitating for a moment, wondering if I should I have knocked. I walked in. Mr Barnes was shuffling under his desk, packing something away. When he heard my call – 'Sir?' – he jumped up, alarmed, and hit his head on the edge of the table. He reappeared, holding the side of his head with both hands, rubbing it furiously with the tips of his fingers. His faced flushed a bright red, and I allowed him a moment to recover from the second most inconvenient pain one could feel; the first, of course, stubbing your little toe at the foot of a table or door.

'You all right, sir?'

Mr Barnes nodded vigorously.

'Shall I come back?' I said.

'No, no, no!' he insisted. 'Do come in.' He stuffed the bag under his desk.

'How are ya, old chap? To what do I owe the pleasure of this delightful visitation?' Mr Barnes went back to his usual self and, for a moment, I wondered why I'd come. But there was something different about him, he was crankier, erratic, wholly different to the 9 a.m. or staff-meeting note-taking Mr Barnes I knew.

'Just thought I would pass through on my way out. We should go for a drink or something, sometime.' His face transformed, a wide smile blossomed.

What have I done? I wondered. 'All right, well, I'll see you later.'

Wednesday: last period. My Year 10 class have settled into their work. They were answering questions on chapters of the book we are reading. It's always the same students who put up their hands to read, until it comes to the chapter with swear words they've heard about, then all their hands go up. I steal their fun by choosing to read those parts myself, then casually skip over any profanity, and give them a stare before I return to reading theatrically.

From my peripheral line of sight, I saw Mrs Sundermeyer enter, in stealth, and go to the back of the classroom. She stood there, statuesque, not wishing to be seen, but also exerting her presence. I felt my body stiffen. My mouth felt as dry as burnt wood. After a few moments she left the class just as inconspicuously as she had entered. Then the bell rang – the sweetest relief.

*

Thursday: lunchtime. In the meeting room that muffled the sounds of screaming children in the playground, Mr McCormack and I sat for our line management meeting during the only free time we both had in a full day of lessons. He was new. I did not know much about him – he kept himself to himself at work. I admired the way he carried himself; he wore the same variations of a short-sleeved chequered shirt – even in the winter – dark trousers, and a large grizzly unkempt beard that covered his mouth and moved as he spoke.

'Sorry to rush, but we both know the routine . . .' he said, in a Scottish accent thicker than his beard. 'We'll have a general chat, and then set some objectives, and your plans.' I nodded along to each word, my eyes fixed on the mouth speaking beneath his beard.

He asked me what my objectives were for the year, what I really wanted out of my job. I gave an ambiguous answer, something that disguised the depths of my apathy: that the thing I wanted out of my job was nothing at all – the same thing I wanted out of life.

After a few moments of back-and-forth work-related banter and fake laughter, mostly on my part so as not to raise his suspicions about me, he asked me if I was happy. The word struck me like two cymbals clashing inside the hollow of my skull.

'Happy?' I replied.

'Yeah, happy. With your job?'

I felt a shortness of breath as if my throat was narrowed to the size of a straw. Happy.

I'm not sure what he meant, or why he had asked. What

was I to talk about? *I'm happier when I am not here, but I spend most of my time here; I must be here. But I'm happy enough with what I know here to still come back; maybe, like ghosts, we only return to haunt what we know; or are we the ones who are haunted? Life is a haunting. Happy? I'm not happy. I don't know what that means. I watched his eyes as he patiently waited for the answer he was looking for.*

'Yes.' I replied, one word, stunted, short. His thin-lipped smile disappeared into his beard, as he got up to leave. The bell rang.

Friday: after a long day – a long week, even – of stomping feet through corridors, screaming children, slamming doors, short naps during mundane meetings, I left my classroom and headed to the sports hall. I crept in unnoticed, at least that's what I thought, but Mr Black had long seen me, even without looking; he had a special ability of being grossly engaged in something distant, while aware of everything around him. He took the basketball club training sessions on Fridays after school. I watched as his voice boomed instructions, and the children quickly followed. He had a presence about him that was eternal, an air of grace that demanded respect.

'Baseline!' he roared, and the players quickly picked up the basketballs and sprinted to the end of the court. He gave commands that children followed and executed like professionals, which amazed me. There were times even when I came in and saw them sat on the floor reading, or doing their homework, instead of playing basketball, which amazed me more, considering how much that was a struggle for them in class. I watched in awe – it was rare to see this kind of submission from students, particularly in this school. I saw the students who were the most feared and aggressive fall in line as if foot soldiers to their general: even Kieron! He happened to look at me at that very moment, as if I had said it out loud. We made eye contact, stared, each letting the other know that they had been seen. Kieron formerly lived by his own rules in school, constantly in and out of provision, roaming corridors during lessons, swearing, disrupting, fighting, but somehow he was calm here, as though a person transformed, and that transformation made its way into his schoolwork. Though our paths had not crossed, we had seen each other, here, and that was enough. He and Duwayne were close. Duwayne used to come with Kieron to basketball practice, but over the years it became a war of attrition; and it was Duwayne who had lost that war.

I stayed a little while. As I walked out Mr Black looked over at me, winking, letting me know that I had been seen. As minute as this gesture was, it felt significant, and deeply appreciated. To be seen. I broke into a smile as I left.

Chapter 14

Peckriver Estate, London; 8.17 p.m.

I walked the dimly lit streets filled with parked cars and trees lurking. Home. It was odd how, over the years, it felt less and less like home, yet it was all the home I had ever known.

I looked up at this tall building – a tower block, in a dull grey colour, breaking the sky. Defiant against its backdrop of flashing city lights, opulence and monuments in the distance; so far in the distance, it was another world. We had lived and seen it all here; no electricity; a room full of candles, no heat; wear your coat inside; a floor with no carpet, the rusted wooden floorboard cutting into our feet. We had seen it all here, drug dealers, smoking and snorting at the end of the steps, police raids at 4 a.m., barking dogs and chases, broken windows, cold air breaking in, burglary and theft, not safe to walk through past a certain time unless you knew somebody who knew somebody who knew somebody, someone who jumped from the fourth floor trying to take their own life but only managing to break their legs. We watched him, laid there, body flat, knees inverted like a bird; his only wish was to fly, fly away from here. And fires blazing, touching the sky – a furious lover scorned.

But we had also seen bread, sugar, milk, shared and borrowed, sitting and eating with strangers until they too became family; children walking to school together every day, until they too became family. Conversations at the bottom of the block, exchanging life stories in the fifteen-second lift ride up, and sometimes longer if you were stuck. We had also seen parties; music so loud the party came to your living room, and leftover food being brought around; Christmas where no one was left alone; Halloween and trick or treats so intense we carried it on for days after. This was the place we all had known, the only place we called home.

I reached the front door of the building, and came in as someone was leaving. 'You all right?' we said to each other simultaneously. I didn't know his name but recognised him and knew he lived floors above us. At the steps of the ground floor were some young guys, tracksuits and hoods up, a puff of smoke lingering above them like a cloud at the peak of a mountain, plant smell wafting through the air. I looked at each one of them; and they looked back at me, not one of us breaking the stare; this act of defiance, this battle we found each other fighting, angry at everything outside of us; and everything including ourselves.

Sat at my desk for lunch, the new week brought nothing but a new heaviness. I could hear the roars and screams of children in the playground. I drowned them out by putting on my headphones and listening to the Ali Farka Touré & Toumani Diabaté *In the Heart of the Moon* album. I closed my eyes and imagined sitting in the hotel room they recorded the album in, being submerged in an air of esoteric magic through the sounds of the kora. I opened my eyes, and just as quickly as I closed them, the Year 11 class was sat in front of me, heads down in their books. That's how time seemed to pass lately, in flashes, moments coming and going in a blink of the eye.

Alex all the As was sat in the left corner front row, nearest to my desk, looking up intermittently, clamouring for attention and receiving none. In contrast to him, in the back-right corner seat furthest from my desk, was Duwayne, slouched on the chair, staring into the distance, demanding to be ignored. He had returned from suspension and received a hero's welcome. His defiance towards everyone save Mr Black was revered, but no one expected him to challenge Mr Black; it was as though he was the de facto head teacher, the authoritarian of the school. All the teachers were given a behaviour support plan on how to engage with Duwayne, and what to work towards. It created an air of trepidation around him, as if he was an explosive device that could be triggered at any moment.

As I stared at Duwayne for just a second too long, my memory flashed back to seeing his eyes under his hood on that bridge. He looked up at me and I wondered if he had remembered, if he had even known it was me. Nothing in his eyes – distant and despondent – seemed to reveal the answer so I returned to normal: classroom, teacher, student. With the class dismissed, I asked Duwayne to stay behind for a moment for 'a quick chat'. He was used to this. He did not move from his seat, let alone the slouched position he sat in, school-uniform trousers falling so low past his waist they revealed the grey tracksuit bottoms he wore underneath. He didn't respond to any of my initial questions: 'How are you doing?', 'Is everything okay?', 'Have you learned from your mistakes?' Instead, he sat there, still looking out into the distance, until I mentioned 'basketball', to which he responded with a twitch of the head, shoulders moving upright, like an alert wolf or soldier on guard.

'What do you know about ball?' he replied.

'I got a pretty mean crossover,' I said, nodding firmly along to reassure myself more than him. He chuckled, potentially showing some teeth and flashing a smile, but it was gone before it came. Truth is, I had not picked up a basketball for years, decades even, close enough to two, not since the London Towers basketball club had come to visit my secondary school, and my premature teenage growth spurt had singled me out as I was chosen to shoot a free throw, which I subsequently air-balled. The free jersey made up for the embarrassment. I wore it every day until the end of that year. I wondered where it was now. I wondered where all my old clothes were.

'Who's your favourite player?' he asked, now sitting up and facing me, eyes coming to life.

'LeBron James.'

'King James?'

'Yeah.'

'You know LeBron James?'

'I don't know him like that ... well, not any more. We fell out,' I said, with such certainty, as if it could be true. Duwayne looked at me with a confused face, unable to tell whether I was serious or not.

'Yeah, I dunked on him when we were playing one-on-one back in the day and we haven't spoken since.'

Duwayne didn't laugh, he just raised his eyebrows up and down. I imagined, in some alternate universe, it was true. Maybe I was the superstar professional basketball player, and LeBron James was a schoolteacher, the G.O.A.T.: the greatest of all teachers.

'Anyway, who's your favourite player?' I asked him.

'I ain't really got one.'

'No?' I replied, surprised. He shrugged his shoulders.

'Not even me?' He scoffed at the possibility. 'I'll tell you what,' I continued, 'why don't we play one-on-one, if you win, no homework ... ?'

'I never do it anyway.' He kissed his teeth, and looked away. 'Think I'm some fool?'

'All right, fair enough. If you win, I'll give you what you like the most ... a fresh pair of Nike Air Max. But if I win ... ' He looked back at me, sat up in his seat again, perked with attention. 'If I win, you've got to go to basketball training with Mr Black ... for the whole season!'

'Aaargh,' he groaned, then placed his hand on his chin, whilst covering his mouth, and sat momentarily in the pose of the thinking man statue. I watched him as the cogs in his brain went into gear.

'If I win, I get trainers. If I lose, I'll go training ... '

'Yes. For the WHOLE SEASON. You can't miss even one.'

'I'll go. But only if you come to the first session with me.'

'Okay, deal.' He stood, and we shook hands firmly, staring into each other's face with competitiveness and compassion.

'When shall we play?' he asked at the door, as he was leaving.

'Next week. I'll give you some time to practise,' I said and sneered confidently. He nodded and left, dunking the frame of the door on his way out.

I saw Jalil less frequently these days, but each time I saw him he exhibited a slight change, only noticeable with close attention. It was like watching a flower, left in a dark room, slowly lean towards the crack of light that had just broken through. However, Aminah was not just a crack of light to him, she was the dawn. We had been invited to Jalil's house for dinner; I was told that, of course, his other friends would also be there, and so would Aminah, an opportunity for us – the closest people in his life – to meet her. But really, it was more than that; it was a chance for Jalil to strategically evaluate how Aminah behaved around his closest friends, and to get an insight into what we thought of her.

I arrived at the front door and steadied myself. A long day's work can leave you exhausted; couple that with an evening of socialising, and you might end up comatose. At least for me, socialising was a drain on the body and the mind, sometimes with disastrous consequences; I remember spending days not speaking to anyone simply because my brain needed to reset. I had always been this way, locking myself in my room, waking up in the middle of the night just to listen to the silence.

As I raised my hands to knock, the door swung open and I was greeted with a bright smile and a very enthusiastic 'Hi' in a singing voice. I was certain it was Aminah, but I did not want to presume. She wore a scarf over her head, and a printed flower dress with long sleeves, and a pair of jeans – she was dressed up, in a casual sort of way.

'Come in. I heard shuffling behind the door, and I thought

I'd open ... I hope I didn't startle you,' she said, speaking so confidently, directing me into the house I already knew so well.

'No, not at all,' I replied courteously, smiling as I entered. I took off my shoes and presented the non-alcoholic glass bottle of some drink I had bought along with some baklava from Woody Grill. I could hear chatter in the living room, combined with the occasional explosions of laughter.

She received my gifts, and just as she began to say, 'I've heard so much about you ...' there came an interruption of 'Yoooooooooooooo!' breaking through the air, as Jalil came rushing towards me. We hugged warmly, patting each other on the back.

'This is Michael,' he said to Aminah, as she reciprocated with a smile.

'And this is Aminah.' Jalil nodded his head and raised his eyebrows at me in a self-satisfied way. I nodded along, validating him.

'I figured. Lovely to officially meet you.'

'Lovely to meet you, too,' Aminah replied, looking up between myself and Jalil.

'You have to tell me everything about him,' she said, placing her arm around Jalil and resting her hand on his stomach, for which I'm sure he would have quickly tensed his abs to impress her just as he'd seen her hand moving closer. I chuckled at the thought of Jalil quickly tensing his abs.

'Well,' I said, 'what can I say? He's a great guy', which seemed really monotone; rehearsed even, not really eliciting a response from either Jalil or Aminah. I continued: 'He paints, he plays the piano, he reads, he's really smart, he's so kind-hearted ... and he's got a motor, with a big engine.' Jalil and I shared a smirk between us.

'Oh gosh, don't encourage him about that bike. I'm trying to find a way to get him to stay off it.'

We entered the living room, where there were fewer people than I had originally thought, which made me feel much more comfortable. Maybe it was the raucous laughter that made me imagine a room full of people all waiting to see who is going to walk in next. At least, that's what I expected from Jalil, but perhaps this smaller, more reserved gathering was an influence of Aminah's. I was introduced to the three other guests, then we took our seats around the dinner table. I sat directly opposite Jalil and Aminah, watching their display of newfound romance. After a few moments, Jalil abruptly stood up, unhooked his arm from Aminah and stormed out of the room.

Chapter 15

Dallas, Texas; 10.09 p.m.

The plane lands. Michael tries to figure a way out of this airport, too quiet for a Saturday evening. He looks up at the information board ahead, and just below is a woman, blonde hair, blue eyes, who is staring at him. There is something behind her cold stare, a fury, a fire, but not of passion; not the kind of fire that warms, but the kind that burns. He looks away and goes to collect his baggage as she watches his every move with intense suspicion. Michael waits outside in the pick-up area, below its large sign. He is constantly checking his phone, now low on battery, for any calls or messages from Rodrique, who promised to be at the airport by 10 p.m. to pick him up – or even earlier, just in case – but has still not shown.

He starts to panic, wondering if he is waiting in the right place, and if his phone runs out of battery, he'll be stranded.

> I've landed. Where you at? I'm waiting by the airport car park.

He sends the message to Rodrique, without any indication that it's been received. Several cars pass by, each one eviscerating the hope he has of Rodrique's arrival. Michael removes the traveller's backpack, heavy on his shoulders, and sits down. It is now 10.45 p.m. He is thinking of making alternative arrangements, but his fatigue, hunger and lack of sleep – having been sat next to a man who took up more than his own space on the flight and snored all the way through – have left him feeling too much in disarray.

A burgundy-red car, with grey-metallic caps, wheels worn, gathering a light brown tinge of dust, pulls up where he is sat. He looks up and realises it is Rodrique as he appears from the driver's seat, towering above the car. Rodrique steps out and towers above the car, walks around it and now towards him. Rodrique takes up space as he walks; this cannot go unnoticed. *When they said everything is twice as big in Texas, I did not realise they also meant people.* Rodrique looks the same as he does in the Instagram pictures; a fade haircut, light stubble covering a well-defined jawline, twisted hair at the top, and a diagonal cut-crease smile.

'Hey, man.' Rodrique walks towards him, chuckling; a soft, vulnerable laugh as if apologising for the lateness that he does not openly acknowledge. They greet each other, wrapping hands, and then arms into a hug. Rodrique appears in real life just as he does in the digital world: a people person, amicable and relaxed – a reflection of all the pictures he posts on his social media. They had gotten to know each other over some years when it was accidentally discovered, through mutual tagged throwback pictures, that they were related; cousins, sort of – distance unknown, a long and complicated history that neither was sure of. Initially, they laughed at how in African families, you gain one new relative a year: a cousin, an uncle, an aunty, and on the rare occasion, a parent. Rodrique, who is also a DJ, appeared to always be the life of the party – and if for nothing else, Michael wanted to know what it felt to live like that. Michael had called him to say that he was coming and Rodrique had willingly and quickly obliged.

After passing the traffic, they are on the highway. Rodrique is talking a lot. Michael notices the twang in his accent, different to California – slower, more relaxed. His demeanour humours Michael. They arrive at a house in a dimly lit residential quarter. They park the car and enter. There is a group of guys inside, music blaring, in a bare living-room space, appearing dressed in what could almost be a uniform: durag, white singlet, basketball shorts, socks and slippers, or Air Jordans. They're playing NBA 2K on a wide-screen TV. Rodrique introduces him as 'my boy from the YOU-KAY'.

'You're from England? Bet. How y'all get around out there?'

'They probably got Uber Horse.'

An eruption of laughter fills the room. Michael joins in, feigning his laughter. He should have anticipated this, the immature jokes, particularly being around college students.

Nonetheless, he enjoys the moment. As Michael sits down, he notices, in the corner of the room, a barber's chair and mirror, with a complete set of trimmers. A barbershop, in someone's house. Smart. In the half-hour they are sat down, numerous people come in and out for a haircut. Bluu, the barber, grins widely – his hair is neatly trimmed and faded to perfection, an advert for the service he offers – as he cuts hair whilst on the phone.

'What kind of girls you got out there in England, man?' This is a bizarre question; Michael is unsure how to answer. But whatever he does say, Bluu responds with 'Bet', and Michael pretends to understand what this means.

Bluu continues, 'I gotta ask you, bruh, who's better, London hoes or Dallas hoes?'

'I don't know, man. That's not really my thing,' Michael answers coyly, keeping it brief.

'What's the moooove?' Rodrique reappears, very timely, interrupting the awkward conversation.

They're on the road once again, driving through the streets. Michael's not sure where they are, he recognises neither sign nor street, however the anonymity of location settles him into a comfortable feeling. The shops are closed, the lights are off in the houses, everything indicates a town gone to sleep, a town at its most peaceful. Rodrique drives with care and diligence, different to his extrovert personality. Michael feels exhausted but the fresh air from the open window, cool breeze rushing in, is keeping him awake.

'You listen to Trap?' Rodrique asks, which Michael responds to by nodding and shrugging shoulders nonchalantly as if he really does. Rodrique turns up the radio until the bassline is so loud and booming, it lifts him out of the back seat. Michael recognises the music but could not tell one song from another. He has learned many of them from his students – a desire to extend his youth and remain relevant. A wave of school and playground memories comes rushing into his mind, hijacking his daydream with sounds of cheering and screaming, playground fracas, slamming doors and echoing corridors. He promptly blocks it out.

They slow down in a picturesque, dimly lit residential area, where the houses have front yards with fresh green grass. They get out and walk towards a house that has the low vibration of a thumping bassline and excited chatter seeping out. A tall, square-framed young man stands in front of the door.

'Just a little kickback,' Rodrique says as they walk up to the house. Rodrique daps the young man at the door, and he lets them in while looking at Michael suspiciously.

Michael acts cool, as if he has been here many times before and knows the routine; he does the universal Black man head-nod as he walks in, which the young man returns. The room is filled with smoke, light and airy, floating, like a winter fog, up to the ceiling. Its smell is botanical, and Michael can feel his eyelids twitch and turn red as he inhales the second-hand smoke. They make their way through the house towards the thumping music vibrating the walls.

Everyone in this room is smoking. Michael has been offered and said no so many times, people are starting to wonder whether he's undercover. He finally hits a blunt, the smoke rises out of his mouth into the air like a cumulus cloud. Rodrique has disappeared again. Michael stands in the corner sipping from his bottle, overhearing vapid conversations about sex, college, money, drugs. *I don't belong here. I don't belong anywhere.*

Miranda has a harmonising voice, the kind that lulls you into a soft sleep. After being the only two left in their corner of the room, she is talking to Michael about nothing, and he is listening closely not because he cares, but because his body is calling for hers; and hers for his. A visceral reaction, like a teenager with raging hormones, a feeling he would otherwise not entertain but at this moment, the only question he asks himself is *Why not?* She strokes his arm every time she laughs, and says 'you're funny', whilst flicking her hair behind her ears. They share a smoke. Her smile is bright, her teeth a pearly white, and her eyes a lighthouse guiding him to shore.

'How long are you in town for? I hope we get to talk some more,' Miranda says, her fingers tracing his forearm. Michael smiles back at her. His lips tremble. His mind flutters at the thought of kissing her, but he resists. *I can't get close.*

'Yo, where you been? Come here.' A deep voice breaks Michael's fantasy. Michael opens his eyes, un-purses his lips.

'This is my boyfriend, Jamal.' Miranda makes the reluctant introduction. Jamal looks Michael up and down, and says 'Whassup?', barely acknowledging his presence. Jamal grabs Miranda by the arm, his fingernails squeezing into her skin.

'Let's get outta here,' Jamal whispers into her ear, quiet but loud.

'No. I haven't finished my drink,' she replies. Jamal takes the drink out of her hand and gulps it down.

'You have now,' he says, digs his fingertips into her deeper, then pulls her with him as he paces out. Miranda looks back at Michael as they leave.

After a few moments, which feels like hours, Rodrique returns, signalling to Michael it's time to go. They're back in the car driving through somewhere else he's not familiar with, but at this point he does not care. It is late, he is tired and wants to sleep. He stirs, quietly and firmly. They park somewhere, and Rodrique gets out of the car and leaves, but not before mumbling something inaudible. He returns fifteen minutes later.

'Ay, you look dead tired, man.' Rodrique laughs. 'I'm going to drop you off back to mine, a'ight?' he says.

'Cool,' Michael replies, with certainty, crossing the border into frustration.

Michael walks back into the house, now empty, not even bothering to switch on the lights. The moonlight creeps through a crack in the curtains that cover the back door to the garden. Michael lies back on the sofa where, just a few hours ago, the guys were playing video games and smoking. But it bothers him not, his fatigue is overbearing.

A flash of light wakes Michael, but he keeps his eyelids closed, pretending to sleep, and it turns the inside of his eyelids a glowing orange. He hears the shuffle of footsteps around him, heavy and with a limp. A hand nudges him and attempts to whisper his name, but the voice has so much bass, it echoes. It's Rodrique. It shocks him upright.

'Yo, let's go get some food,' Rodrique says. 11 a.m.

'Cool,' Michael replies, as if he had any other choice. He looks over and the barber's chair is empty. None of the other guys are here, but remnants of their presence is scattered all over. Dressed in the same clothes as the night before, he puts on his trainers as they head outside.

They're back on the road again, making several stops along the way. Each journey is filled with stops. Nothing here is ever close to each other, even opposite sides of the road feel like separate towns. They halt at the red lights.

'So, are we going to get tea or something for breakfast?' Michael asks.

'Tea?' Rodrique replies, then explodes into a thunderous laughter. 'This dude wants tea,' he mumbles under his breath.

'We'll get you some real food,' Rodrique says. They make another journey, until they arrive at another fast-food restaurant.

$5,981

Chapter 16

Dallas, Texas; 12.15 p.m.

As they exit the car, Michael feels the sun beat him down into submission. 'This is the cooler time of year,' Rodrique says, laughing. Michael struggles to imagine what kind of inferno their summers must be. They return to the house to find it full of the guys from the night before: Bluu cutting hair in the semi-operational barbershop corner of the front room, and the rest, whose names Michael has yet to commit to memory and has no desire to.

'Aay, London!' Bluu excitedly greets Michael with the new moniker he has no choice but to accept. It could be worse, it's a huge improvement on the 'African booty scratcher' or 'freshie', nicknames Michael remembers being teased with when he was at school. Michael feigns excitement with his response as he goes to find a space to sit down. They unpack the food brought back from the Whataburger. It makes sense why Michael was told to wait until they got back home to eat. It feels like he's part of a long-standing ritual, like he is being included in something greater than he could even begin to understand. Michael unravels the burger from its wrapping, and it is so big he needs both hands to hold it together. The rest of the food is shared out, but before Michael takes his first bite, he can feel the eyes of everyone in the room staring at him.

'London gotta eat first. We need to know what he thinks,' Bluu says, which is what everyone else is waiting for. Michael feels the pressure mount, as though he has travelled thousands of miles to participate in the food culture of a sub-group unknown by the wider world; this, his only chance of acceptance. He takes his first big bite of the burger. It tastes like rubber, sand, oil, and other things not meant to be eaten.

'So, what do you think?' Rodrique asks.

'I love it, mate,' Michael replies.

'Mate,' Bluu imitates and laughs. He now starts to add 'mate' at the end of every sentence.

'Next, we gotta get you to smash some Dallas hoes before you leave ... Mate,' Bluu adds, laughing some more.

'It's end-of-semester party tomorrow night too; you gotta roll,' Rodrique adds.

Tonight is the end-of-term dance. They're driving through downtown Dallas, and, for the first time, Michael sees the city come to life; nonetheless, it still carries a lugubrious mystery. Rodrique and Bluu are in the front. Michael is in the back seat. The car slowly fills with smoke, like a fog, from the blunt being smoked and passed around between them.

Michael loses himself in his thoughts.

'Guys, let me ask you something. What do you think happens when you die?'

'What?' Bluu replies, in a surprised high-pitched voice.

'Are you that high already? Barely even started smoking.' Rodrique laughs.

'Nah, nah. I'm not high, man. I'm just asking. What do you think happens? Like, is there a heaven and hell? Is it nothing? Do you come back to life as a bird?'

'I don't know, man,' Bluu responds contemplatively. 'My mom used to say there's a heaven.'

'Used to?'

'Yeah. She took us to church every Sunday. Until she died. I stopped going after that.' Bluu took a long pause, inhales a puff after taking the blunt from Michael and blows out a soft cloud of smoke. 'All I know is I'm alive right now, and I need to make some money.' Bluu laughs, sticks out his hand, and Rodrique daps him, saying, 'I feel you.'

'In my culture,' Rodrique continues, 'when you die, you become an ancestor. And you re-join your ancestors in the spiritual world. There, you live in peace with them.' He looks back at Michael. 'You know what I'm saying?'

Michael nods vigorously as if he understands what Rodrique is saying. He doesn't. But he becomes increasingly interested.

'You ever get curious about it? About dying?' Michael asks.

'What? Why? You can't just die and come back,' Bluu replies dismissively.

'Who said anything about coming back?' Michael says, after taking the blunt back and blowing out some smoke.

'You trippin', man. You need some pussy.' They all combust in laughter. Michael's thoughts drift into Miranda. Her skin, her lips, her body. His urges rise stronger than before; he just wants to fuck, wants to feel, as a raging lust takes over his body. Last night Michael and Miranda spoke in the garden while the guys bonded over video games and smokes. She saw him outside looking up at the stars and decided to join him. Michael knows he cannot let her get close; he remembers the vow he made to himself. That no one else should share his burden but him. It is what he wants. *But what I want is truly beyond wanting. It is not wanting anything that has brought me to what I want – and that is to die.*

They continue through the city and pass a set of traffic lights. Flashing red and blue strobes of light fill the car.

'Fuck,' Bluu exclaims.

'Chill, bro!' Rodrique exclaims.

'It's the cops, man. Fuck,' Bluu says, whilst the flashing blue and red continues. A single siren echoes.

Michael's heart jumps into a panic. His throat has swollen as if something is trying to escape out of his mouth. He starts to splutter and cough, either from the smoke or from the fear. Rodrique reaches across into the glove compartment and sprays air freshener around the car, winding down the windows, letting the old air escape and the fresh air in. There is a sudden stillness in the car.

Michael's hands are trembling. He pats himself down, trying to look for his phone. He starts to pant, mouth open like a dog. Rodrique finds a place and then pulls the car over to the sidewalk. Emerging from the dark, a shadow of a man nears until it reveals itself as the police officer. He is pale-faced, clean shaven, hat tipped low covering his eyes.

'Good evening,' the police officer says, flashing his flashlight into the car, first at Rodrique, who, unlike Bluu, remains immovably calm, and then at Michael in the back. The officer's gun, perched on the leather holster on his waist, glistens underneath the moonlight. It lights the officer's hand delicately placed above it, fingertip of his index finger creeping.

'Good evening, sir,' Bluu replies, stuttering, sweating, noticeably nervous.

'Licence and registration.' Rodrique slowly reaches for his driver's licence. The police officer takes it and walks back to his car. A crackle of voices resonates through the radio. The tension is thick in the air, as if everyone is sharing the same breath. Michael feels his leg begin to tremble as though he were having withdrawal symptoms, a dog abandoned in the cold rain. There is a deathly silence in the car as they wait; deathly is not enough, this silence is a genocide.

'Where y'all off to tonight, then?' the police officer asks, as he returns the licence to Rodrique.

'We're going to the student party downtown,' Rodrique replies, stuttering, his tone tingling with frustration.

'Oh, I figured y'all were college students. I've stopped a few tonight already. Y'all don't look like college students, though, but I figured you were.'

They force laughter at his dubious statement. The police officer pauses and looks around in the car one last time.

'Y'all have a good night now, ya hear? And don't do anything I wouldn't do.'

'Yes, sir.'

The police officer walks back to his car, boots stomping on the tarmac. He gets in, then slowly pulls away. The sounds of the city come back to life like a body resuscitated.

'Fuck!!!' Bluu erupts out of nowhere, taking deep breaths, his cool, collected demeanour shattered.

'Chill,' Rodrique replies, his one simple word setting the atmosphere to calm.

They park the car and get out. Other students pass by, well dressed, going to the same place. Michael looks around. The air is filled with a bitter eeriness. A single tree looms at the bottom of the parking lot, standing in solitary sadness. A loud noise echoes and a flock of birds fly out from the tree, and then go back to it. Birds? Or bats: jet black, tipped wings, hanging upside down. *I have never seen a flock of bats, but it makes sense that it would happen here, now. This city reminds me of Gotham, were it a real place.* Michael looks up at the night sky and imagines a Bat sign across it. *But why would anyone come and save us? Come and save me? I am beyond saving.* Rodrique calls Michael over. He rejoins them.

They enter the club. Everyone is young and pretty, skin clear and hair neatly laid, even the men – especially the men. Michael tries not to speak else he gives away the fact he is an outsider, an imposter trying to blend. He remains quiet and stays close to Rodrique and Bluu as they navigate the room, greeting all who pass, like an entourage of celebrities. It is dark. He can barely make out the faces of those up close, let alone in the distance. He wants to find Miranda. His body calls for her. The heat within is greater than the heat outside. *To deny our impulses is to deny the very thing that makes us human.*

He navigates between rooms, searching back and forth. He spots Bluu in the centre of a large group, dancing with a bottle of drink in hand, waving it through the air. Michael separates from the entourage and goes to the bar. Bluu's voice echoes in his head about 'Dallas hoes', and so, remembering his journey, he plans to live a little. There is a row of girls lined up at the bar, the two closest to him caught up in chatter about the boyfriend who is letting them down. Michael leans over, smiling, and catches their attention. They look at him, as if to question why he is looking at them.

'Can I buy you drink?' Michael says. One girl says nothing, the other lifts her glass in the air, showing it is full, and then looks away. Just as Michael leans in to carry on the conversation, he feels a strong, open palm hand on his chest.

'We good over here, bro,' a deep resounding voice says, as it glides Michael to one side. He looks up to see a basketball player/athlete frame, which his eyes meet at the shoulders.

'Look, I didn't mean no trou—' and as Michael reaches up to pat the man on his shoulders, he accidentally knocks the drink out of the man's hand.

'What's your problem, man?' The man looks down at him.

'I . . . I . . . I didn't mean to . . . ' Michael stutters and feels his heart begin to pound. 'Let me get that for you.' Michael calls the bartender over. 'Whatever this man is drinking.'

'Henny.'

'You weren't drinking no Henny,' the girl says.

'Hennessy,' Michael requests, 'er, make it a bottle.'

The bartender goes to get the drink. The girls turn and face him, shocked, so does the man.

'Actually . . . ' Michael continues, grinning and dramatically slapping his bank card on the table, which the bartender picks up, 'make that two bottles, three even. Make sure everybody at the bar gets a glass. Fuck it, you only live once, right? I have something to celebrate . . . '

Michael is quickly surrounded by a flock of girls, and

guys, who mingle around him, assuming his celeb-like status. Michael feels intoxicated by the attention as much as the drink.

'A TOAST ...' Michael shouts whilst raising his glass, 'to new beginnings.' The flock cheers with excitement as he drinks. 'And the inevitable end,' he whispers quietly to himself.

Michael turns again to order more drinks at the bar. He feels a pair of delicate hands on his shoulders, easing his tension. He turns around and sees Miranda, light, airy, tipsy. Floating like a cloud, she lays her head on his chest as she hugs him.

'I've been looking for you,' she says. 'I missed you.' His heart beats a little faster with excitement, legs shaking out of rhythm as she wraps her arms around him.

'You're not leaving until I have a dance,' she says.

Miranda pulls him to the dance floor, turns around and presses her body into his, feeling all his hardness, synchronised to the rhythm of her softness, moving side by side, hip to hip. Michael lowers his head closer to hers and breathes on to her neck, smelling her skin, scent of jasmine, a flower, a field; the curls of her hair a pillow-like softness.

'But what about your boyfriend, Jamal?' Michael asks, as he presses his body into hers.

'What about Jamal?' she replies.

They dance body on body, the rest of the club disappearing until it is just them.

Miranda lowers her hand from chest to stomach to in-between his thighs, searching.

'Let's get out of here,' she says, and takes him by the hand as they walk through the crowd out of the club. They step outside into the fresh air. They stroll through the dimly lit streets, setting the scene for eerie romance. Miranda kisses him, pressing him up against a wall. Michael kisses her back, searching her body with his hands. She unbuckles his belt, unzips his jeans.

'I can't do this,' Michael says, exasperated, and steps away.

'What?'

'I can't do this. I can't. I'm sorry.'

'What? Why the fuck not?'

'I can't. I just can't.'

Michael breaks free from her and begins to walk away.

'What the hell is wrong with you?' He hears her scream and curse until her voice becomes inaudible. He walks away, faster and faster, picking up the pace until he is running, running, running – away from her, away from himself, away from everything.

$3,711

Chapter 17

Colindale, North London; 7.15 p.m.

I followed Jalil into the kitchen. Aminah had not noticed his outburst. I did not expect her to; learning what is spoken through the body is like learning a new language. She was not yet fluent. And though I was also not fluent, I had at least been around long enough to understand some of the words. I opened the kitchen door and found Jalil pacing up and down inside, cracking his knuckles.

'Are you all right?' I asked, as if I didn't already know that he wasn't. What I wanted to say was, 'Tell me what's wrong', but Jalil does not like having assumptions made about him, particularly ones that make him look weak or out of control. He grunted and paced. I walked to him, placed my hands on his shoulders, forcing him to stand still for a moment until he looked me in the eyes.

'Is it Aminah?' He shook his head.

'So, what is it?'

'He's coming,' Jalil said, his eyes filled with a controlled panic.

'Who?'

'Baba.'

'Oh,' I replied, my confusion self-evident. I was not aware that this was a thing to panic over. I also envied the fact that this was a thing that I could not ever say, that my father was coming home. What a strange thing to envy.

'Is that a bad thing?'

'Yes ... I mean, no. It's not bad, but it's just too soon. He's coming. He hasn't said why. I'm not ready.'

'When? And not ready for what?'

'He'll be here next week. And I'm not ready for him. For everything he's going to do and say.'

'Like what? He'll just be happy to see you.'

'He's going to say the same thing he does on the phone, about marriage, and getting a proper job, and all that ...'

'But you have Aminah, surely that makes things easier.'

'I haven't told him about her.'

'Why not?'

'What am I going to say? "Yo, Dad, I'm seeing this girl, she's cute. Not that serious yet. By the way, you might know her dad, he's got a restaurant on Edgware Road."'

'So why did you organise this dinner?'

'She did. She wanted to meet my friends. I think she was getting suspicious of my privacy and the fact I didn't want to post any pictures on social media. And she said she wasn't sure about coming around when it's just me and her ... too much temptation, apparently.'

'But you like her?'

'Yeah! Of course, I'm not blind.'

'Look, I think you're overthinking it. You're just anxious. It'll be fine.'

I pulled him in close for a hug. His warmth enveloped me. The smell of the scented oils he buys from the brothers outside Brixton station lulled me into a familiar feeling of comfort. I breathed him in, and held him closer, not wanting to let go.

'I was wondering where you two got to?' Aminah said, as she walked in to Jalil and me. We quickly separated.

'We were just having a chat,' I replied, smiling enough for the both of us. We rejoined the guests, who were now eating their dessert: a selection of baklava with tea.

Watching Aminah and Jalil's growing relationship made me think of my own.

'The problem with the West is that it creates the Other, and then resents you for being it; being prejudiced against you for something that emerges from their imagination.'

'They actually believe they were the inventors of civilisa-tion centring themselves in every—'

'No. I don't think they believe it necessarily, but privilege is self-serving, and they must adhere to that which serves them.'

'That's true, they had no problem with Africans or Muslims teaching them maths and science, and our civilisations being the cultural and intellectual centres of the medieval and pre-colonial era, across the Middle East and in Africa, where they came to learn and be educated.'

'But they do have a problem with you covering your head.'

'Or having a beard, or a backpack.'

'Unless, of course, you're in Shoreditch in a pair of skinny jeans and New Balance trainers.'

'Hey, that's not nice ... I wear skinny jeans and New Balance trainers.'

'They were not fashionable to wear in school times. Trust me, I had a pair and got bullied for it. That "NB" sign was ugly.'

'Any sign that wasn't the Nike tick was ugly back then.'

'Hand-me-downs.'

'It still is, to me.'

'I'm about the no-brand life now ... and thrifting.'

'Very hipster.'

'Hipster? Our aunties and uncles have been doing "thrifting" since we first came into this country. We just called it something different back then.'

'Yeah, we called it being poor. And we got teased for it.'

'Now it's "in".'

'But that's just it, isn't it? Everything is in cycles: things come and things go.'

'Then, might I suggest,' interceded Jalil, 'without presumption, that we have overlooked a rather significant detail; that perhaps this ... resentment for the Other has always existed, they merely did not yet have the power to act upon it.' The table went quiet.

'Racism and prejudice are predicated upon fear. And at the root of all fear is awe. They fear you, because they admire you. They want to be you, without being you. Remember, all empires have risen and fallen, but only His is eternal, Alhamdulillah. So, until this empire also falls, let us toast ... ' The room joined in raising their glasses of tea. 'For we have air in our lungs, blood flowing through our veins and love beating in our hearts.' He finished, cup held in the air while looking over at Aminah, and me looking back at him.

*

I'm not sure why I decided to go to church today, but something compelled me, pulled me up and out, something stronger than my fatigue, than my desire to sleep. I was not given the overzealous greeting reserved for first-timers; also, my sporadic attendance touted me as the immovably uncommitted. I arrived in time for the latter part of Pastor Baptiste's sermon.

I spotted Mami sat in the front row of the pews, palms held together, leaning forwards as if each word spoken by Pastor Baptiste was drawing her in closer and closer and closer. I blocked out his voice, muting all noise to an absolute silence and just watched as he flapped his arms onstage and paced back and forth, excited but simultaneously calm and composed. He appeared more entertainer than pastor, the way the congregation was reacting to him.

I caught up with Mami after the sermon. She was less surprised to see me, and reacted with a simple kiss on the cheek, as if we had bumped into each other accidentally at the supermarket or the bus stop. She was no longer seeking surprise visits, they were unsatisfactory, she wanted commitment.

'Pastor, you know my son Michael.'

Pastor Baptiste greeted me enthusiastically, still, his mouth a frame of happiness. I held my smile back. He shook my hand firmly, and let his stare linger a little longer than usual. He did not stay to speak of rain as blessings or prayers, or some other abstract symbolism. I called Mami to go and she told me to wait for a moment as she needed to speak to someone. She went back into the church and through the dimly lit corridors. I could see her talking to the Pastor. She seemed different, jumpy, like a fan at a concert or a crushing schoolgirl. Pastor Baptiste placed both of his hands on her shoulders and looked intensely into her eyes. I could not hear what was said. He kissed her on the cheek as they hugged then parted. Their connection seemed beyond the physical. I felt a heat rise within me, as if witnessing something that shouldn't be happening.

'I was thinking about inviting him for dinner,' Mami said as we left the church to make our way home.

'What for?' I replied bluntly, surprising even myself. Mami gave me 'the look' that only strict parents possess, which, even at this age, I had not yet formed successful rebellion against. I adjusted myself and asked again, correctly this time.

'Because he is our pastor, and I would like to give him thanks for all his work, with a meal,' I noticed the 'our' in her speech, it was intentional – Mami was calculated and obstinate, perhaps the only thing we had in common, 'and I think it would be good for you to meet and, you know, talk. Get to know each other.' The truth reveals itself, once the mask is pulled off. Talk. The word itself is a loaded gun aimed at you from any direction.

'Does he not have plans? A family? A wife and kids who he must prioritise his dinners with?'

'No. He is committed to his work, to his purpose.'

I had no retort. I did not reply, I simply sank into my own quiet. I knew that Mami had told me about dinner not because she sought my approval, she had merely told me to inform me I had to attend.

The following week, one evening, I returned home to find dinner prepared. The cutlery was neatly laid; Mami used the three-course silver knife and forks, and the blue ceramic plates with the white patterns revealing the hills and valleys of an unknown place. She hasn't used these plates since ... I can't remember when, we don't get visitors much nowadays. But I remember the dinners we had with Father. How we would hold hands and pray, and I would look up from between them at their tower of love. Father, the man who I thought more and more of as the years passed; a wound that never heals.

'I'm sorry for my lateness, Pastor Baptiste,' I said, after greeting Mami and settling into my seat. 'I had loads of marking to do at work and got held behind in a couple of meetings.' Those meetings were actually Sandra and I, in my classroom, seeing who could do the Maltesers challenge: lying down on the table with a Malteser at the top of your pursed lips whilst you blow out, keep it hovering in the air and successfully eat it afterwards – my record was eight seconds.

'Oh, no need to apologise,' Pastor Baptiste replied, with attempted grace. 'You are doing good work. What is this food? It's delicious!' he spluttered excitedly, whilst staining the bib he wore. I looked at him, unimpressed. I looked at Mami and could see she was holding back her natural inclination of telling him to 'clean it up', which she would have done were it me.

'Pondu,' Mami replied.

'Pon-du,' he tried to repeat. I hated the way he said pondu. For the first time, I noticed his torn accent from the Islands. The food was special. It was Father's favourite food. And Mami only used to cook it when I came home to visit from university. It was so rare, and exciting. But she hardly ever cooks it now, not since I moved back in; who knew moving out again would take this long. It deflated me, being so behind in life; no partner, no place to live, no kids. Where was my life going?

'So, Pastor, where are you from?' I asked, with urgency, and regret, for I wanted to know, but did not want to hear him talk.

'Well ...' he chortled, before wiping his mouth with the bib under his chin. 'You could say I'm from all over,' he continued, impressed at his quip.

'Where would you say you're from?'

'I was born here.'

'And your parents? Are you married? Did you go to university?' I asked.

'Michael, that's enough questions. Pastor did not come to be interrogated.'

'It's quite all right,' he replied, laughing nervously before continuing. 'I was born here, but my family are from the Caribbean, by way of Jamaica, if you will. I spent most of my childhood there, with my grandparents, and then came back here during my teens. Hence, the slight twang in my accent you have probably noticed – my mother could not get rid of it completely no matter how much she told me to "speak properly".' He chuckled to soften the tension in the air. I looked at Pastor Baptiste with the expectation that he was going to continue his life story.

'And ...' I prompted impatiently.

'Well, when I came back things were a bit rough during my teenage years. But I was lucky enough to attend university and come out with a degree. I did all kinds of jobs, from cleaner to stacking shelves at the supermarket to security guard to teacher. I loved it. But I had to move on, I got wrapped up in some issues that were unresolved, let's put it that way. And then I found my calling . . . '

'Which is . . . ?'

'Which is what I'm doing now.'

'Okay, Michael, perhaps you could now give Pastor a chance to finish his food?' Mami said. The tone of her voice was a question, but the look in her eyes was a threat.

'Michael could always come to see me at church if he ever wanted to find out more,' Pastor Baptiste said invitingly. After the Pastor finished eating the food, and wiped his mouth and lips delicately with the napkin he had tucked into his shirt, Mami cleared the plates and returned with tea.

'Well, there's something we wanted to talk to you about. There was a reason for this dinner.' Mami spoke after moments of silence and slurping, mostly from the Pastor.

'We wanted to tell you something . . . ' she continued; her tone changed into something more propitiating.

'Pastor Baptiste and I are . . . we are . . . ' Mami stuttered through her words. 'We have the intention of marrying. And have come to you to let you know – for your blessing.'

They reached across the table and held hands as if they had rehearsed this moment. I was in shock. My face remained still, frozen, immovable, as if it had been carved into resistance from alabaster. I said nothing.

'The guy is an absolute madman,' I said exasperatedly to Sandra.

'Mr Barnes?' she replied, unconvinced.

'Yes, Mr Barnes.'

'Mr Barnes from Barnes who hums "Ride of the Valkyries" whilst he's waiting for the microwave in the staff kitchen? Who cycles on one of them folded bikes, and wears a helmet and hi-vis jacket? The same man who is always offering to make everyone tea and goes on weekend trips alone to check out the different valleys of England and then uploads pictures of him with his thumbs up on Instagram?'

'Yes. Weird that you know him so well, but yes, the same guy.'

'Okay, so what happened?'

'First thing, you abandoned me. I'm sure you knew this would happen, but we'll get to that later. I thought I got there first, but there he was, already waiting, popped up out of nowhere. We didn't quite know what to do as we were both expecting you to lead the day, seeing as it was your bright idea we all hang out, so we went to get some food and then noticed a pub where they were showing the football. We decide to go in. I thought it weren't a bad idea, at least we won't have to talk much. Now I haven't watched football since . . . never mind, you probably wouldn't know.'

'Why wouldn't I know?'

'Do you watch football?'

'No.'

'See.'

'But that doesn't mean I wouldn't know.'

'Ugh. Let's stick to the story. So, we're sitting down together, watching. At this point, I don't even know which teams are playing, but I'm supporting the team that everyone else in the pub is – because that's just the smart thing to do.

And we are absolutely surrounded by them, and they're doing the chants and all.

'Mr Barnes keeps reacting to every missed opportunity or close call for THE OTHER TEAM. I'm looking at him like, "What the hell are you doing?", but he continues relentlessly.

'Now, I thought he didn't support either team because he was talking about "if they were showing Barnes, you'd get to see some real football", or something like that. Does Barnes even have a football team?'

'How would I know?'

'At this point, the other fans are starting to look at us really uncomfortably and aggressively. I'm obviously trying to ignore, sinking my face further into my drink, but I can feel their stares on my skin.

'Then the other team scores, 1–0. Mr Barnes pumps his fist and comes out with "get in", and there is a deadly silence in the room. The score remains 1–0 and with each passing minute, the tension increases; the air gets thicker in the room. I develop a cough; I think it was the anxiety of it all, which only drew more attention to us.

'Wait, why are you laughing?'

'Because I can imagine where all of this is going. And that is so something you would typically do, just make the situation worse.'

'I haven't even done anything yet. Mr Barnes says he's thirsty again and offers to get some drinks. I say yes and decide to join him. As he gets up and walks, he bumps into this big, burly bald guy with tattoos, who was carrying three drinks with both his hands in a kind of triangle formation. The drinks spill all over his jeans and shoes, but he doesn't drop the glasses. "Watch it, mate," he says. Mr Barnes replies with, "Oh, fuck off!" But that's not all: please tell me why his accent changes from bubbly northerner to east London Cockney! The other guy puts down his glasses, squares up to Mr Barnes, obviously Barnes is small, so he's looking at the guy's chest.

'He says, "You got a problem, mate?" and Mr Barnes replies with, "I ain't your mate. You call me 'mate' one more time and I'm gonna slap the tattoos off your forehead."'

Sandra looked at me with her jaw hanging southward half-way to the floor.

'Listen, and then he—'

There was a knock on the door, which jolted both Sandra and me into the air. Mr Barnes appeared, peeking his head through the door. He was his usual self: shy, awkward, reserved, stuttering a greeting, uncertain whether it would be received.

'I didn't see you in your classroom . . . was going to pop by and say hello,' Mr Barnes said sheepishly.

'I'll catch up with you later,' I replied.

Mr Barnes nodded, swivelled his head back out of the door and left.

'Did you see that? The madness in his eyes.'

'Ha ha, yeah, a proper hard-nut he is. Finish the story, then,' Sandra said in a fit of laughter.

'No point, to be honest,' I huffed.

'Yeah, make up stories that make your boring life seem more exciting than it really is.'

Chapter 18

Grace Heart Academy School, London; 4.15 p.m.

The pitter-patter of feet and the sound of leather balls bouncing on the wooden floor echoed through the double doors where I stood before going in. I had gotten changed as fast as I could but was still late. I wondered if Duwayne was already there. I had beaten him in the one-on-one. After a week of intense gym, running and going to the park to shoot, he was beating me easily so I simply resorted to using my height and weight, after all I'm 6 foot 1 and he's 5 foot 9. I just backed him down and shot over him, using my grown-man strength like any logical person would. It was a close call, down to the final point, me winning 11–10 on the last shot; I claimed I took it easy because I did not want to embarrass him, but inside I felt as though there was more pressure on me playing this one-on-one game than being called 'The Chosen One' before you've even played a professional game.

Mr Black roared, 'BASELINE,' and began counting down, 'five, four, three . . . ' – the students ran to the end of the line – 'two, one.' I saw Duwayne at the opposite end. He was focused ahead. He broke his focus once he noticed me looking at him. He smiled. I nodded at him. I could not recall the last time I had seen him smile, if at all. 'GO!' Mr Black yelled, and the students broke off into formation, whilst I followed, confused.

Training was hard. At the end, I sat down, drinking water, lungs pumping, trying to capture as much air as possible lest I faint. I had achieved my ultimate objective: do not embarrass yourself. And perhaps gone a little bit further.

'Sir! Sir! I didn't know you could dunk! That was AMAZING.' Some of the children came over to me excitedly.

I laughed nonchalantly, playing it cool, *say nothing, say nothing.* 'Don't beg it, sir. It's just a dunk. You were sick, though.'

In the last few minutes of the practice session, I had found myself on a fast break, just me and the basket. I ran as fast as I could, and flung my entire body upwards towards the hoop, eyes closed, ball in hand. Before I knew it, I had dunked it, hanging on the rim for effect. 'So cool, so cool,' they ran off, high-fiving and cheering.

I noticed Duwayne talking with Mr Black and I went over to join them.

'It's good to see you here,' said Mr Black, towering over Duwayne, and me. He turned to me. 'He's got potential. I want him to keep coming and join the team. We've got an important game to get into the cup final coming up soon, and we're going to need all the help we can get.'

Duwayne looked up from the ground, beaming. 'I think he's ready for it,' I said, patting him on the back, whilst he nodded. It felt as though I was talking to a different boy to the one who sat in the back of the classroom, slouching with one hand down his trousers.

The change I had been hoping for all along was just starting to show.

'Tu as rien dit,' Mami said, as I navigated my way around her
standing still in the middle of the kitchen.

'You said nothing,' she repeated.

'So?' I replied.

'Tu ne vas pas parler?'

'Why should I speak when I have nothing to say?'

'Rien du tout?'

'That's right. Nothing. Nothing at all.' I finished washing
a plate at the sink and gathered a knife and fork. I realised
how much noise I was making, the clanging sound of metal
against metal in the sink and the clapping of the wooden
cupboards, but I did not care. I was angry, apoplectic, blood
boiling with a venomous rage, but I could not be angry at her.
She was my mother and so I directed it towards everything
else and, most crucially, towards myself – letting the rage
burn inside.

Mami had cooked loso, soso and pondu. I prepared a plate.
She hardly ever cooks pondu these days. Says she hasn't the
time, but she knows how much I like it and I knew this time
was her attempt to make peace. I stormed out of the kitchen
into the living room, sat down to eat and switched on the TV,
raising the volume loud enough to drown out the potential
for any conversation.

'And on today's CNN news: AN UNARMED BLACK
MAN WAS SHOT DEAD BY POLICE in what appears
to be a routine traffic stop. The incident occurred
between ...' I sat watching the news, chewing my food

with grinding teeth and a clenched jaw. Mami came into the room.

'Can you turn down the volume? I am trying to talk to you,' she said. I ignored her and carried on eating. She picked up the remote and turned it down. We both watched in silence as the news replayed the footage of the young Black man's body, lying lifeless, on the ground.

'But please, tell me, why you are not saying anything?'

'About. What?' I replied, in staccato, voice a broken shadow of itself.

'About me and ... ' she hesitated, 'the Pastor. It has been one week. And you said nothing.'

'I have nothing to say of you and that man.'

'We have decided to be together. I thought you would be happy.'

'*Happy?*' I bolt upright to standing, as if an electric surge had entered my body through my feet. 'Happy for who?'

'Happy for me ...'

'How can I be happy for you?' I walked around the small coffee table over to the cabinet where she was stood.

'What about him!' I grabbed the framed picture of Father and shoved it in her hands. I watched as she held it delicately in-between her palms, a single tear falling from her eyes on to the glass of the framed picture like a raindrop from a cloud of a thousand memories.

She looked up at me with eyes turned red, between rage and sadness, her lips trembling. She slapped me, hard, across my face. So hard, I heard the echo ring in my ears for a few moments after. But I did not flinch like how I would cry when I was boy. I am a man now. I just looked at her with fury. I sat back down, transfixed by the TV, while it showed residents being interviewed about the shooting; I could feel the pain on their faces as they spoke.

'So, this is what you want to remind me of . . . ' she said. 'Have I forgotten?'

'Maybe you have forgotten. He was your husband, my father.'

'It has been twenty years . . . twenty years! And there is not a single day I do not think of your father. There is not a single day that I do not wish I could have told him not to go back.'

'Then why are you marrying this man? Why?'

'Michael, I loved your father. But your mother is old. I am an old woman, growing older. I need to be taken care of.'

'I would be here to take care of you.'

'You have your own life.'

'He didn't do nothing. That was my dad. He was unarmed. He was innocent. The police shot him. They shot him.' I watched the young girl break down into tears, live on camera. She could have been a student of mine. I wondered how it would feel, to have to walk in to school tomorrow, and see her sat in my class, and ask her meaningless questions, 'Did you do the homework?' or, 'Can you face the front?' It would feel so inhumane, so brutal, so callous. This world.

'Michael, I want you to live your own life, to have your own family.'

'I cannot accept you and this man.'

'He is not some man, he is a pastor.'

'I do not trust him. I do not want him in your life.'

'But this is what I want. We have decided. We have already made the announcement at church, everybody knows.'

'Then you must decide between him and me. If you marry him, then you will have no son, and I will have no mother.'

'It's been going on too long. There are too many families who are being torn apart just because—' I picked up the remote, switched off the TV, and stomped out of the room.

I had left the house so fast I'd forgotten to take my coat. I felt the breeze slap against my neck like a playground bully. I lifted my hood up, wearing it tight around my head. The wind colonised my bones, which made me want to go back home, but if pride hardens the skin, then I was wearing enough layers to protect me from a blizzard. Still, inside I was soft; on the edge of sadness. The streets were filled with looming lament from the dwindling orange glow of lamp-post lights. I decided to walk the canal, the path I would sometimes run, and found it a bit darker than usual.

I couldn't believe Mami wanted to marry, and that Pastor of all people. I didn't trust him. But, how could she? What about Father? How could she forget about him and just move on?

My phone vibrated in my pocket. I saw three missed calls from Mami, and a string of messages.

What you up to? Call me asap, bro – Jalil.

Hey, you alright? – Sandra.

Sandra had a peculiar way of timing her messages as if in direct correlation with what was going on in my life. She would always, unbeknownst to her, message me asking how I was at the time I needed to be asked the most. I'm all right, you? I replied. Yeah, boyfriend troubles. We should chat? She answered quickly. I left Jalil's message, to be considered another time, and switched off my phone. The cold had become unbearable. I decided to cut back and make my way home. The bridge was just up ahead, and I could see the phantoms lurking in their group, just as before. I saw Duwayne. His nose peeked through the puffer jacket he wore, with the outline of the hood layered with fur, his hands inside the front of his tracksuit bottoms that he wore sagged low. I felt betrayed. I wanted to run over there and drag him away, as if I was his parent. But this was not something we had spoken about. I wondered if he had not yet seen me, so I decided to keep it that way.

We were walking along Edgware Road – Jalil, his father and me – past the Hilton hotel, past the pharmacy and along to the many restaurants where, sat outside, were young mostly Middle Eastern men blowing shisha smoke in the shape of circles into the air. Just before, I had gone around to the house after work to meet his father, calling him 'sir'. I was stuck between words, and he replied, 'Please, call me Baba. You too are my son, I have heard much about you.' He kissed me on the cheek and hugged me, his warmness enveloping me, filling, even if only a little bit, a long-standing void. Some things come to you in ways you do not know you need. His accent was heavy as I sat and listened to stories that Jalil would have heard a thousand times before. However, Baba eventually had gotten restless and wanted to eat, so we all left to find somewhere, and ended up on this side of the city.

'Does he always do this?' I asked Jalil. He looked at me,

thin lipped, and nodded a yes in response. He knew exactly what I was asking about. Baba paced ahead of us by several steps as we were looking for somewhere to eat.

'Even if he doesn't know where he is going, he still walks ahead of everyone else just to get there.' I chuckled because this is how I saw Jalil: if we were out in a group he always, somehow, found himself at the front leading the way.

'Where are we going to eat?' I asked.

'I don't know. Let's just find the restaurant with the fewest people inside, that way he's less likely to cause a scene.'

'Makes sense. Do you know which one is Aminah's family's restaurant?'

'No. I just know it's somewhere on this road, but she refused to tell me which.'

'Oh my gosh, imagine the one we go to is actually her restaurant,' I said, laughing at the possibility. Jalil looked at me sternly, startled and unamused.

'That's not funny, bro. What about if this actually happens?'

'It won't, don't worry. Chances are like zero.'

After walking down to the end of Edgware Road, and in and out of many places, we found a restaurant to eat in that was bare and poorly decorated: sporadic pieces of Arabic contemporary art and a soft touch of sitar music to give it an 'authentic' feel.

'It's clearly for foreigners,' Jalil said, trying to reassure himself, 'and plus, it hasn't got any of Aminah's touch, the colours are too dull.'

I took a quick glance at Jalil and thought how Aminah's touch had affected him as well, primarily around the house – a touch of flowers, a framed picture, scented candles – but his wardrobe appeared brighter too; he wore a fire-orange sweater over a light blue shirt that contrasted his eyes, with khaki-coloured chinos and brown boots.

We had enough food to feed the whole restaurant, never mind just the three of us.

Baba devoured the food, folding the naan with his bare hands and strategically attacking like a predator, while Jalil put on his best act of faux sensibility, eating with a knife and fork.

After beginning with a knife and fork, I changed and followed Baba, eating with my hands instead.

'Son ...' When Baba would call Jalil, I imagined he was also talking to me. It came at the beginning of each of his sentences like a fanfare.

Jalil replied, 'Yes, Baba' after each sentence about this family member or that, or what was happening where, his tone becoming flatter and flatter, and quieter, until it was only a dull whisper.

'And finally, what are you waiting for?' Baba asked, stopping eating and looking up at Jalil, hands coming together, fingers interlocking.

'Waiting for what, Baba?' Jalil asked, his confusion genuine.

'For marriage! Eh, do not pretend with me,' Baba scoffed. Jalil groaned. I remained a spectator in-between.

'You have to. Your time is up. I will expect you to be married by the end of this year. To start your family.'

'Baba, it is not the right time—'

'No buts. When I was your age, your mother and I had already started. You were already a growing boy.'

'But what's for you doesn't mean it's for me.'

'I said no buts.'

Jalil fell into silence and lowered his head.

'I say you must marry . . . because I want to give you the house, everything in your name. To you, son. You are the only thing keeping me coming back. I do not want to come back here, to this place. It is not my home.'

Chapter 19

Downtown Chicago, Illinois; 6.39 p.m.

'Ay, this my shit, man,' Banga says excitedly, turning up the volume to the Afro Trap that plays with a bassline so strong it vibrates the car doors and sends the two dice hanging from the rear-view mirror swinging side to side. Michael had got into the cab, and when Banga had asked, 'Where to?' he'd told him to just drive. Banga can tell Michael is a tourist, not of a holiday, but of life – that he is a man looking for something.

'Aight, man. Chi-town, my city. I'mma show you around,' Banga says in his accent mixed of the thickness of two places burning: the fire of his African roots married with the heat of the banlieues of Paris that raised him.

Banga speaks incessantly. Comfortably unloading to Michael, who listens intently and pays attention to even the most mundane detail, from the woman he almost married to get a green card to what he had for breakfast that morning. They are now in downtown Chicago, Banga eager to point out all the attractions they have passed: the United Center, the Michael Jordan statue, the DuSable Museum of African American History, the Museum of Contemporary Art, and so on.

Chicago is a city that gives itself back to you, it is the friend that calls you just to see how you are doing, it is the stranger who has time to listen to your problems whilst you ride the metro, it is the gentle smile of a passing face, it is the 'let's do this' for an idea or project, the open arms of a hug, it is all the warmth felt in spite of the bitter cold of the lake, that could even freeze the tear on your cheek, but the seasons pass and glory always comes with the sun.

'How you doing, man? You seem kinda stressed. You too quiet. I don't like it when people are too quiet. You talk, I'll listen,' Banga says.

Michael looks up into the rear-view mirror at Banga, who is looking back at him with a wide grin, and then looks away. Stressed. *This is taking too long. This walk towards death, it is slow and arduous, more painful, even, than the death itself. We live as if we are free, because we do not know the day it will meet us. But I have made a pact, a decision where I do not wait for the end day to arrive, the end day waits for me. Each day until then is an agony; an obsession for the mind.*

Stressed. It is easier to kill another than it is to kill oneself. The most powerful instinct in nature is survival; to stay alive, and whomsoever overcomes it has great strength, not weakness.

'Let's get some food,' Banga says, interrupting Michael staring out of the window.

It is late. They stop off at a Caribbean fast-food restaurant and get some curry goat and patties. They eat the food in the cab. The meter has run up into the hundreds, but Michael doesn't care – 'keep it running' is what he told Banga about the meter when he asked.

He feels pangs of nostalgia in his heart like thinking of a

past lover, through all of their times good or bad. It reminds him of the Caribbean restaurants in Dalston or Tottenham High Road, and how there's always something endearing about the way the servers behind the counter never smile at you, or tell you 'we nuh ave that', and yet you keep coming back because you love it. And you could say that it is love, but only a certain type of love known by a few – a love only for us.

Michael feels vulnerable and alone. To be close to those who know him is too much, but to be with a stranger is not enough. Banga drops Michael in the South Side and pulls into the downstairs parking lot of the apartment off 82nd Street where he is staying. It is snowing again, mixed with rain; puddles fill the potholes in the road like lakes. The streets are empty. The hardware store across the road, the barbershop, the nondescript restaurant across the street from the martial arts studio that shares the same building are all closed.

Michael reaches into his back pocket, pulls out his wallet and pays Banga with multiple bills without looking. Banga reluctantly takes the money. He looks at Michael as if there is something greater that he would like to give back.

'Yo, listen, I'mma pick you up tomorrow. 9 p.m. When I finish my shift. Meet me here, aight?'

'Cool.' They dap each other as he parts.

The apartment gloom is broken by the bright light of the tall lamp-post on the street. Michael is restless. Wide awake, sat up on the living-room sofa, staring out of the window into the nothing outside, breathing, breathing, breathing.

*

The bus is taking too long to arrive to catch the L train, so Michael decides to walk. He walks past large houses and apartments, each with their own shade of faded paint and broken windows, letting light into a broken world, past the barbershop, and the convenience store on the corner, where an armed security guard serves the store, usually late at night, Michael learned when coming home past 2 a.m., and saw the hand gun on his waist like a symbol of honour, past the mural paintings of the community heroes, some who he knew, some he did not – all with faces resembling his – then past the church, past the Caribbean fast-food takeaway restaurant, where he stops to get some plantain before continuing, towards the bridge, to Cottage Grove station.

As Michael arrives, he sees a petrol station to the right with a cash withdrawal sign.

He walks over to the machine, checks his bank balance – $3,211. Michael realises for the first time just how much his money is running out, just how much the inevitable is moving closer and closer. He mumbles expletives to himself and slams the side of his fist on the keypad of the ATM. Exhausted, he breathes out and feels a little bit of life leave him. He withdraws $200.

A man approaches Michael. The man looks lugubrious; tall, dark, baggy clothes, unshaven, a reflection of Michael through another's eyes.

'Yo, brother,' the man says in a higher tone of voice than expected, 'where you from?' The man pauses. 'Are you African?' he asks.

Michael looks at the man, unsure how to respond; *aware of how our histories have shaken us, two branches from the same tree, fallen, leaves blown by two thousand seasons of violent winds, scattered seeds in barren soil.* Michael replies, 'Yes,' with all the normalcy his voice could muster.

The man reaches forward, and they shake hands and hug, as if a reunion of a lost brotherhood.

'I could just tell,' the man says, 'there was something different about you.'

Different. Michael wonders what that difference was, because whatever the man saw in him that was different, he saw in the man that was the same. They then spoke, about their lives, filling each other in on their years since birth, about family, about home, about country, and no country at all, and how 'they didn't teach us nothing about our history, man'.

Michael notices the tattoos on the man's neck: pyramid, cross, Africa. The man's head is wrapped in a durag, crowned with a cap, and for a moment he becomes the man, looking back at himself, seeing through the eyes of another the face he was beginning to forget. He feels what the man is feeling, that within him, too, is a battle for life – a struggle for the will to live.

Banga pulls up, screeching his dusty green and yellow cab to park as if it were a sports car. He has a big smile on his face.

'I could tell you like your books, and your smart shit,' Banga laughs as he drives, 'so I thought we could go to this open mic.'

'Yeah?' Michael responds with genuine surprise, and wonders why he underestimated Banga showing interest in something cultured and creative.

'Yeah! They have writers and poets and people who just go

up and read their work and share stories. It's at this café-bar, so we can get food as well ... on me.' Banga looks away from the main road and back at Michael and smiles.

They enter the café-bar, passing the bar and going into the café tucked away quietly at the back. They order food and drinks, then find their seats. It is quiet and warm despite the chill creeping in from outside. The room starts to fill up and the open mic begins, with the host, a rugged man named Pete, whilst Banga continues to talk incessantly about the passengers he picked up that day. Michael is nodding and listening, feigning attention. The host lays the path for each poet to walk the audience on their journey; each poem a story; each story a universe.

He introduces the next poet, who emerges from seated within the audience, and stands, looming, over the microphone, hat fitted to the skull, beard neatly unkempt; a man of worlds, travelling, with words, through each one. Banga continues to talk, but then is also compelled to listen. The audience faces the poet, who brings the room to silence.

'This poem I'm going to share is one I wrote when I was going through one of my lowest periods of my life, when each day was littered with bitter monotony, when I felt trapped in total darkness and I did not want to wake up to see the next day.' The room shifts slightly, settling into itself, into a silence of mouths closed and hearts open.

'Most days, I spend my days trying to figure out what the days mean, and I'm stuck.

'Stuck between caring too much and not caring enough, between holding on too long, and letting go too easily, feet stumbling beneath me, trying to follow this narrow path. I look around, and all I see are faces that laugh, grass greener on the other side, eyes wide, brimming smiles and full hearts, music on blast, and the nervous excitement of the accidental touch of two lovers at the start. I look at myself, and I'm going nowhere fast.

'Maybe this is just a façade. A shallow mask to cover up the fact that we are all hurting inside, that no amount of pride could dry the sea of tears, years of pain, waiting for the clouds to clear, fear settling like dust. And you know what? Some days, I am just tired. Some days, I'm barely strong enough to carry the burden of my heavy heart, let alone the weight of the world on my shoulders, some days I need space on my own, no internet, no mobile phone, and some days, I just want to run away from it all. But then on some days, I hear a voice call in the back of my mind, each syllable sounds like a little droplet of light and it says to me, "Why would you want to run when you have wings for feet? Fly." So, this is to all those with wings for feet who keep on running, please do not run. Fly.

'Fly like the poet's pen across the page, fly, like it was your twelfth birthday, and you just made the biggest wish, and blew out a candle with a flame the size of the sun, and the darkness of the universe is now your living room. Fly, like a midnight, moonlight, city cyclist going downhill, headphones on with no hands. Fly, like a runner, in the park, racing against the sunset, no regrets, like every mistake you've ever made has just been washed away. Fly, like your new crush has just noticed you, looking fly, and has walked up to you holding roses and chocolates to ask you out on a date, and they're paying. Fly, like you never stopped believing in love. Like you weren't the only one. There was a time, when everything you imagined was real. Your mind is the most powerful instrument you will ever own; only second to your heart, which you feel, and they are made of one and the same so, fly.

'Fly like you are not worried about the days, the months and the years of getting older, because each day that you live is the youngest you will ever be, and we live eternally, in each dream, in each sleep, we keep a piece of ourselves just to give to each other.

'So, this is to all those with wings for feet who keep on running, please do not run, fly.'

$3,011

Michael walks out and quickly heads to the bathroom while the crowd applauds the poet. He rushes to the sink, opens the tap of cold water and splashes it on his face. He stares into the mirror, stares at the face staring back at him – the face he is forgetting – the face he wants to be forgotten. His eyes start to well up as the tears begin to fall, from single stream to flowing river. *I am scared. I can feel it getting closer, I can feel the sword dangling above my head, ready to fall, at almost any moment, and I am scared. But what am I scared of? There is no other way.*

The decision had been made, and it was mine. And I stand by it. But what is this feeling? I feel lighter, lightness, free. This way is the best way because, unlike everything else in my life, this is what I have chosen.

Someone opens the door and walks in. Michael splashes more water on his face to camouflage the tears. He returns to his seat next to Banga, who asks nothing, and may not even have noticed the momentary absence. Michael looks around the room for the poet, but he is gone. The poet is gone, but the words remain.

'I feel light, man; a weight has been lifted,' Michael says to Banga as they drive in a taxi back to the South Side. The streets are calm and laced with a layer of peace that he projects on to it, falling like moonlight through a clear dark sky.

'What you mean?' Banga replies, grin widening.

'I don't know. It's just a feeling. You know that feeling?'

'Yeah, man.' Banga laughs and nods, leaning back, right hand on the wheel, looking back and forth between the road and Michael. 'Yeah, I do.'

They're close to home, passing the store with the armed, oversized security guard.

They approach the parking lot by the apartment, where they would usually slow and turn in to park the car, but Banga maintains his speed and carries on.

'Let's head out,' Banga says, before any objection could be made. 'I wanna take you somewhere to hang out, it's still early.' 1 a.m. And though it is not still early, Michael follows Banga's plan.

'Cool. Where are we going?'

'Somewhere chill. A bar. Get a few more drinks and go home,' Banga replies.

Michael says nothing, after all, the poetry reading, where his soul was lifted, turned out very well and so maybe it was something to go by for the rest of the evening.

They drive further and further south of the city, eventually passing into the suburbs. The eerie, leafy silence makes every sound that breaks feel suspicious. They pass three-bedroom white-picket-fence house with front lawn and back garden after three-bedroom white-picket-fence house with front lawn and back garden. Banga slows the car and pulls into an industrial estate; there are trucks and lorries parked in the distance, the whole area is lined with warehouses, large bins and empty boxes. Banga parks the car and they get out.

Weird place for a bar. But this is America, anything can happen here. The moon is full and bright up above. They walk to the front of the warehouse, around the standing metal dividers leading to a barely visible door in the form of make-shift iron shutters, guarded by two security men who appear as though they wasted the best of their years in a dark cell.

Banga walks straight up to one of the security guards – the other, paying them no attention, talks through his earpiece. The security pats Banga down, front to back, and waves him through. Michael is next. He follows Banga. His heart beats with apprehension. As they enter, there's a reception area where Banga says a word and slips the lady some money.

They walk through a small corridor to the next door, through which loud, thumping music can be heard. Banga opens the door and they go in. Michael looks at the bar, and there are dozens of bikini-clad women, all shades, dancing and gyrating, their bodies firm, toned, sexual, the kind you only see in music and other videos too. The bartender, a woman, serves up the drinks that they take and pass across. Michael follows Banga in and they find a place to stand unnoticed but close enough to the centre where some more women pass them in bikinis, serving drinks. Michael looks at the centre stage, and there is a pole planted in from the ceiling to the stage floor, and it glows like it is magic metal. A strip club! A fucking strip club!

Chapter 20

South Side Chicago, Illinois; 1.15 a.m.

Michael tries not to make it look as though he feels out of place, but he does. The discomfort makes his skin feel as if insects were crawling all over. London strip clubs always appeared to be a who's who of pervy, middle-aged, mediocre businessmen attempting to escape their mind-numbingly dull lives of boring job, boring wife and boring children, but here, it is different. Everyone in this room looks and acts like him: young, fresh, cool. The room slowly fills up. Some are young men, flashing cash; some are groups of women on a night out with friends; some are even couples. Banga returns with more drinks. He looks at Michael with an ever-familiar grin, and says, 'I knew you wouldn't come if I told you where we were going.'

There's an ATM in the corner. Banga walks over to use it. A woman approaches Michael for a dance. She turns around and slowly backs up into him. He feels her soft body against his hard. It startles him, and he steps back. Banga watches and giggles, holding his drink up to cover his mouth. Banga whispers something in the woman's ear, which she nods to, and he hands her something. Michael then also walks over to the ATM to withdraw some money; he places it in his wallet.

Lust leaps from Michael's eyes as he makes a playground of their bodies, but he remains far within himself.

There are spotlights flashing on the main stage, which everyone now moves around. The compere – a barely 5-foot middle-aged man in sunglasses and an oversized five-button suit that makes his core look long and legs short – hypes up the crowd. Women arrive on the stage and start to dance on the pole, showcasing their Olympic-level athleticism. A woman in an orange bikini spins at the top of the pole, holding an outright stretched position as if a superhero in flight. She drops all the way down, evoking gasps from the crowd as she stops within an inch of the stage floor. Michael watches in awe of their bodies, akin to art.

Banga moves closer to the stage and is cheering and whooping. He pulls out a wad of cash and sprays it on the stage to the women. Everyone around him is doing the same. Michael realises it's not just about the dancing, it's also about the overzealous display of wealth. So, he, too, joins in throwing money on the stage. The women on the main stage finish the show, yet the night continues. Banga says, 'Follow me,' and leads them away.

'Where are we going?' Michael asks anxiously.

'Don't worry. We going to the private party,' Banga replies, even more excited than before. They go through doors that Michael was oblivious to, as if a hidden passageway to another world. They enter a room, and the music and smoke submerge them like a fog; loud and thumping. The room is dimly lit, with a burgundy-red tinge of light, which covers them like the sky above. There are a few guys around, tall, morose, clothed with money, standing in their cool.

'Yo, this is my boy Michael.' Banga introduces him to a guy, who nods his head, and does the handshake that only they know; showing as if he, too, is from here. They sit down on a large leather settee, divided by a table, with champagne on ice and glasses atop. Banga pops the bottle and is surrounded by women. He pours the drinks. There's a young woman sitting on the leather settee in the seat directly parallel to Michael. She is staring beyond him, beyond the room, staring into a universe of her own; she returns and makes eye contact with him. Her eyes are fierce, her face is fire and fury, rendering all things in its path to dust. He imagines the storm inside her, raging through a desert, through the abandoned city of her soul, and never settling.

She stands up in the light and stretches her body, her hair bouncing. The silk garb she wears hangs loosely from her shoulders, lightly covering her nipples. What the light does to her skin, only the mystics understand; she is the shade of the canvas of the stars; Black is essence, Blackness, then, is essence manifesting. Her eyes are two colliding nebulas, her mouth swallows constellations whole.

Michael watches her as she stands and joins in with another woman, dancing. She pulls the woman in closer, closer, close, until they are hip to hip, navel to navel, breast to breast. She kisses the woman, but just ever so lightly on her lips; enough that they touch, but not too much; leaving only enough room for the dim light to break through. She looks at Michael, her face a cry for war; a journey between life and death.

Michael looks beside him and Banga is gone. He keeps cool. But inside, his heart flees with panic. Another woman approaches Michael, smiling; her hand stretches out, reaching for his.

'You want a dance?' the blonde-wigged woman says. *No,* he thinks nervously. But he stands regardless and follows her. The woman stands in front of him, and then slowly turns, rubbing her perfectly sculpted body into him. Michael is surrounded by one, two, three, he loses count. She takes his hand and says, 'If you see something you like, follow me.' Weakened by urges, overcome by loneliness, he obliges. She leads him and a few other girls into a dark room. The bassline of the music is muted but the vibrations shake the bed he now sits on. The women dance sensuously in front of him. *These are the stuff of teenage fantasies, stories that I would run to tell the mandem, but here I am feeling confused, disassociated and alone. I don't want to be here. And yet, I don't want to leave.*

She is in there too, with her warrior face. She looks at him as if looking through him.

'So, what would you like?' the blonde-wigged woman says, pushing her chest up against him as he feels her through his shirt. Michael leans down and whispers. The blonde-wigged woman looks up at him and smirks, nodding, and places out her hand. He reaches into his pocket and passes her some bills without looking. The blonde-wigged woman then signals for her and the other women to go, leaving but one in the room. She.

$2,611

'So, you just gon' stare?' she says, as she stands in front him. Her voice is just how he imagined it, a revolution; peace to a nation at war.

'I don't know how these things usually start.'

He motions for her to sit down next to him and she does. They remain in silence for a while, the only sound, the beating of their hearts, matched with the beating bassline of the music.

'What's your name?'

'Savannah Jade.'

'Your real name.'

'Oh,' she chuckles, 'you don't get to know that.'

'Why are you here?'

She laughs at the question. 'Are you okay?'

'I mean, why are you here?' Michael continues. 'Doing this.'

'I could ask you the same thing,' she says, and he has no answer for her.

'I'm here to earn a check, to make money. It's a job, just like how you have a job ... apparently.'

'You seem so much more.'

'Yo, where you from?' she asks, which, in his ears, translates more so to, *Who do you think you're talking to? You don't know me.* She leans away from him, closing her silk garb.

'London,' Michael replies.

'Oh,' she responds, with a new kind of understanding. 'That's why you're askin' all these dumb-ass questions?' She chuckles.

'What about you?' he asks. She hesitates.

'New York,' she answers eventually. 'Are you one of them weird niggas who are shy and into fetishes and shit?'

'No, no . . . '

'Good, cos I don't get paid enough for that.'

'No. I'm sorry. I don't mean to alarm you . . . '

'Alarm me?' She laughs. 'Nigga said "alarm".'

'I just want to talk . . . ' he says to her. She stops laughing and falls silent.

'Can we lie down?' Michael continues. He goes first and lies down. After a few moments, and a deep sigh, she joins him. She is far from him, on the other side of the bed; the space between them a canyon.

'Are you okay?' she asks.

'No,' he replies. She looks over at him. He looks up at the ceiling. He remembers his promise. That he cannot and will not come close to another, but she, she is different; he is desert, and she is ocean, and somewhere on land they were destined to meet.

'You ever wish that you could die . . . but without all of the dying?' he says. 'Like, not die, but just cease to exist, disappear, be invisible, every trace of your life, even the memories of you in other people's hearts and minds, all gone.'

'You need to be on a therapist's coach, not in a strip club. I don't get paid to deal with all this . . . ' She sits up as if she is about to walk out but then stops.

'Life is so hard, and I know it's hard for everybody, but I can only make sense of what is hard for me; what I feel, in this mind, in this body, and I don't want to feel this way. Not any more.'

She lays back down and breathes deep, reaches her hand out and touches his with her fingertips – electric. As if by instinct, their fingers entwine, bringing their hands together.

He feels her pull. He rolls towards her, she moves closer to him, and the distance between them is no more. She is cupped into him, his arms now wrap around her; she uses his arm as a pillow, his fingers stroking her hair.

Their breaths synchronise, his chest rising and falling in line with hers. They speak for a while. They speak of death, and aliens, of multi-dimensional realities, omniverses and time travel. She says, 'Do you know that once you travel faster than the speed of light, time ceases to exist,' and he replies, 'So is that what this feeling is?' They speak of sex and of love, of home, of where they would like to go, of their favourite books; his of a journey of many seasons, hers, of heroes and heroines; his, a man he knows not well enough, hers, a woman who turned the tragedy of her skin into triumph. Of Blackness, and their different forms, of how their journeys have transcended both time and space, and that if they are both here it is because of the amalgam of infinite possibilities; that somewhere along the line an ancestor fought for them to live; even though they were only imagination and not yet memory. They speak of here and now, and of nothing; nothing at all. In the silence, Michael pulls her in, closer again, and feels her warmth. He wonders how close Icarus got to the sun before his wings started to burn, and if ever, his falling still felt like flying.

Michael wakes up. He reaches out on the bed to the space beside him. It is empty. He sits up, and slowly comes to the realisation that he fell asleep. Where is she? He frantically searches his pockets for his phone and wallet. They're not there. *Fuck!* He jumps out of the bed and flings the duvet off. He rubs his hands across the bed searching, under the pillows, throws them off, under the headboard, the mattress, the bed, but does not find them. *I've been robbed. I should have known.* Defeated, Michael sits back down on the bed and looks across to the bedside table. He switches on the lamp. He sees his phone and wallet. He also finds a note: *If you're ever in New York – 332 483 1182.* He breathes a sigh of relief and clutches the phone, wallet and piece of paper to his chest, grinning. He opens the wallet, and checks in-between the compartments. The money is gone. He kisses his teeth, but smirks and is humoured by it all. He remembers where he is and that he is alone. He is desperate to leave. Where's Banga?

Michael leaves inconspicuously, navigating his way out of the club back to the industrial wilderness. He finds Banga in the car park, leaning against the cab, smoking his last cigarette.

'Where did you go, man?' Michael rushes towards Banga, who is startled and throws the cigarette on the snow-covered floor.

'Yo, man,' Banga laughs, 'the question is where did YOU go?'

'I was looking for you. One minute you were sitting there, and the next you were gone.'

'Had to take care of some business. I knew you'd be good. I wanted you to have fun and enjoy yourself. I thought I'd just wait for you out here.'

'But what if something happened?'

'Well, did it? Damn, chill, bro. You're here now. Let's go,' Banga says, shivering in the cold. They both get into the taxi, with its old, vibrating heater that blows out cold air before it gets hot.

'So, did you like it?' Banga asks, grinning. Michael shrugs

his shoulders. 'I come here all the time, man. You see the girls in there? Fine as hell.

'Tell me you got some, bro?' he carries on. Michael does not reply.

'You did, didn't you? Ha ha, that's my dude.' Banga reaches out for a high-five, or something of equal affirmation, and, seeing the non-responsiveness, clutches Michael's shoulder instead, big brother to little brother.

'I just wanted you to have some fun, man. You seemed like someone who just needed to have some fun.' Michael huffs resentfully.

They drive through leafy, suburban Chicago back towards the South Side. The moonlight falling on to the snow makes it look as though it's glowing. Banga blasts blues music from the radio and sways his head with a loose rhythm while singing along. Michael thinks about the girl whose name he does not know, 'New York', and checks his pocket to make sure the paper with her phone number is still there.

$1,811

Chapter 21

Colindale, North London; 5.46 p.m.

Baba was watching videos of long-forgotten memories and listening to his favourite childhood songs on the iPad, head bobbing up and down, mouth widened, showing a cheek-to-cheek, toothless smile, when his body jolted in an unusual way. Jalil did not notice. He was on the PC, headphones on, eyes so intensely close to the screen his long eyelashes almost flickered against it. Baba jolted once again, this time falling out of the chair. He dropped the iPad on the floor and clutched his chest. I shouted Jalil's name. He turned around slowly, unsure if he had heard something. He looked at me, before looking down at his father.

'Baba?' Jalil whispered. Baba tried to muster the strength to sit back on the chair, but he stumbled back on to the floor. His breath became slow and stingy. He looked as though all the colour in him was fading.

'It must be a heart attack,' I said. I grabbed my phone and immediately rang 999. 'Sit him comfortably and get him some water.'

Jalil placed some pillows underneath Baba's head.

'Hello, 999 Emergency, which service do you require?'

Jalil returned with a glass of water, giving it to Baba in small sips.

'Ambulance.'

I watched as Jalil's face began to sink with worry. The burden of his father's presence began to shift into compassion and fear of loss. He had never imagined life without his father, as I could not imagine life with mine. His father, particularly in recent years, had always been a reference point, like a map when you're lost, but always tangible, always real, and mine, an idea, a memory. We waited for the ambulance to arrive. Baba sat up, trying to make light of his pain. The ambulance arrived swifter than anticipated. They placed Baba in the back of the ambulance, wrapped warmly in a blanket, face in an oxygen mask, blood pressure monitor around his arm, lying back in his kaftan.

'I'm afraid only one of you can come with us in the ambulance.'

'It's okay. I'll get a cab and meet you at the hospital,' I replied. I hugged Jalil and gestured a wave to Baba that he did not see.

This relaxing Sunday had taken a direction none of us had anticipated. I arrived at North Middlesex Hospital and walked into the reception area from the foggy autumn cold. I looked around, trying to find my way to cardiology, and saw tired faces. I found the room where Baba was kept. Jalil was standing outside. He saw me before I said hello, and we hugged, holding each other longer than any other circumstance would usually allow.

'How is he?'

'He's okay. He's in there now, being assessed.'

I breathed a sigh of relief – a gust of wind strong enough to set a ship to sail.

'Thank you for coming, bro.'

'Of course. I'm here for you. For both of you.'

Jalil nodded at me with affirmation, and then stared into an invisible abyss beyond me.

'Don't you have work tomorrow?' he asked, looking back up at me. I did have work, but I was not thinking about it. Besides, it would be such a lack of compassion for me to leave my best friend without anyone to support him.

'Don't worry about me.'

'Aminah was going to come tonight as well, but I told her not to. It'll be better for her to come tomorrow. I told her to spend the evening with her father and cherish him as I have failed to cherish mine.'

His words resonated like a gong in my heart, causing a loud, sensitive vibration. Spend the evening with her father. I envy the wrong things sometimes. I placed my hand on his shoulder, and offered some words to affirm him, and, perhaps in turn, to affirm myself. The door to the room opened and the doctor appeared.

'Hello, I'm Dr Patel,' she said, looking back and forth between Jalil and me, her voice a measured tone of empathy.

'Your father is in a stable condition. He is in good hands and being well taken care of. We do have concerns, though, which will require further examination. We do not want to alarm you, but simply want to make sure we cover every possible base.'

'Thank you, Doctor. Can I go and see him?'

'Yes, you may.'

Jalil walked towards the door and signalled me to follow him. I walked in tentatively behind. Baba was lying flat on the bed, angled slightly upwards, eyes closed; a deceptive imitation of sleep.

'Baba ...' Jalil whispered as he slowly approached. He kneeled beside the bed. Baba's breathing was deep, laboured.

Jalil held his head in his hands. Two tear drops fell in succession on to the floor. Baba reached forward and touched Jalil; they delicately held each other. Baba removed the breathing apparatus from his face.

'Baba ...' Jalil said, panicking.

'It's okay ... don't worry,' Baba said, his voice groggy. He squeezed Jalil's hand a little tighter than before. Jalil nodded.

'My son ...'

'Yes, Baba ...'

'You have to ... fulfil my wish.'

'Yes, Baba.'

'It is my last wish ... for you ...'

'Yes, Baba.'

'Promise me.'

'Yes, Baba.'

'It is time.'

Baba's breathing quickly became heavier, which was followed by coughing and spluttering. The nurse came in instantaneously.

'It's okay, he just needs to rest,' she said, placing the breathing mask back on Baba. 'It looks like you need to get some rest, too,' she added, patting Jalil on the back. Jalil stood and slowly walked towards me at the door. We left the room together.

'Come back tomorrow. We will call you if there's a change.'

'Thank you,' Jalil said graciously.

'This is too much. I don't know what I'm going to do,' his face a pale version of himself.

'It's all right. It'll be all right,' I said as I held him tightly.

I woke up with a resounding headache. My body ached as though a set of bricks had been lifted to 100 feet above and released down on me. I did not want to move, but the headache became a migraine; the unbearable kind, an ailment of the soul. I got up to search for some food and aspirin.

It was quiet in the house, and cold. I had called in sick, not caring how often it had been lately. I went from the kitchen with my plate, glass of water and packet of paracetamol, to the living room, and found Pastor Baptiste sitting on the sofa, reading a newspaper. He looked up at me, surprised and startled. He scrambled to close his newspaper and stood to greet me. He said hello, switching on the charm and enthusiasm he afforded to others. I gave a reserved response, choosing instead to sit down and eat my food as I had intended. I looked the Pastor up and down, analysing every strand of his being. Nothing gave. The thought of him and Mami sneaking around like teenagers, desperate to be together at the first given opportunity, was repulsive.

'Please do not misunderstand my being here, Michael,' Pastor Baptiste said after a long moment of silence. 'I did not spend the night,' he stuttered, 'I am simply passing by on my way to the church.'

'Frankly, Pastor, I'm beyond caring.' I stared at him with eyes like two clenched fists.

'You know, Michael, I know that tough exterior you are putting on is only skin deep.'

'Oh?'

'Yes. I know, I feel the world of trouble that is disturbing you. You don't have to talk to me about it, but you are always welcome to.'

'Really?' I replied with as much cynicism as my mouth could carry.

'Of course!'

I scoffed.

'And, if you don't feel comfortable speaking to me, the Lord is always there to listen. He hears all.' Pastor Baptiste smiled and returned to silence. Mami came out from her bedroom and froze in her steps as she approached, increasing the exploding awkward tension.

'Michael,' she said, 'What are you doing here?'

'I live here,' I replied.

'Well ... ' Pastor Baptiste said cheerily, trying to break the tension in the room. 'I should be going.' He stood up, grabbed his briefcase and folded the newspaper under his arm.

'Have a great day, Michael.' I looked up at him, offering nothing but a thin-lipped smile, then back down into my bowl of cereal. He walked over to Mami to say goodbye. I kept my eyes fixed on them, ready to pounce if I saw something I did not approve of. He opened his arms wide, then placed his hands on her shoulder, awkwardly positioning his mouth from a kiss on the lips to one on the cheek, until neither manifested. It all eventually collapsed into an awkward side hug.

He walked out, the heels of his leather loafers click-clacking against the laminated wooden floor.

'Take down your hood, man,' I said to Duwayne, as he and the rest of the class entered. The 'man' came out inadvertently, it was layered with bitter derision and discontent. The class felt it too. Usually, they were jovial and engaging, giving back to you what you gave to them whilst also doing the work; however, there were times when they could sense you were not in the 'mood' and would approach you like a ticking time bomb hoping you didn't explode, at least not on them. The rest of the class settled into their work, silently scratching their pens into the paper. I watched Duwayne lounge at the back, his hands tucked into the front of his trousers. I saw flashes of him on that bridge, hood up, hands down, phone waving in the air for pictures, middle finger to the world.

'Get your hands out of your trousers,' I snapped, startling him so much that he quickly lifted them out.

'Are you going to do any work today?' I walked over and slammed his book, which he had left behind in a previous lesson, on to the table. I could feel the rest of the class stop working and lift their heads to watch. Duwayne shrugged his shoulders nonchalantly.

'Get out of my class!' I erupted, roaring so much my voice echoed. Duwayne got up and walked past my pointed finger leading to the door.

'And the rest of you, get back to work.' I could feel the class quickly lower their heads and continue working. I joined Duwayne outside the classroom.

'Come here,' I said, as he was walking away, my voice

assertive, strong. 'Do you want to explain to me what's going on?'

He chose to remain silent, exercising a right that I did not grant him. I stared at him more intensely, urging him to speak.

'I'm waiting.'

'I ain't do nothing.'

'Can't you see that's the problem?' I said, almost in a growl, using all my will to hold back the expletives that were punching their way out of my mouth. He shrugged. I went back into the classroom. The students were watching the door, as if it would help them see through to the other side. They quickly returned to their work once I entered. I picked up my desk phone and made a call then sat in my seat, looking out into the back wall. Moments later, Mr Black arrived at the door, his head rising above the door frame. He had to duck his head to enter but I saved him the effort and joined him outside.

'Sir,' he said, towering above myself, and Duwayne, making him look like the parent of us both.

'Duwayne here, sir,' I said, 'seems to think it's okay for him to come into my classroom and not do any work.' Mr Black alternated his head between me and Duwayne as I spoke. 'I just don't know why he thinks this is okay? Especially when he wouldn't dare to go to basketball practice and do nothing. I know this because I've been watching him the past few weeks.'

We both fixed our eyes on Duwayne. He lowered his head, and if, in that moment, a hole appeared in the ground, he would have placed his head inside it. He appeared vulnerable, timid, exposed. A shadow of the boy on the bridge or the boy in the back of the class or grabbing the other children and pushing them against the wall in the corridors.

'Do you have anything to say for yourself, Duwayne?' Mr Black asked. Duwayne moved not even a muscle in his body, offering not a shrug or a frown.

'Okay. I'll take him with me, sir, and maybe he can have a moment to think about his actions.'

Chapter 22

Grace Heart Academy School, London; 6.59 p.m.

Is everything all right? Sandra. I picked up my phone from the desk to reply. It was 7 p.m. on a Friday evening, at the end of a long and frustrating week.

No. My life is falling apart, and no matter how hard I try, nothing seems to get any better.

I almost sent the message but quickly erased. I started again.

Do you ever wish you could leave everything behind? For good? Leave it all, your job, your house, your name, your identity, who you are, whoever you are, and just go and disappear, unknown to the world? Another message that I ended up erasing.

I'm fine, I finally replied.

It's just that you've not been your usual self lately.

I didn't know what she meant by this, but it shook the tectonic plates of my core. It was true. I had not been myself. I felt something. At least something within me, though I could not give it a name; it felt like when you're on a ship in the middle of the ocean, during a rainstorm, water is slowly filling it up, and you've got a small bucket, and you're frantically throwing it back out into the ocean, but unknown to you, there is a hole at the bottom of the ship rendering your efforts futile. And at the worst of times, that you are not *in* the ship, but the ship itself – doomed to sink, doomed to wreckage.

Are you still here? she double texts.

Yeah. You?

Yeah. I figured you'd still be here, so I stuck around.

As I was walking to the door to leave the classroom, Sandra walked in. She smiled tenderly, her cheekbones lifting her face, and my spirits.

'What are you doing after?' she asked.

'Nothing,' I said.

'Not going to the pub?' I almost laughed; the corner of my lips shifting slightly upwards, which was enough for her.

'Let's go eat, maybe? And chat?' she suggested. I was not up for it, but I also did not want to say no, and I did not want to be alone. I did nothing. 'Just us,' she added. She leant in closer, parted my coat and gently placed her hand between my chest and my stomach, roaming as if searching for my wandering heart. She looked up at me, and I, down at her.

She reached up, tiptoeing ever so slightly, and softly

touched her lips on mine; it was a kiss, of sorts, a message, perhaps, a letter.

'I should go,' I said. She landed back on the flat of her feet, and nodded, while looking down at the ground.

I stomped out of the building, not even acknowledging the pub crowd who were gathering to leave, the guys who had returned from five-a-side football in the playground, the receptionist and the caretaker who always flirted at the welcome desk and were clearly sleeping with each other but so adamantly denied the rumours. It was raining, but I did not care about the rain, or anything else. I felt the water drip down my forehead, covering my face as I walked to the station. Clenched fists with nothing to hit, there was an all-encompassing rage simmering on the end of my fingertips. I used to punch walls when I was younger, or even get into fights, but now I have nothing to direct this rage towards, nothing and no one but myself.

If I go home, it's going to make me angrier. I don't want to risk seeing Mami, or even Pastor Baptiste's face. If I have to put up with his fake charm right now, I will surely lose it.

I decided not to go home, instead choosing to get on the tube and go alongside the canal. The sun had long set, and it was now dark, the canal bringing with it an extra cold and gloom. Surrounded by the druggies and the homeless, the four-storeyed houses of the rich and the canal boats, there was nothing here, nothing but a glimmering void, an irides-cent vacuum; the feeling of everything alive but dying.

I stared into the endearing darkness of the canal for hours. Its voice invited me to come in for a while and stay. I walked all the way around and back out aimlessly on to the high street, and was met by hundreds of people, boisterous, joyful, loud, masking their ambivalence with the elixir of soon-to-be-forgotten memories, and the sweat of the soon-to-be-regretted sex. I looked at them, and myself equally, with disdain, wondering why I could not be more like them, wondering why I was stuck in this body, like a prison cell, a life sentence, and whether I would ever be able to escape it.

I hid behind a van parked on the pavement. I peered out slightly to see, but not to be seen. Was that Mr Barnes? I noticed someone with his combination of a slightly odd shape, diminutive stature and bowlegged walk, head upwards towards the bridge. I followed, keeping a safe distance behind. He arrived at the bridge, walking up to one of the boys in the group, with their hoods up and sagging tracksuits. *What is he doing?* I knew what he was doing: same thing everyone else does on nights like this that keeps these boys around here waiting. The cycle stays the same, it's only the faces that change. I had seen it several times, been among it several times. I had just never seen someone I worked with come here too, not to this part of the world; an underworld that operated on an underground economy, where the most expensive thing that could be taken was your life.

The boy, with his puffer jacket and hood up, nodded, signalling the rest of his crew.

Duwayne! There he was, emerging from the few. His face wrapped up around the mouth, with a pulled-down balaclava, his head covered in two hoods – one from his tracksuit, the other from his jacket. I only saw him from the eyes, and I knew those eyes well; I recognised the despondency, the fear. They led Mr Barnes down the path to the canal. Barnes.

Don't go, you idiot. He followed, either fully oblivious and naïve or fully aware, as if not for the first time. I know their routine, where they hide the drugs. How they hollow out a part of the wall, where they put their stash, and line it with bricks to make it look natural. And there's always one person on watch, and they stay far enough from it so if they're ever caught, it's not on them.

I followed them, wrapping the scarf I wore around my head like a makeshift hood. I watched and waited. They walked to the underside of the canal, by the second bridge, where the hollow of the tunnel makes the acoustics echo. The tall, hooded boy who Mr Barnes had first spoken to went behind somewhere and then emerged with something in his hands whilst Duwayne and two others waited. Mr Barnes reached into his own pockets and handed over some cash. The tall hooded boy looked at it, counted, and then handed over the drugs to Mr Barnes.

'What's this? Is that it? Fuck off,' Mr Barnes said, muffled, from a distance, as he held up the bag to the nearest light. 'You owe me.'

The tall hooded boy responded with something I could not hear and pushed Mr Barnes. *Just go, man. Get out of there.* I pleaded, praying, to some god, any god, who would hear. Mr. Barnes pushed the tall hooded boy back, hard, with both hands, knocking him to the floor. A fist came swinging through the air and landed on the side of Mr Barnes's head, knocking him to the ground. I could not tell who was who, whether it was the tall hooded boy, Duwayne or any of the other boys, but they jumped on him, punching and stamping into him, a thunderous flurry of blows landing on his body, curled up in a ball. The tall hooded boy ran away, and the others, before they ran, checked Mr Barnes's pockets, picking up his phone, wallet, keys and spare change, then they ran, like athletes competing for a scholarship, into the dark of the night. I grabbed my phone and keyed in 999. I hesitated to press the call button. I could hear Mr Barnes groaning and writhing in pain on the floor. I pressed call, but before it could ring, I cancelled it. I put my phone back into my pocket, wrapped the scarf around my head a little tighter and walked away. I reached the high street, relieved I had just returned to civilisation.

'Did you hear that? Over there?' I said to the first person I saw passing. A woman, going for dinner with her husband. 'I think someone's been attacked.' I left and never looked back.

I walked into the house gasping for breath. It was dead silent. All the lights were off. I went straight into my room, took off my jacket, scarf, and threw everything that was weighing me down on to the floor. I was alive.

Maybe this is it, all hell, all fire, all fury. This is the only warmth we feel, all that we are destined to feel in this place. This city doesn't love us. It grips us with its shark-like teeth, rips the meat from our bones and spits us out. This city doesn't love us. It imprisons us, condemning us to sentences that we do not know we serve; our cells are the streets, the blocks, the tower buildings, the back-alleys, the underground tunnels, the canals, the swamps, the early mornings and the night shifts, the factories, the bottom of the stairwells, these life sentences we are handed, that we inherit. This city doesn't love us.

We make this city, but this city breaks us. We take this city, and tattoo it on our tongues, speaking its name like a fanfare wherever we go, saying, 'This is where I'm from,' but this city doesn't love us. We give to this city. We live for this city. Only, after all you've done, for it to turn around and say, 'So what?' For it to kick you out or wave goodbye every time you threaten to leave. You cannot leave. This city is all you know; this place is all you have ever known. Even a prison becomes a home if you have known no other place. This city doesn't love us. There is no song, no lament, no prayer for us. No god to hear our woes. We know no heaven, and we fear no hell. This city doesn't love us; this city, this country, this world.

Part III

La Belle Dame sans Merci

Chapter 23

Harlem, New York City; 7.15 p.m.

Michael exits 135th Street subway. Cars pass by in silence and the trees, blown side to side by the unrelenting wind, sway in either praise or redemption. Walking along Frederick Douglass Boulevard, he feels the history of these streets in his bones. He's meeting She soon and begins to feel all the traces of her evoked in the memory of his senses: her smell like a field of unnamed flowers, her touch like a shaman healing an afflicted soul, her voice the trumpets bringing down the walls of his guarded heart, and her face, her face like the laying down of arms; an unexpected declaration of peace.

Peace is what he feels here, he is closer to it. He walks the streets and blends in with the people. He feels peace because here, they do not know his name, they do not know his face; here he is unknown, a child of no mother, a friend to no one. Here he carries no weight. He is blown in the wind like dandelion seeds. He is caught and wished upon. He is a shooting star, unseen in the skies of this bright and luminous city.

As the moments to their meeting draw closer, like the

meeting of the sun and the moon for an eclipse, he feels a wave of emotion, this act of pure ablution, a swim in the holiest of rivers.

He walks back down the street, past the shops, and the loud men in front of their tables selling books and DVDs, and other things. He sees She, standing outside the Schomburg Center; Harlem Hospital hangs on the other side of the street like a painting. She's looking into the beyond; a diviner, a seer of the future, an esoteric wanderer of other worlds. If only he could stop and watch her, and watch her, and just keeping watching. She sees him and tries to hide that she is surprised by his presence. He notices how different she looks, different but not unfamiliar.

'I didn't think you were going to come,' Michael says.

'Neither did I,' she replies.

He's unsure how to greet her. She sees his uncertainty and mumbles something under her breath. She offers her hand as if they are in a business meeting. They shake hands and her touch alone sends tremors to his core.

'You look . . . ' Her hair is no longer bouncing at the shoulders, she wears it up instead, curls tied tight in knots around her head. He looks her up and down, takes her in: hooped earrings, big scarf, torn black denim jacket, matching skirt, fishnet tights, with black, laced-up Dr Martens boots.

'I look different?' She laughs. 'Not what you were expecting from that li'l girl you met at the strip club before, I bet.'

'I was going to say you look beautiful,' he replies. She falls silent, offering nothing in return.

'I would suggest taking you somewhere, but I don't really know New York like that at all . . . '

'There's nowhere you could take me in this city that I don't already know. And anyway, New York would swallow you up. Whole. Let's just . . . go for a walk. You said you like walking?'

So they walk, past the hanging yellow traffic light in the middle of the road, past the beige tower blocks with aligned trees below, past building, after building, after building, with black metallic staircases on the outside, past food shop, nail shop, pawn shop, Chinese restaurant, beauty supply shop, laundry shop, past man on the corner trying to sell them everything, past man on the corner begging, past bookshop, church, gym, young girl on the corner, waiting, waiting, waiting, past the mosque, where in the distance, a silhouette of the bright city skyline against a sky of crimson purple and noir starts to appear.

'This is Malcolm X Boulevard; you know who Malcolm X is, right?' she says playfully. He does not dignify her question with a response, his face an expression of faux outrage, to which she laughs and replies, 'Just checking.'

'I know a bit about Black history, but not enough,' Michael replies. 'I mean, who really knows enough about Black history? None of us do. There are, and have been, Black people for centuries, all over the world, since the beginning of time, but people still don't know enough. People act as if we're aliens that landed yesterday, and they've still gotta figure us out.'

'Okay, so I have to ask, I know you're from London, but where are you from from?' she continues. They both laugh.

'I'm from Congo.' He answers her question. 'We speak Lingala.' He smiles and she stays silent, as if giving him space to say more – as if she knows he doesn't like to talk about himself.

'I was born in Congo, but we came to London not long after.'

'We?'

'Me, my mother . . . and my father. We fled the war.'

'Oh.'

'Where are they now?' she continues with curiosity.

'My mother is in London . . . ' Michael hesitates, his mouth feels drier than charred wood, 'and my father is dead.'

'I'm so sorry.'

'It was a long time ago. I was young. I barely remember. One day he was here, and the next he was gone. All I know is he had to go back . . . back to Congo. Something was happening, still to this day, I don't know what. But I miss him, or maybe I just miss who he would have been in my life.'

I'm often reminded that I come from a place at war; and that I live in a body at war, a mind at war. I am suffering from memories.

'You see your mother . . . '

'Yeah?'

'Hold on to her.'

'What do you mean?'

'Whatever you have with your parents, you only realise when it's gone that you can't get it back.'

'We didn't leave things on good terms.'

'It's never too late to fix it.'

But it is too late.

'What about your parents?'

'I never knew my dad. And I didn't get a chance to know my mom.' As they walk, soft winds blow by them, passing like ancestral spirits.

'I'm an orphan. I have no parents.'

Michael does not know how long they have been walking for, but it feels like he's never taken a step without her.

'I want to show you something . . . ' she says.

Michael imagines doing this with her as though it is ordinary: coffee shops, walks through Central Park, watching the stars at the Hayden Planetarium, flicking through the pages of their favourite books at the Strand, playing chess in Union Square, going to watch the Knicks, or more so, the visiting team, and watching her instead of the game. He slides his hand into hers and holds it. It feels as natural as the passing of the seasons, as the turn of dusk to dawn, as a wave in the ocean. He can see her in his future, more than he can even see his own future; a future that does not even exist.

'You know you still haven't told me your name . . . your real name.'

'I know.'

'So, are you planning on ever telling me?'

'Probably not, if I'm honest.' She laughs. 'What?'

'Why not?'

'Cos, I don't trust you.' She continues to walk ahead, all the while still holding hands.

'I'm sorry . . . ?'

'I. Don't. Trust. You.'

He walks beside her, mouth agape, unsure what to say.

'Anyway, pay attention, we're almost there.'

They're deep in the city, in-between rows and rows of buildings that seek attention. They pass a pair of police officers standing in patrol.

'Do you know where we are?'

'I mean, this is where ... this is Ground Zero ...' Michael says as he follows her ahead, slowly.

'Yes, it is ...'

'Oh, my gosh. Do you remember where you were when it happened?'

'I was in school. The teacher pulled in the TV and we watched it. We watched, but it was happening just outside ... the cloud of rising smoke, the falling buildings ... it felt surreal, like a movie.'

'I remember I was coming home from school and some kid from our estate, Peter, was running around screaming and shouting. He was always off his head, so I thought he was chatting shit. I got home and switched on the TV, Mami was in the kitchen, and then we just sat and watched it together, in total silence. We both knew that this day would change the course of the world for ever, and not for the better.' They both fall silent for a minute.

'But I brought you to see this ...' she says, lightly taking his hand and leading him. 'Do you know what it is?' she asks. He looks at the grey monument with a map of the world etched into the stone floor in the centre. African Burial Ground National Monument. Michael can feel his stomach turn itself inside out.

'This is where the remains of 419 enslaved African people were found. Some remains were found with broken bones, lacerations, and other wounds. They had African ornaments in their possession, too. And they were buried here, under the buildings, where above people just went to work, made their money and got on with their lives. Meanwhile, the dead were buried beneath them. It's a kind of un-poetic metaphor for America, for the world, even,' she says with a tiredness in her breath that he too knows so well. 'So when you ask me where I'm from, this is one way I know how to show you.' They walk away from the monument with a sombreness too heavy for their hearts.

'It's late. I have work in the morning,' she says. The clock strikes twelve, revealing how, that evening, time had been a fleeting, untraceable thing. Michael stares deeply into her eyes.

'What?' she says nervously, 'I have work.' She starts to laugh.

'I thought you ... ' he hesitates, unsure of how to place his words together to form the sentence.

'Dance?' She laughs, louder than before. 'Yeah, I do. And?'

'No "and", I mean ... I ... just ... ' he stutters; his words fail him.

'I dance. Sometimes. That's a job. But I also got an office job that I need to get up at 6 a.m. for. You know, we can be more than one thing, right?' She laughs at his naivety and pats him on his shoulder as if to console him for failing to grasp something so simple. But she's right, and he wonders why he never thought about her being more than a dancer, more than one thing. They board the train and, though it is full, they manage to find space in-between a group of inebriated women on their hen night.

'Oh, which reminds me, you have my money, right?' Michael asks.

'Your money?'

'Yeah. I had around five hundred dollars or something that night in my pockets, and by the time I woke up, it was gone.'

'Whoa. I don't have none of your money. In fact, come to think of it, you owe me.'

'You literally took my money . . . '

'You ain't paid me for my time.'

'It's my fucking money. I need that back. I got plans for it.' Michael remembers, his breath shortens, chest tightens; clamps on his lungs.

'Whoa, yo, you buggin' right now, son. Listen, why would I rob you, give you my number, and then meet up with you?' She laughs.

Michael settles himself, realising that maybe She is right.

'How long did you sleep for after I left?' she asks.

'I don't know, I just remember waking up and you weren't there, then the money was gone. But my phone was still there.'

'That's because no one wants your brick phone.' She laughs, finding this more and more amusing. 'Ha. You got robbed by one of the girls. I think I know who would have taken it . . . blonde wig. She got you good, man.'

'Wow. At least she left my wallet. It's where I keep the only photo I have of me, my mum and my dad, in Congo, before the war. It reminds me of a peace I've not known since.' *A peace that I will never know again.*

'She got you.'

'It doesn't matter. It's not like I'm ever going to a strip-whatever-it-was type of club again, anyway.'

Michael's facial expression remains stunned while She full-belly laughs, almost to the point of tears.

'I'm glad you're finding this very entertaining.'

'Oh, my, God,' the woman sitting directly in front of them says, her streaky ginger-blonde hair falling to the side of her face, 'you guys look so beautiful.' Her speech slurs. 'How long have you been together?'

Michael looks at She, sitting next to him, and it's the first time he's noticed her look flustered.

'We're not together. I'm single,' she replies to the woman.

'Oh, my . . . you look like you been together for years. How long y'all known each other?'

'Not long.'

The woman yells, and says 'Honey', then gets up, leans over and whispers something into She's ear. The woman sits back down, raising her eyes and pointing. The train stops at the next station and the woman leaves with her entourage, all the while looking back, still raising eyebrows, still pointing. Another crowd replaces them. The noise lowers and the world disappears until it feels as though it is just the two of them, riding a magical underground train to freedom.

'You're single?' he asks.

'Yeah,' she says matter-of-factly. 'You?'

'Yes.'

'I guess what I should ask you, cos you're a guy, is if there is someone out there who thinks they're your girlfriend.'

'Wow. No. I'm single. That's what that means, right?'

She scoffs. 'You never know with men.'

'What?'

'I don't trust men. For all I know, you could have a wife in another country.'

'Come to think of it, I have a couple of wives deep in the villages of Congo.'

'Not funny.'

'All this sounds like you're projecting to me . . .'

'You're lucky I know what that means otherwise I'd think you were insulting me. And no, I'm not projecting.'

'So, do you hate all men because of your ex? What happened, did he cheat?'

'No. She ... didn't cheat.'

'Oh.'

'We were going to get married, but it all got too much. I got depressed, she got abusive, and we destroyed each other. I don't hate her; it just wasn't meant to be.' She looks down at her hands, fingers layered with jewellery, and anxiously rubs them together.

'I need to get off at this stop,' she says, as the train pulls into the station. She quickly gets up to leave.

'Wait ...' he shouts. 'I still don't know your name ...'

'Belle.'

$1,631

Chapter 24

Grace Heart Academy School, London, 9.17 a.m.

I arrived at work a bit later than usual on Monday morning. I skipped the staff meeting and the awkward chatter and went straight into my classroom. A morning of no classes afforded me the momentary solitude I desperately needed. I sat on my desk. I could not stop thinking of Mr Barnes; the image of his head landing on the ground, then bouncing, once or twice, replayed in my mind every time I drifted. I had been doing a lot of that lately, drifting, going through the motions, each day feeling a little less special than the last, less meaningful – less alive.

I checked my emails, figuring the deeper I plunged myself into my work, the more I'd be able to forget this feeling. Click. Delete. Click. Delete. Click. Delete. *Staff Announcement: Christmas Party*. Delete. *Mr McCormack: Meeting – Important*. Click. I wished I could delete them all and get my inbox to zero. Surely, hell must be an eternity of never-ending emails. Break time approached; there was still no sign of Mr Barnes. Usually, rumours spread around this place like wildfire, so if anyone had heard anything, it would be around the school by now. I remember the time a new teacher completely lost their temper and punched a wall in the classroom. The word got around faster than the school bell. And it wasn't even from the students. I suspect he had been eyeing up that wall for weeks and knew just where to hit it. To be fair to him, I had often thought about punching a wall, but I could not find one deserving enough to be hit.

I walked through the corridors, past the sports hall, the canteen, the library, up the stairs, around again. Still no sign. His classroom was empty. As I walked back to my classroom, I saw Sandra walking towards me. She looked at me, holding my gaze, but showing no signs of slowing down to talk. She rarely did this, if at all. We would always stop in the corridors for a chat, or at least a joke that would often lead to staff members gazing at us with suggestive suspicion, or the students making comments. The boys saying, 'Is that you, sir? Go on.' Or the girls asking, 'Miss, is Mr Kabongo your boyfriend?'

My eyes screamed at Sandra to stop. I wanted to talk, to tell her everything, but she kept walking. I went back to my classroom, slumped into my chair and waited for the bell.

'You all right there, pal?' Mr McCormack came into the room. I shuffled some papers around on my desk unconvincingly to make it look like I was working. He wore a puzzled expression on his face as he sat down on the table in front of my desk.

'Look, is everything okay?' he asked, with a hint of concern. I was taken aback by his question, not by the question itself, but by the fact he was asking.

'Yeah?' I replied, more a question in response to his, than an answer.

'It's just that you haven't been yourself lately, or really at all as the year has gone by. I just wanted to make sure that you knew you could come to me if there's anything you wanted to talk about ... ' I hated how genuine he sounded. As if the idioms 'my door is always open' and 'if you need a shoulder' were true. In this case, it was and this saddened me. Mr McCormack always made time for you – to talk, to listen. He was a married man, with three kids, and he always made time. Yet here I was, alone and living with my mum, and barely able to stop each moment crumbling into the next. I wanted to tell him it was me, that I was the thing with poison. But my mind blocked my mouth before I could speak, and I simply muttered, 'It's okay,' as the bell rang, signalling the end of break.

The day passed. My thoughts grew heavier. I did not leave my classroom. Mr McCormack's question had sent me on another drift; this time of isolation and doubt, contemplating the inevitable futility of my future. I did not even stop to think about Mr Barnes, not until Sandra walked in and said, 'Have you heard what happened?'

'What?' I replied, surprised.

'Apparently, Mr Barnes got robbed or something. He's in hospital. He was on a night out with friends, got separated from his group and then got robbed ... '

'Oh, no ... where did you hear this?'

'Gina told me.'

'Separated from his group ... ?'

'Yeah.'

'Ah, that makes sense now ...'

'Wait, what do you mean that makes sense?'

'Don't worry.'

'Are you going to visit him?'

'I don't know. I literally just found out.'

'Wait, you didn't know?'

I shook my head.

'Well, aren't you going to go see him?'

I thought about the best way to answer this question, without lying. I couldn't.

'Yeah. I will.'

She went on a rant about how unsafe it is these days, and how there's violence everywhere in this city, and gangs, and knives, and how you can't even have a peaceful night out any more, and I listened and validated her woes – not because she was right, that was irrelevant, but because I wanted her to stay. She left as soon as the conversation ended.

I heard a basketball bouncing and rubber sports shoes squeaking against the wooden floor. I went into the sports hall. There was a basketball game on. An opposing school was visiting, their plain red and white uniform an eyesore against our chrome-blue and gold. I stood against the wall watching Mr Black waving his hands through the air giving instructions. He seemed to grow larger with every movement and move in sync with his players, as if he was their master puppeteer. Duwayne sat on the bench, completely consumed by the game; cheering, whooping, supporting his teammates. I watched him and wondered how many sides there were to this boy.

There was less than a minute left in the third quarter. Mr

Black called Duwayne from the bench, and he went to the sideline, preparing to sub in. He high-fived his teammate coming from the court, and went to defend number five, on team red and white, bringing down the ball. Duwayne hounded him. Team red passed the ball around, fumbling but avoiding the defence. Duwayne stole the ball and sprinted with it on a fast break towards the basket, the defenders chasing behind him like the police. They slowed him in his tracks, and with the few seconds left on the clock, he took two wayward steps, and threw the ball up one-handed into the air and fell on the ground. The ball floated up high with a rainbow arc, tail a shooting star trailing its path, and landed, like a stone thrown in a river, into the basket: swish. Duwayne pumped his fist as the buzzer went. His teammates ran over to him. He looked at me as he passed, a brief glimpse, eyes asking for someone to be proud of him. I quietly left the sports hall.

The week was long and labouring, some days an uphill climb, others a downward tumble. I made my way into the church mid-week. The main area was empty. I followed the sound coming from the side room. I knew Mami wouldn't be there today. Thankfully, she was at work. I knew that if she saw me here, she would see this as approval, though it was the furthest thing from that. In fact, I'm not even sure what it was, but here I was, walking quietly through the side door into a half-empty room with Pastor Baptiste at the front.

He jumped up when he saw me but managed to disguise and convert it into one of the many natural movements he has while preaching that leaves people saying, 'He's so energetic and passionate.' He acknowledged my presence with a nod, and I acknowledged his by not responding.

'Let not your hearts be troubled. Believe in God – believe also in me. In my Father's house are many rooms. If it were not so, would I have told you that I go to prepare a place for you? And if I go and prepare a place for you, I will come again and will take you to myself, that where I am you may be also.'

Pastor Baptiste very delicately closed the Bible he was reading from and began speaking as if addressing an audience of thousands. I tried to listen to what he was saying, but every word that came out of his mouth filled me with indignation; his voice was fuel added to the rageful fire of my burning heart. After a half-hour of intense prayer, which I had walked out of, I returned to find the evening session had finished and Pastor Baptiste was left alone, packing away the chairs.

'Michael, I welcome your presence, but if I'm honest, I did not expect to see you here tonight.'

'Why?'

'Well, it's just you don't often attend so I did not—'

'No. That's not what I'm asking you about.' Pastor Baptiste stopped in his tracks and stood upright.

'So, what is it that you are asking me about?' he said, looking over, stern and focused.

'Why? Why do you do this? All of this?' I replied, waving my hand across the room.

He chuckled, and then continued packing away the chairs.

'That conversation is for another day.'

'Well, I'm asking now. I deserve to know, don't you think? Especially as you intend to marry my mother.'

'She told me about what you said, about your ultimatum, Michael.'

'And?'

'And do you think it's fair?'

'I don't know about fair, I only know about what's meant to be.'

'And what's meant to be will be.'

'So, answer my question. Why?'

'Why? You want to know why? I do this because I love the Lord . . . and because people need hope. Without it, we have nothing.' He finished his sentence like a sermon.

His simplicity and elusiveness frustrated me. He wasn't magnificent and esoteric. He was simple. I huffed.

'Michael, I sense much pain in you. You must learn to let it go, otherwise it will eat you up inside. Trust me, I know.'

His words sent me into an internal flying rage. Pastor Baptiste slowly walked away and there I stood, a dilapidated building, falling apart brick by brick by brick.

Chapter 25

Colindale, North London; 7.17 p.m.

'Where are you?' a panic-stricken Jalil said, as I answered the phone.

'Is everything all right?'

'I need you to come, quickly.'

'Okay, sure. I'm on my way.'

I'm sorry. Something has come up. It's urgent. Can we please reschedule? I texted Sandra as soon as I got off the phone. We were supposed to 'talk'. I'm not quite sure what that meant, but it made me feel as though there were a thousand spiders nesting on my head. After a week of not speaking, she had emailed me saying that there was something she needed to get off her chest. She only ever emails me when it's serious, like when she got called into to a meeting by Mrs Sundermeyer and was scared she was getting fired but ended up being offered a new role, or when she suspected me of sneaking into her classroom and taking from her 'secret snack drawer', which I did, but that's beside the point. I rushed out from work and made my way across town to Jalil's.

'What's going on?' I said as Jalil opened the door to let me in.

'Yooo,' he gave a stunted greeting, 'you got here fast.'

'I know. You said to get here quickly. Is it Baba? Is he okay?' I said as I walked into the living room and found Aminah sitting there, arms crossed, one leg over the other.

'Baba's fine,' she replied. Her voice, two discordant chords attempting to harmonise.

'I thought it was an emergency?'

They both hesitated to respond. I looked at Aminah, and she was sat as if the warmth of her body was fleeing her. Jalil looked nervously around the room, eyes shifting until his met mine.

'It is, bro . . . ' he said, in a pleading tone. 'Listen, you know how Baba is in a bad state, it's not looking good. And I'm trying to explain to Aminah.'

'No. What you're not about to do is use one of your preambles to make it seem like—'

'Can I finish?'

'Like you're justified in what you're asking.'

'But can I fucking finish?' Jalil yelled, plunging the room into a barrel of silence.

He cleared his throat before continuing, 'Sorry. As I was saying, it's a difficult time,' his voice returned to its pleading tone, 'and you know how much Baba wants me to be married—' His voice started to break, and a single tear fell on to his cheek.

'He's asked me if I would marry him,' Aminah cut in, 'but not actually for real, just a kind of pretend marriage for—'

'Baba has a serious heart arrhythmia. It's not looking good.

I've been spending all my days at the hospital. I should have told you.'

'It's not fair. You can't use your father's illness to manipulate me into a fake wedding.'

'It's not manipulation, habibti. I'm trying to fulfil my father's wishes, I want to make him happy.'

'I would have more respect for you if you actually asked me to marry you.'

'We're not there yet, we're not ready yet.'

'But we're ready for this?'

'What difference does it make if we're going to get married eventually anyway?'

'The difference is I won't be some dumb woman to go along with your stupid plan. Who do you think I am?'

'But I love you.'

'I ask that you respect me first, before you love me. You would not ask this of someone you respect.'

Jalil lowered his head.

'Have you got anything to say for your friend?' Aminah asked.

I stood there with my mouth half open, the fury of Aminah's eyes slowly burning through me. She scoffed.

'Oh, I'm leaving,' she announced, before pacing out of the door and slamming it loud enough to shake the walls. Jalil looked at me with bitter disappointment.

'Why the fuck didn't you say something?' He paced around the room, hands gripping his hair, almost tearing it out.

'What was I supposed to say? Tell her to marry you?'

'Bro, I'm going to lose everything. Everything!'

'What do you mean?'

'I'm broke, man. Broke. I've got no money, not any real money. And getting a job, a real job, is hard, so I've just been doing whatever. You know, buying and selling stuff . . . '

'What do you mean?'

'No, nothing like that. All legit. Kind of.' Jalil huffed as I looked at him suspiciously, not knowing what to believe.

'And now Baba thinks I'm living some wild lifestyle,' Jalil continued, 'He says he doesn't trust me to take care of everything on my own, so he'll give away the house and my inheritance unless I marry. He says a wife and family will humble me. Help me learn the true purpose of my life. But I know that what he really wants is to see me in a suit and tie. That's what he thinks being responsible means.'

'I don't get it. Why don't you actually just ask Aminah to marry you though?'

'Because I'm not ready. I'm scared, okay? I am scared. And now all of this has come along, it's too much pressure. And it's too soon. Would you marry someone you met after three months?'

'Maybe. I would if I knew that I was going to marry them anyway.'

Jalil quietened, lowered his head and placed both his hands on his waist.

'It's not too late. Do you love her?'

'I think so.' His thick eyelashes flickered as his eyes blinked rapidly. 'I mean, yeah, I do. I don't want to lose her. She's amazing.'

'Are you sure?'

'Yeah.'

'You don't sound like it.'

'What do you mean, man?'

'Bro, what do you want?'

'What?'

'Out of life, like, what do you want?' I asked Jalil, as though I were asking myself.

'I don't know, I guess I've never really had to think about that. I've just been okay with moving from one thing to the next, and not taking things too seriously. I've used staying in university as a way to seem like I'm doing something, but I don't really care about all that. I just want to be okay, you know?' Jalil looked away, breaking the eye contact we held. 'I want everything to be okay. But I don't know what I want to be or do.'

'Well, that's what you have to figure out for yourself, you can't just go around letting life happen to you, otherwise it'll eat you up inside.' Jalil nodded as I spoke and as soon as the words left my lips I wondered if I was speaking to him or to me. 'Then it isn't too late to do the right thing.' I brought my words to a close, sounding like the ever-confident counsellor; there for others, for everyone but himself.

If there ever was a moment to watch the weight of the world fall upon a man's shoulders and collapse him, this was it. What a good problem to have: marry the love of your life for a windfall of your father's cash. What a privilege it is, even, to see your father die. To know where he is buried, to know where he can be found. What a privilege it is to inherit more than just absence, more than loss or trauma. But we all carry our burdens no matter the weight. They are heavy because they are upon our own shoulders. Who among us would swap our burdens for another's if we knew not the weight?

Jalil sniffed and dropped his head into his hands and started to cry. I reassured him, taking him into my arms like an orphaned child into adoption, a rough sleeper into a home.

I walked into my classroom and threw my coat, scarf, gloves, bags, every weight I had on me, on to the floor and crashed into the chair. I felt my body, stiff, joints clicking and squeaking like rusting metal, limbs ready to snap as if elastic stretched too far, and a migraine thumping the side of my head. But deeper than this, I felt an intrinsic tiredness, not just of the body, beyond the mind, and deeper than the soul; a fatigue yet to be named. Luckily, it was an inset day so there were no students in. The quiet and peace throughout the building was self-evident. I decided to avoid the staff team-building activities and spend the entire day in here, my classroom; a prison or a sanctuary from the world – on days such as this, I knew not which.

I'm sorry I had to cancel yesterday. I know you wanted to talk and how important it was to you. Are you around today? X. I replied to Sandra's email. I knew she was in, not because I had seen her, but because other people would have come to me if she wasn't.

I spent most of the day staring into the back wall, watching the hands of the clock move but not at all. The minutes passed, but the moment seemed to stay the same. I printed out what I had been writing, stuffed it into an envelope and into my pocket. I walked through the corridors of the school, this time with a different feeling; of ambivalence, and vacillation, between two minds, between two worlds.

I knocked on Mrs Sundermeyer's door before I went in.

Her face remained serious, as if posing for a portrait. She had already begun listening before I even spoke.

'If you've got a minute, I just wanted to talk and let you know ...'

'Of course,' she said reassuringly.

'I don't know how to say this but ... I am leaving. I am quitting my job.' I took the envelope from my pocket and slid it on to the table.

'I haven't been coping. Each day that I come in, it gets worse. I feel like I'm breathing in this smog, its dark and grey. I can't see it. But I know it's there. I feel it on my skin, in my lungs. I cough it up, I spit it out. It never goes. It's always there, some days more than others, but it is always there. Lately, it's been there more and more: when I wake up, before I go to sleep, in the middle of a lesson, always. I find myself randomly staring into nothing, feeling empty, and I won't know how much time has passed, sometimes a minute, sometimes an hour. I can spend the whole day just staring into nothing.

'I take long baths just to feel the warmth, but it's only so long before I start to feel as though I'm drowning. I don't know what to do, but I know that I can't be here any more, because it makes it worse.

'Imagine there's something trapped inside you, a sharp clawed animal, and it's running out of air, so it's scratching away, trying to break free. And the more the air runs out, the more it scratches at you, inside, trying to escape, and it hurts you more and more. And all you can do, on the outside, is just stay calm, because no one knows you are carrying this thing; no one knows, and sometimes you don't even know.'

I was shocked at myself saying all of this to her. I regretted it instantly. I tried to hold it back, but couldn't; every memory, every pain, every cramp of the heart, every ache of the soul, every tear of the spirit, came rushing back to me. Even the happy memories, the joy, the laughter, the smiles, made me cry some more, for I knew that I would not see them again; this ship had sailed, and I was left on an island alone. Mrs Sundermeyer remained in the same portrait-like position that she had when I walked in, as if she was unmoved, indifferent, or yet to take in what I had said. She doesn't care.

'So, I have to go. That's my notice. But I don't want anyone to know, none of the students, none of the staff. No one. I don't want any leaving cards, or cake, or goodbyes or anything else. I just want to quietly disappear, move on and do what I need to do.'

Chapter 26

Brooklyn, New York City; 8.08 a.m.

Michael's eyes open to a solemn silence. He lies on a single bed, surrounded by white walls, in the room of a Brooklyn apartment with no windows. There is a two-seat sofa next to the bed and a desk on the other side, with some art, which makes the room feel less temporary.

He sits upright on the bed, legs stretched out across the mahogany laminate floor. There is no sound from the other side of the door, so maybe the people he's sharing with have all gone to work. He met two of them yesterday, a man and a woman, both of whose names he cares not to remember. The man was short and kept trying to make up for his lack of height with awkward jokes, which Michael validated with awkward laughter, and the woman kept talking about her ex-boyfriend, who she was still sleeping with; both conversations forcing him into a daydream, mostly about Belle. He can say that now, Belle. He knows her name. It fills him with the feeling of the flutter of a bird's wings against the brow of his heart.

The living area is so spacious he could run in it. He walks up to the window, to look at the view, and it is blocked by the next building, with spray-painted art on its side, and fallen snow, pure, soft and white, on the sidewalk. He sits down on the sofa with a cup of tea, and the guitar in the corner of the room makes him wish he'd kept practising. He feels a serenity here that has eluded him for a long time. Maybe it's here; maybe it's her.

Michael leaves the apartment and walks to Morgan Avenue subway. The snow is soft and delicate under his feet, but it quickly freezes his toes. He walks past the row of converted apartments that were former industrial buildings, past a bas-ketball court, filled with snow, and wonders what it would be like to play a game there. Sitting on the train, during the day, making his way uptown feels surreal. It feels as if he's making an ordinary trip, part of his usual weekly routine. He looks around at the other passengers in the carriage, and they do not look at him any differently.

New York City metro is confusing, the map looks like a dia-gram of the human central nervous system. Only New Yorkers know how to get around without getting lost. He gets off the train, and transfers to the red line, up to 135th Street. He calls the lines by their colour: Red line to Harlem, Green line to the Bronx, Grey line to Brooklyn. Belle told him it was a ridiculous way of remembering the lines when he asked her for directions to get to hers, and instead tried to explain the letter system to him, which he found even more ridiculous, especially when she mentioned something about the trains going 'local'.

Michael first gets off at 116th Street and looks around. He remembers Belle saying – when they went on their long and mysterious walk – that there is a soul food restaurant on this street that does amazing cake, and he thought it would be a good idea to get some. Chocolate, for her persuasion, and carrot, for his. As he walks down the road to the restaurant, he sees a cash machine. He stops, inserts his card and checks the balance: $1,452. He takes a deep breath. He feels neither panic nor calm, merely an acceptance of what is and what is coming. *I cannot forget what I came here for.* Michael gets the food from the restaurant, then gets back on the metro and back on the Blue line until he eventually arrives at 135th Street station.

'You can't miss it. It's a tall brown building, three blocks from the station.' Her instructions were clear, and simple, yet, he still gets lost. He looks up at the tower blocks. In the end, he gets there with the aid of the maps on his phone. Michael takes the lift and knocks on her burgundy-coloured door. She opens.

'Hey, you,' she says, her voice a song. 'You made it.'

'Made it just fine.' He smiles.

She's wearing a long, loose-flowing printed dress that hangs against the slenderness of her body. Her hair is wrapped in a silk scarf. She turns around, leaving the door open, and says, 'Come in' as she walks through her living room, into the connecting kitchen.

'I was just feeding my cat,' she says, as he looks around and sits on the leather sofa, trying to make himself as small as possible. The wide-screen TV in front of him is switched off. Her bookshelf to the left calls out to him. There are paintings, some on a canvas, some on the walls, of silhou-etted, esoteric, god-like figures with wings, each somehow resembling her.

'You have a beautiful apartment.'

The cat steps out from behind a large far-eastern ornament on the floor. It has an odd limp, and a little bell that rings from its collar.

'I put a bell on her after she kept wandering out and getting lost. She got hit by a car and the vet had to amputate her leg.'

'Oh, that's so sad,' Michael says, hoping his concern appears genuine.

'That was before me. I picked up her at the shelter. It was love at first sight.' She laughs. 'Her name is Monica.'

'Oh, like Monica from *Friends*?'

'Nope.'

'Monica Seles?'

'Nah.'

'Monica Lewinsky?'

'No . . .'

'Okay, I'm all out of Monicas.'

'Like Monica the singer.'

'Oh. Of course.'

She picks up the cat and strokes it.

'You're okay with cats, right?'

'Yeah, totally,' he says, trying to convince himself rather than her. She stretches out her arms and motions the cat towards him as if he should come and pick it up.

'Maybe next time,' Michael says and smiles nervously. Although it is a bright afternoon outside, inside Belle has the curtains drawn, candles lit and sage burning, which gives the room a midnight séance type of feel.

'You can take off your coat, you know,' she laughs, 'and get comfortable.'

Her laughter makes him settle. He relaxes and takes off his

coat, scarf and boots, and spreads across the sofa, taking up a lot more space than before.

'Okay, but don't overdo it,' she says, chuckling, as she comes over, extending a hand with a cup of warm brew.

'Tea?' He smiles, then she smiles, which reminds him of how long it has been since a smile was for him.

'I brought some cake.' He passes her the box and she excitedly grabs it and returns with the cakes served up on a plate. She sits next to him on the sofa, with her feet curled under her legs. The music of a raspy-voiced, acoustic folk singer serenades them in the background. They drink tea, and eat cake, and bask in their momentary solitude.

'Michael,' she says after taking a slurp of tea, 'we've seen each other more than a few times now, and I don't know enough about you.'

'What do you want to know?'

'You never talk about yourself.'

'Okay, so what do you want to know?'

'That's not the point, don't make me ask.'

'So, I'm just supposed to start talking?'

'Yeah!'

'About myself?'

'That's right.'

'I don't know. I'm just not used to it. I never had anyone to talk to. I mean, I had people, but I felt alone, no matter who was around.'

'I've felt alone too. Well, at least mostly alone.' She stops and sighs, looking into her cup of tea. 'I had a big extended family. I grew up with my cousins and my grandparents, then I was fostered, but you know all that. But that's because I actually talk.'

'Yeah, but it's easier for you because you're a ...'

'Because I'm a what?'

'Nothing.'

'You were going to say woman, weren't you?'

'No.'

'Yes you were. You were going to say that because I'm a woman, I talk a lot more.'

'I wasn't! I was going to say because you're ... you're ... an artist; you're more creative and expressive than I am. You paint and all that.'

'So, not only are you a patriarchal, sexist misogynist, you're also a damn liar. Ugh. Men are trash.' She punches him playfully on his shoulder and he feigns pain.

'And you're a misandrist; that was violence based on gender.'

'No, that was violence based on you being a dumb ass.' She lunges at him with cat-like swiftness, but he anticipates it and catches her mid-air, bringing her back down towards the sofa, until they tussle. He wraps his arms around her and locks her in.

'You do know I've got you trapped, right?'

'Maybe. Or maybe you've got me right where I want you to have me.'

'Ha!'

'Maybe I'm a masochist and all that's left is for me to get the handcuffs, whips and chains I have hidden under this chair.'

He slowly unravels her from his hold.

'That does sound kind of exciting, though,' he smirks.

'You nasty.'

She returns to her side of her sofa, gets her tea, and extends her legs across his middle, smiling sinisterly. *I enjoy every*

moment with her; all the joy and the laughter. Every moment.
He looks at her, looks into her.

'What?' she says, feeling evidently self-conscious.

'Nothing.'

'I want to know more about you, though ... like how you grew up?'

'Well, I grew up on an estate ... the same estate we still live in now.'

'Wait, on an estate?'

'Yeah.'

'With horses and fields and shit?'

'What? No.' He laughs.

'An estate?'

'Yeah, an estate. You know, social housing, the hood, what do you call them, Section 8, the projects?'

'Oh! Wow, that means something totally different here.'

'I figured.'

'And what was that like?'

'You know, just the stereotypical stories of growing up poor ... and Black, but it wasn't all negative. I loved so many things. I remember always being told to read by my dad, so that's what I did. Even after he was gone.

'And you know, we wore the whole FUBU, and Fat Albert, Sean John, Rocawear, four-XL baggy jeans, sagging low, Air Force Ones ...'

'YOU?' she shrieks. 'No way.' She explodes with laughter. 'I just can't picture it.'

'Trust me, you don't want to. Thank goodness we didn't have camera phones in those days.'

'I know, right.'

'What about you? What were you like?'

'I was a little punk goddess, metal dog-collar, spiked hair, wearing anarchist T-shirts, and holding fake witch séances to curse my high-school bullies whilst listening to death metal.'

'So, you haven't changed, then?' he says and watches her smile turn into laughter. He wishes he could capture it in a jar and take it with him wherever he goes; maybe multiply that smile by the thousands and release it into prisons, into drug-infested street corners, into places of conflict and war, into abusive homes, and other places in need of hope.

'Do you ever think about how different life could have been?' Michael asks.

'All the time. I'm always questioning whether I made the right choices, or if I did the right thing, even if there's nothing I can do about it.'

'Sometimes, you just got to accept fate?'

'Fate? Fuck that shit,' Belle answers unequivocally. 'I don't believe anything in this world is meant to be. Just look at it. All the death and the destruction, somewhere out there a new-born baby is going to die, families will be separated at a country's borders, all the meaningless wars, hundreds of people will die in a part of the world that won't make the news, and everyone will go on like normal.

'And I'm supposed to say it's fate cos I got a new car or a new job, a salary increase, or because I have a reciprocated infatuation over some other brainless member of our species?'

'But there is some beauty in this world.'

'Does it necessitate the existence of all the ugly, though? You know, we humans are supposed to be the most intelligent species, made in the image of some omniscient, lazy-ass god, too bummed to use his powers, a god who'd rather watch wars than end them, and we still can't come to terms with the one fundamental thing that we all know: that we have no idea what the fuck we're doing here and, one day, we won't even be here to try and figure it out.

'We live on a rock, spinning around another larger rock that's on fire, in a universe so vast, full of billions and trillions of rocks, and yet we are so arrogant to believe our lives are significant.

'We puff up our chests with importance, but we forget that it's in our insignificance where we find value, it's in understanding that none of this matters that we find out what does matter. Therein lies the beauty. That's where we find ourselves.'

Michael stares at Belle. He is entranced under her magic spell: voodoo queen, shaman, priestess. She stares back at him, and her eyes transport him to otherworldly destinations.

'Sorry,' she says, 'I tend to go on long hyperbolic rants.'

'Tend to?' She looks back at him, slightly embarrassed. 'Never apologise for being who you are.'

Her eyes lower. He watches her disappear into herself for a moment. She is calm and peaceful on the surface, but beneath, thunder rumbles.

'There's this documentary we should watch. You like documentaries?'

'I love them!' he says, with a cheer, changing the mood in the room. The sun starts to set in the sky, taking with it its blended canopy of cerulean and crimson.

$1,426

Chapter 27

'DNR,' Belle says, noticing the tattoo on Michael's ribcage, just below his chest. 'What's that?' she asks.

'Oh, er, it's just the initials of someone – a reminder.'

'That's why it's tattooed close to your heart?'

'Something like that.'

'You're obviously lying, but it's okay, I ain't gonna probe.'

'You're too smart for your own good.'

'I'm too smart for anyone's good.'

They lay in a comfortable silence, the kind of silence shared between lovers.

'I thought you would have a problem with it,' Belle says, her head on his chest, stroking his stomach, his hand reaching upwards, twisting the curls of her hair. The moonlight shines through, transforming the white walls into a dark fluorescent blue, like the darkest hue of skin, the opposite of sin. Her room is a sanctuary, a respite from the bitter cold of this world.

'That's why I got off when I told you. It wasn't even my stop. And if I'm honest, I never thought I would see you again.'

Michael continues twisting her hair, watching her as she breathes deeply, watching as her eyelashes flicker, counting each one in the shimmering light of the candles.

'You didn't have to worry,' he says, trying to reassure her.

'But I do. You don't get it. A lot of guys switch up on you once they find out. It's all jokes about threesomes at first, but then, after a while, they feel pressured. They start to think about what their guys would say, their friends or their family.'

'Look, you loved someone, it didn't work out. You don't have to bring the past into the future.'

'It's hard not to . . .'

'I understand.'

'Especially with men,' she hesitates and breathes out a long, heavy sigh, before speaking again. 'I'm attracted to y'all. But I don't like y'all. I haven't been with a man in a long time.'

'I don't know how I should feel.'

'You should feel lucky,' Belle says, as if in awe. 'You are just different, a calm energy.'

A silence passes between them, heavy and beleaguered. He stays quiet and waits for her to speak again.

'I just don't get why men are like this. Why the world is like this. A girl in middle school from the Bronx getting cat-called by grown men cos her body's getting thick, immigrant west African women standing on the streets of Paris having to sell their bodies just to make extra money to provide for their families back home, women raped in South Africa, raped in Congo, raped in Sudan, raped in Crenshaw, raped in Honduras, raped in Bahia, raped in Myanmar, raped in India, raped in Spain, raped in Ireland, raped, raped, raped, raped, raped, raped, raped, raped, raped, raped, raped, raped, raped, raped . . .

'What becomes of a word that is used over and over again? Does it lose all meaning? Does the poison turn into such sweet nectar it becomes normal? That we do not see how it is killing us? How this poison is killing all women? Gay women, bi-women, transwomen, and to be Black, on top of all that, you know? Do you really know?

'Do you know how it feels to see and know all of this, but to still have to carry on, to still carry on in this world knowing there is no one else for you but you? I would sooner throw this world into the same fire they use to burn the effigy they made of woman, they made of Black, they made of gay, and watch the world go up in flames and just leave it all behind.'

Michael pulls Belle in close. He feels her tears. He knows she is crying though he does not see it. He knows she is crying because he is crying too. And in this moment, this moment of unbridled emotional synchronicity, he is one with her. He feels how strong she has had to be all her life, how much she has had to endure, with no chance for respite. *I do not wish to give her the world; instead, I wish to take it from her, take it off her shoulders, and lay it down. I wish I could tell her that there can be a life without burden, a life without suffering, a life where each day is not a trial, a test of endurance or a thing to be overcome. I wish I could bring the hope of future generations to this moment, and show her that one day, everything will make sense. All the pain endured, all the suffering, that one day we will live on the fingertips of those who declare themselves free. But I can't, all I can do is be here; I have nothing to give her, nothing left to give even to myself. My hands are emptier than my heart, this heart that has bled itself dry.*

Belle looks up at him, the tears in her eyes a Cressida-formed waterfall; winged lover unfaithful to the world, flying upwards to the burning sun. If only they could leave this place for ever. They kiss. Her lips, so soft and tender, evoke forgotten memories of how it feels to be alive. Michael feels the dark cloud, the smog surrounding him start to lift. It falls into the wayside, drifts back into the unknown from which it came. She lays herself on top of him. Her warmth is everlasting. Her heart is a lighthouse and he is a lost ship in the ocean.

She mumbles words in a tongue unknown to his ears and slides her hand delicately with the tenderness of each finger-tip, from his belly button, up his abdominals to his chest, and spreads her hand out as if exploring the territory of his body.

Belle lifts her leg over Michael's middle, and gently strokes her thighs above his. He feels himself harden, a log, and it rubs gently on her. She starts to stroke it as she kisses his neck. A small pocket of air escapes from his mouth. She kisses him again. His breath becomes a wild flutter. He watches his chest rise and lower, each breath faster than the last. He can hear her soft groans. They echo in this moonlit room.

She raises her kisses to his cheek. He turns and faces her, his mouth on her mouth; their lips share the dance of the sacred. He rolls over on top of her. She wraps her arms, her legs, around his body. They are at each other's mercy, at each other's freedom. He lowers his kisses on to her neck, she moans in a higher tone, and he cups her breast in his hand. She unravels as he raises her loose-flowing, printed dress over her head, and throws it across the room. He kisses her nipples and feels the soft tissue of her breast. He lowers his kisses, his mouth moves nomadic across the land of her body; lower from breast to sternum, sternum to stomach, stomach to navel, lower to in-between her thighs. Their hands lock, fingers entwined as she raises her legs up above his shoulders. He goes down and kisses her lips, separating them with his tongue, searching for the jewel of her crown. A queen with no empire; a kingdom not won by war. Blessed are the holy who sit among us; blessed are those blessed enough to touch, blessed enough to love.

You are an enigma, a mystery, the aurora borealis of my darkened skies, the childlike imagination of my adult mind. You are the moon's harmony, composed in the key of tranquillity, an orchestra of violins playing into ten burning suns; you are the tears of the last sun that shines. You are a kalpa, captured in a single breath, my heart finds rest, this senseless sensation, you give me vibrations like ancestor hands on a djembe drum.

With no legs, to you I would run; with no eyes, your face I would see; with no ears, your voice I would hear; with no hands, your skin I would touch; with no mouth, your jewel I would taste; with no nose, your scent I would smell; with no heart it is you I would love. You are my person.

The apogee of her moans rises above like a tidal wave in the ocean and falls over them, cleansing like ablution from the high priestess; they are loved, they are loved, they are love.

The train runs local as he rides it back to Brooklyn. He sits and watches the tired and worn faces with him. It is 4 a.m., a time he knows too well. He gets out at Morgan Avenue and walks home to the apartment. The streets are quiet, cold and eerie; the melted snow resembles a liquid pool from another planet.

He opens the big, red, heavy front door of the apartment

as quietly as he can, and ventures into his bedroom through the darkness. He closes the door, and slowly takes off all his layers. He sits on the side of his bed staring, staring, staring.

$1,351

Chapter 28

Peckham Rye Station, South London; 7.58 p.m.

Thunderous rain poured down from the grey clouds covering the sky. I waited at the station. The few who were brave
ventured out. After my patience expired like curdled milk,
I walked left out of Peckham Rye and up through the high
street, past the McDonald's, past the Poundland, past the
charity shop, past the hairdressers.

'I can't believe he lives around here,' I mumbled to myself,
as the rain seeped through the scarf I was using to cover
my head. See, fifteen, even ten, years ago, someone like Mr
Barnes would have never lived in Peckham. He would have
been too intimidated by the number of languages people
spoke in that he didn't understand or how loud the churches
were on Sunday afternoons or the number of young boys
who walked around with their hoods up and tracksuit bottoms sagging. I used to be one of those boys. We'd end up
getting into fights in the McDonald's, or some back streets
somewhere, only the most athletic of us able to run away to
tell the story, which is all we wanted to do – let others know

that there was something going on in our lives. But on other days we came here, with our parents, our uncles and aunties, to buy the foods only we knew, and to speak the ways only we heard, and to praise the Lord how only we could. We'd have fun and make friends and though it wasn't perfect, it was ours.

I barely recognised this place. I walked to the end of the road, and then turned right past the library, past the Prince of Peckham. I carried on through an array of back streets until I came upon his door. 276. I stood in front of the door, catching momentary respite from the rain that had refused to ease. I knocked on the door three times, tentatively. Footsteps creaked down the wooden stairs and shuffled along the floor until a light switched on and the door swung open. Mr Barnes. His face was a canvas of primary colours: the blue of the bruises above his cheeks, the red of the blood that emerged from his split lip, and the green from the envy in his eyes that never seemed to settle. He stared at me, as though unable to string together a coherent sentence.

'What are you doing here?'

'I came to visit you,' I replied, while moving forwards, suggesting being let in. Mr Barnes hesitated, then waved me through. I sat down in the living room and looked around at the walls painted a colour between white and cream, and the Ikea furniture.

'Can I get you a drink?'

'Tea, please.'

He returned with a cup of tea for me, and a glass of something else for himself. I looked at him, but he kept looking ahead at the TV on the wall that was switched off.

'Are you not going to say anything?'

'Say what?' he replied.

'Are you going to tell me what happened?'

'Why? You must have heard something. So, you already know. That's why you came down here.'

'Everyone at work was so sad for you – "Mr Barnes got attacked, he got robbed" – but I know what you're really like. So, I need to hear the truth.'

'What for? What the heck has it got to do with you? It was nothing.' His voiced raised a little, as he stared back at me.

'You're lying. I know because I saw you! I saw you, okay. I saw you on that bridge.'

'What!' He stood up.

'What the fuck were you doing there?'

'You were there?!'

'The question is why were you there. You know that place is only good for one thing. Were you trying to get your latest fix or something?'

'Oh, fuck off. You don't know about anything, you saw me get attacked and did nothing ...'

'You were getting drugs, what the hell was I supposed to do?!'

'Call the police.'

'And get arrested when they arrive? You're an idiot. Don't you know how things work in this city?' He remained silent.

'And there were students from our school there.'

'No there weren't.'

'From our fucking school.'

'Did they see me ...? Shit. I could lose my job.'

'This is more important than your job, they could lose their future! Don't you know you're trapping them in that same fucking cycle?'

'But I was just—'

'To you it's just another night out, but to them they don't see a way out.'

'And I'm to blame? You were there, and you didn't do anything.'

'You're still part of the problem.'

'The problem? Who the hell do you think you are? You don't know anything about me, about where I'm from, and how I grew up. Who are you to judge? Shall I tell you about my abusive dad, or my alcoholic mum? Or did you just come all this way to lecture me? You don't care. You're a prick, coming here trying to sound all wise, all high and mighty, when you're no different from me. You're here for yourself. You're here because you felt guilty, and you couldn't handle it. The difference between you and me is I can handle it.' In one gulp, Mr Barnes swallowed whatever clear liquid filled his glass.

He was right. I didn't care, not about him. I came here because the guilt I was carrying felt too heavy, and by being here, the little voice in my mind would lighten the load by saying I did the right thing.

'If I find out who that boy was,' he continued to roar, 'I'll shop him in. And I'll shop you in an' all,' he said, pushing his finger into my chest.

'Man, fuck you.' I wanted to punch him in the face, but instead, I pushed his hand aside and left, slamming the door on my way out.

*

I had not seen Sandra for a while, perhaps she was avoiding me. Or I was avoiding her. At least it felt that way, but as I walked through the corridors, I craned my neck in hopes of seeing her. I walked to my classroom to find a few students already lined up, Alex all the As at the front. I opened the door for them to go in, and the rest of them followed in to sit down as the second bell rang. Duwayne was at the end of the corridor, running towards me.

'Sorry I'm late, sir,' he said, panting, with a look that sought validation. His apology surprised me; this wasn't late by his standards at all. He had once arrived so late, it was the end of the lesson, and he popped his head in saying, 'Safe, sir,' before telling one of his friends to go with him. His audacity then surprised me as much as his apology now. I nodded him in. He stumbled into the class with gracious relief.

'Today, we're looking at the book *The Kite Runner*, but before I continue, how many of you did the research?' I asked, with little expectation. The usual suspects put up their hands. Duwayne also slowly raised his hand. I looked at him suspiciously, with quiet disbelief.

'Okay, so then who can tell me what a refugee is?'

From the back of the class, Duwayne raised his hand. I noticed the difference in his body language, how upright he sat, how his hand was straight up in the air, his entire demeanour, unrecognisable from his former self. I looked around the class in hope that someone else would raise their hand to answer. I stared at Alex, sat at the front, almost imploring him to speak instead. He reluctantly raised his hand.

'Alex!'

'Is it kind of, like, when someone goes to a new country for better opportunities?'

'Well, good attempt, but that's not quite right.'

I hesitate before asking again. Duwayne had remained unmoved from his former position. I was obliged.

'Yes, Duwayne?'

'Sir, I think a refugee is someone who is forced to flee their home country because of the political circumstance, like war, conflict or fighting, or because of persecution.'

'Well done.' I tried to downplay my surprise. A part of me still resented him; I knew this was wrong of me, but I had decided that he would have to work much harder to win back my favour.

'So, moving on, I want you to do a simple writing exercise. I want you to imagine the life of a refugee, what it would be like if you were forced to leave London to go to another city or country because of conflict or persecution. How would you feel? What would it mean for your family? What would you take with you?'

They put their heads down and began writing in their books. I watched Duwayne.

He was working as if moving at double speed compared to the rest. His focus was immeasurable. While he worked, I kept seeing flashes of the old him leaning back on the chair, hands down his trousers, eyes screwed up at the brow.

'Pens down.'

'Now, does anyone want to read out what they wrote?'

A hand flies into the air.

'Go ahead.'

'I would be scared. London is my home, the only place I

have ever known. My memories and the people I love are here. My family are annoying, I argue with them all the time, but I would cry and miss them if we were separated. I would want wherever I go to accept me and treat me fairly because I would be hurting too much.'

'Thank you, Johnson.'

'So, class, I heard this interesting quote about identity and stereotypes, similar to what we were discussing the other day: "They create the Other and then resent them for being it." What do you think is meant by this? What are they trying to say?' I asked as I wrote on the board. The class remained with their hands down, the hesitation and subtle resignation evident in the air.

'Maybe it's about fear . . . sir.' I recognised the voice. I slowly turned around and there he was, Duwayne, with his hand up, ready to expound on his answer.

'Go on,' I said, curious.

'Well, people fear what they don't understand. And so, if they don't ever try to understand something, they can pretend it doesn't exist. That way, they can ignore it and hope it never happens to them. Like, the way homeless people are ignored on the streets is the same way refugees are ignored in this world. We see it, but hope it never happens to us.'

Duwayne slowly lowered his hand as if it were a weapon. The bell conveniently rang in my momentary silence after Duwayne's response. I was caught unaware of how much time had passed. I quickly dismissed them.

'Duwayne,' I called to him as he was at the door, leaving. I nodded at him to come to my desk and he left his friends and walked sheepishly towards me.

'Great answers today,' I said, as casually as possible. 'Where did this come from?'

'I read bare, you know.'

'Read ... bare?'

'A lot. I read a lot. You're always telling us to read, and get knowledge, so I thought I would try. It's amazing what you can learn by yourself.'

'Seriously. Well done.'

'Thanks, sir.' He nodded at me, lifted his hand up to fist-bump me. I looked down at his fist, and then back up at him. We fist-bumped. He smiled a smile I had yet to see on his face before, of acceptance, of joy. It's the little things.

'By the way, Duwayne, did you guys win your basket-ball match?'

'Yeah, sir! We're in the cup final.'

'Oh, congratulations!'

He started to walk off, but then stopped mid-way, turned and said, 'Sir, I just want to say thank you.'

'What for?'

'You know, for encouraging me in school. And not talking to me like I'm dumb or just another troubled yout'.' The frustration in his voice was palpable. 'People act like they care but they don't, but with you it's different.'

'That means a lot to me, Duwayne. I appreciate that.'

'Yeah, yeah, but don't get too gassed, still.'

I exploded with laughter at his insouciance.

'I'm going to prove you right.'

'What do you mean?'

'One day, after one of those long mad speeches you gave, like you're the president of some country, you said to me how "we're all shooting stars, who are we not to shine?" – I'm going to prove you right. I'm going to do well in school; I'm going to get my grades. And I'm going to shine.'

He walked towards the door to leave, 'Sir ... ' he said, looking back at me.

'Yes, Duwayne?'

'Are you going to come watch the finals?'

'When?'

'Next week ... '

'Wow! Of course, I'll be there.'

I felt a surge of pride from the bottom of my feet to the top of my hair. Duwayne was out of the door in a flash. I cried at my desk, literal tears of joy. I quickly moved on to check my emails to distract myself from the overwhelming emotion.

Michael,

I've been thinking about you a lot lately ... more than a lot. I don't know how quite else to say this. It's weird because any time someone else tried to hint about you, or suggest that there was something, or could be something, going on between us, I would laugh it off like it was the most ridiculous thing: 'Ha! Who, Michael? That big head? No!' At first, I just thought it was people trying to make something out of nothing because they saw us talking a lot, or because we were the only two Black people in our department, so obviously, we have to get married. But then, as time passed, I gradually started to see things differently. I started to see you differently. I started to notice you, how you would talk to people, to students, to staff. I noticed how you would walk through the corridors, I noticed if you weren't in that day; your absences made me sad, but your presence brightened me up. I developed feelings for you. I found myself wanting to be around you, to walk home after work with you. I imagined we were going back to the same place – you would cook and I would go and do my woodwork in the shed – so it would make me sad to snap out of that fantasy when we went home separate ways, and I didn't even know why.

I realised that I liked you that day when … well, I won't even say when. If you've already forgotten, it shows how much (or how little) I mean to you, and there's no point in carrying on. That day revealed a lot to me, it revealed a lot about you, but also about me. And in the past week since, you haven't even tried to get in touch, no call, no text, not even come to see me, you haven't even suggested for us to talk and figure this thing out. I don't know how quite else to say this but I'm really dis-appointed in you. You didn't seem like the type of guy to play mind games or to be fooling around, but if that's what you're on, I'd rather be left alone.

Sandra

I pushed the power-off button on the computer as soon as I finished reading the email. If I could scream, it would be loud enough to smash the glass windows into a thousand pieces. I felt rage spreading through my heart like a forest fire; it was seething through my veins, ready to burst. On the surface, my face appeared calm as I walked through the corridors and out of the building, but inside I dreamt I held the most brutal instrument of violence that could wreak havoc on the world. I felt wronged. I felt betrayed. I felt violent. I felt rageful. I turned these emotions in on myself. This rage wasn't just for Sandra, it was for the growing weight of burdens accumulating in my life: Mami and the Pastor, Jalil, Duwayne, work, and myself. To exist, even in my own body, was taking its toll; I wanted to escape from it, leave it all behind; I wanted to be free of it. I wanted to live where there is no consequence to this body, where I am not named, where I am not known. Where I am passing, invisible, like a breeze, or a gentle gust of wind, light through broken windows, moving from one life to the next. I did not want to know others. I did not even want to know myself.

Chapter 29

Peckriver Estate, London; 10.17 p.m.

I walked into my building and, upon opening the door, was met by the same group of youths sitting, smoking; cumuliform clouds hovering above, playing music, exploding with laughter and profanity. The loudness went quiet when they saw me, my eyes locked into a stare with each one of them. I walked to the left to get the lift, but it was out of service. I thrashed on the 'call lift' button. Taking the stairs up to the sixth floor seemed a mountainous task, as though Sisyphean eternal damnation had been cast upon me.

I bashed the button harder. The sound of my fist against it echoed through the air.

I turned around and saw all their eyes staring at me, still – them and me, frozen in a moment. They were blocking the narrow stairway that led up: one leaning on the dusty-grey metallic handle rails, one on the front two steps, with another just behind him, and two more standing on adjacent steps at the back. Nobody moved. I walked towards them, brushing past the first two on the steps. I took another step up towards the last two who were standing; it seemed as though the first had made himself wider. I continued on to the next step and the next, and our shoulders collided, the weight of my body overpowering, causing him to lean back on the stairs, as I took the next step up. I felt a hand grasp upon my shoulder with firmness, and say, 'Ay, big man,' in a deep, bass voice. I clenched my fists, ready to hit, as I turned around. This moment felt like it had been coming, and I welcomed it. I walked into this violence, this destruction, as if it were a cross I had chosen to bear. My eyes began to twitch, filling with a watery overflow. My heart beat like two pummelling fists against its own body.

'Big man,' the voice repeated. I turned to look at his face. It was covered in a woolly hat pulled down to just above the eyes, with a hood above it, and a black-and-white bandana over his mouth. All I could see were his eyes, I saw through his eyes into another world, a world that I also lived in – a world that I had truly yet to escape. He lowered the bandana covering his mouth.

'It's all right, big man. It's all right,' he said, his hand now a light touch on my shoulder, sharing a compassion I thought void of his soul. The compassion I had been seeking in a myriad of places and had yet to find. I had nothing to offer him in return, not even words, for his touch alone had struck me to silence. It is a mystery of life how a single touch can make you feel like you are human, like you are somewhere you belong. How the people who are closest to you understand you the least, but those who know you the least can understand you the most.

I nodded at him, a gentle nod of appreciation and fatigue,

as I continued to take my steps up the narrow staircase. I opened the front door to the flat, quiet and empty, then, without switching on any lights, went into my room and lay on the bed.

This sadness, how it falls upon you, like mist or fog, not there, then sudden and all at once; a greyness, enveloping you, submerged underwater. This sadness in your bones, each step heavier than the last, raises questions: how much longer is this journey? How much longer can I walk? The days pass into weeks, into months, into years, and your flying turns into running into walking into crawling, into laying still, unable to move, for no other reason but this heaviness upon you. This sadness, you wonder why it haunts you like a ghost, as though you were responsible for a death other than your own. This sadness, the push and the pull of it, how it whispers into your ear and speaks the language of melancholia that you know so well, lulling you into an eternal sleep. Oh God, I feel so alone. Loneliness is the empty space between the heart and the chest, the space where you are close enough to feel, but not close enough to touch, the space that grows, and grows, only ever into a chasm, a vacuous abyss, a hollow passageway through which hopelessness crawls. Loneliness is being there for everyone, everyone, in the hope that someone will be there for you. But no one ever is. You are the sun, lighting the world of another, whilst setting yourself on fire. And they just watch you as you sit in your darkness; in your solitude and burn. Loneliness is solitude starved. A solitude void of touch, void of sweetness; a bland existence, void of love, the love that you give to others that is never returned. Here you are, then, an un-replenished thing, flower withering in the ice-cold darkness you grew in, waiting for a break of light through the crevasse.

We sat in near silence, in his cave, I, distracted by the new paintings and Jalil, by whatever video he was watching on his laptop. It all felt bland and dutiful, as if I was fulfilling an obligation of friendship by being there.

I continued staring at the new paintings: a shooting star across a night sky of constellations, eight phases of the moon, and a silhouette of a man walking into a horizon of clouds broken by a bright streak of shining sun. I wanted to ask who the man in the painting was, whether it was him or Baba. He had not said anything, and I had not asked, neither of us comfortable with the weight this conversation carried. I assumed nothing had changed of late but Jalil had become so good at disguising even the most troubled parts of himself, it was difficult to tell. Maybe that's why we were such good friends; we hid the worst parts of ourselves and gave each other what we thought the other needed. It was the kind of friendship that floated on air, thin air that was inevitably bound to expire.

'You all right?' I eventually asked, as he looked up and caught me staring. He raised his eyebrows, an unconvincing affirmation.

'I'm all right,' he replied. I pointed my head at the laptop he held.

'Oh.' He hesitated.

'You still trying to find a good Muslim wife, yeah?'

He didn't laugh, not even a subtle smirk. I had touched a nerve, one that was bare and exposed. He tried not to let it show, but I could see I had unsettled him.

'I was actually looking at this story.' He turned his laptop screen to show it to me.

'Basically, in America, a man with a DNR tattoo – "Do Not Resuscitate" – was brought into hospital after being found unconscious, and the doctors debated about whether or not it was ethical to save his life . . . '

'What happened in the end?'

'The doctors honoured the tattoo and left him. He died.'

'Wow.'

'Not sure how he ended up there, I think he tried to shoot himself and it backfired.'

'Really?'

'Probably, I mean, that's just how it is out there, there's just guns everywhere.'

'Where did you hear that story from?'

'Oh, I'm in this email chain with my old philosophy classmates where we discuss different issues from this, to euthanasia, to poverty and capitalism, and all that. Last time it was veganism: one guy was going on and on about the benefits of a plant-based diet.

'Everyone else was going at him but I had no retort, he was probably right, more ethical, better for the environment. The thing is, I know I'll never give up meat because I love me some chicken, you know what I mean?' He laughed, searching for validation. I looked at him blankly, pulling my lips in to form neither a smile nor a frown.

'Those shawarmas, can't get enough of them,' he continued awkwardly, then returned to his laptop.

'You know, you didn't tell me about what happened with Am—' I said, barely finishing my sentence. His neck snapped up and gave me an intense look that terminated the question.

'Nothing, don't worry about it.'

'Okay.' He wasn't himself, but was trying so desperately to be. In the same way that you would attempt to tighten your grip on something you were losing control of.

'Look, Jalil, I really care about you, like really,' I said. He stopped typing and looked over at me.

'That's a strange thing to say, out of the blue like that.'

'I just wanted to tell you.'

'Okay, but I don't know why you're saying it.'

We returned to near silence. The room was empty of sound but heavy was the feel of our hearts. I traced the lines of his face with my eyes, knowing it would be the last time I saw him. And with him and Baba in mind, as well as Aminah, I began to let go and make my peace with it all, like a faithful on a pilgrimage, a fasting monk or an abstaining priest, my footsteps treading lightly on my journey.

I stood at the bottom end of the football playground on duty, watching the older boys play their games as if it were life or death, or rather reputation or humiliation; the pushing, the fouling, the arguing, while the girls watched on the sidelines, texting and taking selfies on the phones they shouldn't be on; save but one girl, who would join in playing with the boys. I had no energy to stop them. A couple of students would glance at me, expecting me to rush over as I usually would and then go on a rant, but I simply shrugged my shoulders – the apathy had long set deep in my bones.

I reminisced on the times Sandra would join me. And we

would laugh for the rest of the afternoon until the bell went. It was an informal pact that we had made with each other, something to keep our hopes up and away from the all-encompassing work despair. But I had still not seen her. The bell rang. Mr Barnes was outside of his classroom at the end of the corridor, trying to get the children to line up. His demeanour was so rigid, it surprised me to think he could be any other way. He looked up at me. Our eyes locked for a moment. He looked at me as if his stare would tear me into pieces. I looked back at him, daring him to. He turned his attention back to the students as they walked into the classroom. Sandra appeared from the bottom of the corridor. I was filled with small hope, like the pocket of air between two palms clasped in prayer.

She approached me at her steady pace. I stopped, hoping to talk to her. She seemed simultaneously to be looking at me and looking through me, I could not tell which. As she got closer, she moved faster and faster until she stomped past me. I felt as though something sharp had cut the air I breathed and had cut me.

I entered my classroom and crashed on to my chair. My breath drew shorter and shorter. A wave of heat came over me. I could feel trickles of sweat down my forehead; ants crawling over skin. My heart pounded against my chest, each hit harder than the last. I closed my eyes and placed my head in my hands to escape this onslaught of dizzying discomfort. I took full breaths in, and out, and in, and out, and in, and out, and in, and out, and in, and out, and in, and out, and in, and out, and in, and out, and in, and out, and in, and out, and in.

I opened my eyes to the bright light of day. I felt my head pounding. My phone vibrated on the table.

Smh, you couldn't even stop me to say hello.

Sandra. I felt another rush of blood through my veins to my head like a herd of stomping elephants, a bare-knuckle punch to the face. I began typing a reply.

If you must know, I've been dealing with a lot of things and I don't know what to do. On the surface, it looks like everything is fine. I come to work, I smile, we joke around, and text, and email, and go to meetings, and do all of that, but what people don't know is every time I'm in a room, every time I stand in front of a class, it's suffocating. I feel as if I'm climbing a mountain and the air is thinning, to the point where I'm lightheaded and could faint. I have to fight so hard just to do the minimum; getting out of bed takes so much energy, sometimes I don't know if I'll ever make it through the day. And then at night, I can't sleep because all I can think about is how I've got to do it all again tomorrow. It's affected every aspect of my life, my work, my friendships and relationships, my family, in every way, even something as simple as answering a phone call, sending an email or being around people. I don't know why I'm feeling this way, I don't know what has happened, I don't understand it, but I hate it, I hate it all and I want it to end.

I'm sat here on my desk crying while I'm typing this message, because it's become that overwhelming. And so yes, that was why I couldn't even come and say hello. Some days, I don't know what to do. Some days, I don't want to do anything. These kinds of days are becoming more and more frequent. I would have preferred not to keep it all bottled in and just get on with things, like how I usually do, but that hasn't been doing

me well, and I need to find a way to sort this thing out. In fact, I
have found a way. And will sort this out, once and for all.

I reread the message over and over again.

CTRL + A.

Fingers hovering over backspace, tears falling on to
the keyboard.

Chapter 30

Harlem, New York City; 8.03 a.m.

Michael wakes up to the symphonic sounds of roadworks and car horns. The bright light of the sun flashes into his eyes, turning the inside of his eyelids a glow of orange. He lies on Belle's bed. He is submerged in her scent, covering every part of him as if he was taken to the river and baptised. He stretches out his arms to the space across the bed and remembers she is not there. He recalls watching her through the faint of his eyes as she dressed in the morning, the silk garb that flowed against her skin, her curls wild and free, her transformation from something divine to something human, taking the form of those whom she walks among. She stopped to stare at him, standing above him, over the bed, like some otherworldly visitation until she was no longer there.

Last night was a blur, but all he can see in his mind is her; an image of her, like a renaissance painting, sprawled out on the bed with the formerly clean white sheets wrapped around her. Last night was a blur, save the moment when the senses came alive by the heat of her touch, the harmony of her sound, the intensity of her stare whilst he bowed on his knees before her, whilst he covered her, like the constellations above cover us. Belle. He wishes time would stop. Rather that it did not exist all; that it could be suspended in that moment, to be repeated again, and again, and again.

Michael wakes up again and feels himself sink deeper into the comfort of the mattress; his body like driftwood floating on the water, drifting into pieces. After a long bath, Michael gets dressed and makes himself breakfast. He finishes the food and sits on the sofa in the living room and waits. He imagines a role reversal, a 'Honey, I'm home,' as she enters, he jumps up with excitement to ask her how her day was and let her know that dinner will soon be ready. It feels like something he could quickly get used to.

Michael chooses a random book from her shelf. And sees a few books he remembers from his university days. It was a strange time for him, university. While everyone was out getting drunk and having sex, he spent most of his time in his room staring at the ceiling contemplating his life and its eventual meaninglessness. In the three years he spent there, even the only girl who paid him attention got tired of it. She would always come to his room to check on him, mostly because he spent months not getting out of bed, and missing lectures. Michael can barely remember her name now, he just knows it was more common than not. Stephanie or Tiffany, a name that sought not to be remembered.

They would stare at the ceiling together, asking questions, having philosophical debates, which would lead to him telling her how much he would be satisfied with dying at that moment and she responding by laughing, and laughing, and laughing saying, 'It's funny because you sound as though you're being totally serious,' until one day he replied, 'I am,' and saw the look on her face, drained of colour, as if she had witnessed a death.

Michael learned from then on to keep it all within. He was not sure how long this sword had dangled above his head, but he knew that he would sooner cut the string that holds it than wait for it to fall.

Michael opens the nondescript book he chose arbitrarily to a random page and begins reading about a man called Gaspar Yanga, an enslaved African man who fought for freedom against his slave masters in 1570, liberating himself and his people and establishing a free town in Mexico, which was named after him.

Yanga. It sounds wildly familiar in Michael's ears, echoing a resonant vibration within him. Michael wonders where Yanga was from, what led him to keep fighting, and fighting, and fighting for a freedom, uncertain whether he may even live to see it. Yanga. It resembles a word in a language he should know, a language that he was never taught, but watched his mother and the elders around her speak to each other in. He remembers their laughter whenever he would try to talk, saying how his language is broken, how he speaks like a mundele, how it is shameful when someone cannot speak the language of their country, as if they weren't the ones who didn't teach him. He wonders then, what we lose when our names and our languages are not given back to us, he wonders what parts of us remain dormant when they should be pouring out into the world.

Hours pass by like minutes, as Michael remains sat on the

sofa, engrossed in the book. He hears the metal click of the key in the door. He stops reading, perking up in anticipation whilst simultaneously trying to remain calm and poised. The door swings open and Belle walks in carrying a load of shopping bags.

'Are you sitting in the dark?' Belle says, as she flicks on the light. Michael realises he had been sitting in the dark. During the time he was reading, day must have passed into evening, and taken the light with it.

'Why didn't you call me?' he says as he rushes up to help with her bags. He stops and stands above her and kisses her on her lips as her neck arches up to reach his face. He wraps his arms around her and explores her mouth.

'Hmm,' she groans, 'okay, but these bags are heavy.'

'Sorry.' They laugh. As he takes the shopping bags and carries them into the kitchen, he thinks about how hauntingly familiar this all feels; amazed at how something so foreign can so quickly feel like home.

'You bought all this food?'

'Yeah . . . '

'Why?'

'So, we can eat, what kind of question is that?' She chuckles.

'I mean, you didn't have to.'

'You're a guest, I wanted to cook.'

'You're going to cook?'

'Yes.'

'Wow.'

'What?'

'You just didn't seem . . . '

'The type?' she scoffs as she arranges the groceries.

'Did you clean up . . . ?' she asks.

'Yes.'

'Oh.'

'What?'

'You just didn't seem . . .'

'The type,' they say at the same time and laugh.

'You shouldn't have, you're a guest.'

'Well, I was going to clean and cook, but you haven't put a ring on it yet, so I can't let you be getting too comfortable.'

Belle slaps him playfully on his arms, and he pretends to be hurt. She pulls him towards her and wraps her arms around him. He feels taller, looking down at her, as though somehow he has grown, not simply in height but in spirit. They kiss in the small space in her kitchen, her lips raising his blood pressure.

'You go and relax, let me get started on dinner.'

'I could give you a hand,' he says, but she looks at him as if he has made an absurd proposition.

Michael sits on the sofa and starts reading again. The aroma of Belle's cooking flows through the air. She looks over, and their eyes meet, their glances sending little messages of happiness to each other.

'So how was work?'

'You know, just the usual. I hate working with incompetent people, and it's even worse when the incompetent motherfucker is your boss, you know?'

'Yeah.'

'That's not even the worst of it. When I was walking home from the station, some guy try holla at me, talking about "Yo What's Good Ma", blah fuckin' blah, and followed me for like five blocks.'

'What? Really?'

'Dead ass. I got fed up and had to turn around and cuss him out. He just stared at me like a little child who should know better and didn't even say anything.'

'Oh, I'm so sorry; I don't even know what to say.'

'I had to walk around three extra blocks just to make sure he wasn't still following me.'

'Damn.'

'Sorry, I didn't mean to unload on you. It's just frustrating.'

'It's okay. I can imagine . . . '

'I mean, some women get killed over shit like this.'

Michael looks at her with the saddest face he knows and motions for her to come and sit down next to him. She stops cooking and joins him on the sofa, bringing with her two cups of tea.

'How did you know I like green tea?'

'You seem like a tea drinker, you pro'ly got a library that you sit in too.'

'Ha, I wish. Maybe I'm into cough-fee.'

'Coffee.'

'Corf-fee.'

'Coffee.'

'Caw-fee.'

'Are you trying to impersonate a New York accent?'

'That's how you lot say it. Core-fee.'

'Boy, if you don't get . . . ' Belle hits him playfully several times, which turns into a semi-wrestling match as he wraps his arms around her and holds. She lays her head down on his chest, and he watches it lower and rise as he breathes.

'I'm rude; I didn't even ask you how your day was?' she says, as she lifts her head to look at him, then lowers it back down.

'It's okay, I didn't do much. I stayed in the apartment all day. Oh, and I did some reading. You have a lot of books in Spanish, do you speak it?'

'Why, yes I do.'

'Really? Say something.'

'Tú tienes una gran cabeza.'

'Wow, that sounds so sexy.'

'Don't you want to know what I said?'

'What did you say?'

'You have a big head.'

'Oh my gosh,' Michael replies, as she starts to laugh. He tries to push her off the sofa, leaving her hanging over the side as she scrambles to hold on. She shrieks and screams and laughs, until he lets her climb back on top of him.

'I was just kidding.'

'I know.'

'Dumb ass.'

'I know some Spanish too.'

'Oh, do you?'

'Guapa.'

'Which girl were you trying to impress when you learned that one?'

'I know some more ... "Bailamos, let the rhythm take you over, Bailamos, te quiero, amor mío."'

'So, you're just gonna sing Enrique Iglesias song lyrics? Is that what you're doing? Corny ass.'

'I can be your hero, baby!'

'Okay. Wow. I did not see that coming. In English, too. You're not even trying any more.'

'I don't think you're appreciating my efforts, to be honest.'

'There's nothing to appreciate. You really cannot sing.'

'I haven't heard you try . . .'

'And anyway, that's not my kind of Spanish.'

'J-Lo? Shakira?'

'My Spanish is more, I dunno, Amara La Negra.'

They both sit in a moment of quiet.

'The food!' With a cat-like quickness, she leaps off him and heads into the kitchen; the sound of clanging pots and pans and closing cupboards takes to the air.

'It's called hudut,' Belle says, as Michael scoffs the food down his throat, saving little time for chewing. He looks up momentarily with a blank stare in his face.

'It's a dish from the Garifuna.'

His face remains blank. 'Everything is a history lesson with you, isn't it?'

'Ugh, obviously, I have so much to teach you,' she adds.

'Well, either way, it's amazing,' Michael says, mouth full. Belle looks at him with delight and satisfaction.

'Just something I prepared last minute. I'm glad you enjoyed it.' He nods and looks at her with the same kind of awe a child does to a magician.

'Go ahead,' she says, knowing how much he wants to go for seconds. He rushes back from the kitchen with a full plate.

They sit on opposite ends of the sofa, facing each other; exchanging looks of longing and wonder. She swirls a glass of red wine, and he sips on a cup of chamomile tea. Melodious acoustic music plays in the background, the singer with a voice of a thousand broken hearts trying to heal.

'You got a dick.'

'What!' Michael responds, almost spitting out his tea.

'You have ... a penis,' she says, waving her hand through the air as if providing an elaborate explanation.

'I'm pretty sure this isn't the first time you're noticing.' He looks at her smugly, smirking.

'You're so different. I'm sometimes in shock that you're not a woman.'

'Okay ... I'm pretty sure I'm a man but go off.'

'Well, gender is a social construct anyway, but shut up and let me finish. I'm just so comfortable with you, and so soon. A man. A whole ass man. Y chromosome. Male phallic organ. Penis. Balls.'

'Last time I checked.'

'This is moving fast like a lesbian relationship.'

'What do you mean?'

'If we carry on this way, we could be married in a few weeks.'

Michael shrugs his shoulders. 'Why not?' he replies, but is then quickly struck by the reality that he will not be here in a few weeks. Belle laughs at the fact that it doesn't freak him out.

'You have no idea, do you? It's funny, straight people have no idea what happens outside of their own relationships, especially men.'

'Yet here you are.'

'A man. I feel like I'm betraying myself, I said I wouldn't do this again. I was really done.'

'Oh, you've dated men before?'

'Yeah.'

'When was the last time?'

'Years ago, I'm talking years. I was probably in college …'

'What was that like?'

'College or the man? Well, let's just say they were both a let-down.' She quickly answers her own question. 'Ugh. What is it with men thinking they are giving you greatness, but in reality, it's just disappointment?'

Michael shrugs his shoulders.

'When we'd fuck, he would finish and just lay there, and I would go to the bathroom and get off myself.

'But you …' she continues, 'you're like a woman, the way you touch, the way your body hears and listens.'

'Surely, not every man or woman …'

'Shhh, I know that. Just let me talk.'

'You or the wine?'

'Ha, you real funny, my guy. You ever been in love before?'

'Love?'

'Yeah, love. I know you heard me.'

'You first?'

'Fine, I'll say it. Yeah, I have. I'm not embarrassed to admit it. Your turn …'

'Well, I don't know …' Michael hesitates, losing himself in a world of memories. 'Sometimes, I think I have, then other times, I'm not so sure. I don't know if I've been in love or if I've even been loved. I feel more like people were obligated to me.'

'What do you mean?' Belle asks with genuine concern.

'Like they had to be with me, bound by a duty rather than a want – I've never been chosen. I've never felt like I've been loved the way I want to be loved, or the way that I see love.'

'And what way is that?'

'Well, to me it's a home; the home you build for you and your love. It's like, in my language, they say "na lingui yo", which means I love you, but it also means I like you. It's like someone saying they'll be with you for eternity, but also for today. It's like saying I am your love, but I am also your friend. And I don't think I've ever had either. Maybe I've been in love with one person. But I've always felt alone.'

'Oh, Michael . . . '

Belle stands up and holds her hand out to him. He takes it as she leads him to her room. They passionately kiss as they arrive at the bedroom door. He lifts her up and carries her to the bed. He turns around to take off his clothes; he unbuttons his shirt, and removes his jeans, with the belt; a poor choice of clothes for a day spent lounging in an apartment. The lights are off, the moon and the gods their only witnesses. He joins her on the bed under the covers. He slides up behind her and kisses her on her neck. He can hear her deep breathing, her frame rising and lowering, her breath a small pocket of wind. She's falling asleep. She responds and moves towards him, guiding him so that she can rest her head on his chest. And in that moment, she is gone, into a sleep full of sweet dreams, and health, and quiet breathing. He holds her delicately, stroking her hair and the smooth of her skin. Maybe if there is a god, it is simply the amalgamation of moments such as this.

Chapter 31

Harlem, New York City; 6.30 a.m.

Michael is woken up by the sound of Belle banging and clattering around the room, wardrobe doors flung open, items thrown on the dressing table, clothes littered across the floor. He feels a sense of urgency, panic; something unfamiliar that he had not seen in her before. He sits upright on the bed and continues to watch her.

'Are you not going to work today?' he asks. She looks at him.

'No,' she replies, sighing deep and heavy. She sits on the edge of the bed. 'They didn't call me in, said they won't need me for today and all of next week.'

'Oh? Okay, so you get some free time.'

'Yeah, but I'd rather have the money.' She stops still for a moment, looking down long and hard at the floor as if looking into another world.

'Look, let's get some breakfast in you first. We can sort out life stuff later.' Michael moves over and holds her. She lays herself into his body, and he kisses her on the cheek. He feels a sense of relief; quiet, sweet relief.

Michael's in the kitchen, frying up some eggs, making his special blend of avocado, tomato and onion to go in a wrap. Belle sits on the sofa, knees folded up to her chest, warming her hands with a cup of coffee that she has not yet taken a sip of, staring into the television even though it is switched off. He brings the food to her on a plate. She seems surprised to see him, and the food.

'Ah, you didn't have to,' she says, her voice subdued under its own weight.

'I know. I wanted to,' he says, perky and enthusiastic, as he sits next to her. She barely touches her food; she unwraps it with her fork and takes a bite, and fiddles with the rest.

'I have to go out later,' she says, 'and sort a few things out.'

'Okay. Can I come with?'

'What?'

'Yeah, I'll come with you. We could get lunch after.'

'Oh ... okay,' she says, with a slight stutter. 'Okay. You would do that. Thank you.'

'Of course.'

They leave the apartment and walk down towards 135th Street station. The cold air reminds him how much of a privilege it is to have known warmth. The sun is bright in the sky. Belle paces ahead of him, her small, staccato steps always two ahead of his. They enter the subway and get on the train, eerily empty for a weekday afternoon. They get out at 116th Street. Michael follows Belle into the CVS pharmacy. She comes back with only a few items and stuffs them into her large shoulder bag. He follows her out.

They walk to cross over to the other side of the road. She holds him back and says 'Wait', until it is time to cross. They cross and head into the bank. He tells her he'll wait outside. She goes ahead. He looks out into the street, watching the myriad people passing by, indifferent to his existence. Maybe he seems more like them than he thought; a mother and child, rapturous teenagers, men standing on the corner. In the places that he knows the least, he blends in and disappears, and feels more at home. *I guess home is wherever you are met as if you never left, wherever you see a reflection of yourself.*

Belle walks out of the bank, head lowered in dismay. Michael catches up with her and places his arm around her, and gestures for food. She nods. They walk into a soul food restaurant, where they are playing 90s RnB. His head bops to the music, but beside him Belle remains still. They sit at a table in the corner next to the window.

'Are you ready to order?' Jackie the waitress says, with a spark in her smile. Michael looks up at her, then back down at Belle, who has not responded at all.

'Hellooooo?' Michael says and waves his hand in front of Belle, frustration in his tone.

'What?' Belle replies sharply.

'Ready to order?'

They make their order. The food arrives, met by their silence.

'Aren't you going to eat?'

She looks up at him and then back down to her food.

'Is your meal okay?' the waitress asks, passing.

'Everything is perfect, thank you.' Michael replies for himself and Belle, who does not even move.

'Okay, so are you going to tell me what the hell is going on?'

Michael drops his knife and fork on to the plate, the clang of cutlery echoes.

'What do you mean?'

'You've been sulking since this morning and haven't even eaten anything all day. It's like you're a completely different person.'

'SO?' Belle roars, causing a few heads to turn.

'I don't know what's going on, but you've got to talk to me, babe.' Michael reaches over to her hand across the table. She moves it away as he touches her.

'Wow. So, it's like that.'

'It's not like anything. You wouldn't understand.' She sighs deeply and folds her face into her palm.

'Tell me . . . '

'Look, I'm broke. I need to make rent this month, I'm already behind, and I could end up being kicked out of my apartment. Then my job calls and says they don't need me. It's too much.'

'What? Why didn't you tell me?'

'What for?'

'So I can help you.' She says nothing and looks away from him again.

'I don't need you to do that. I can take care of myself.'

'How much do you need?'

'I said I can take care of it.'

'And *I* said how much?'

'At least a grand.'

'How much?!' Michael nearly coughs up the orange juice he is drinking.

'A thousand dollars . . . it would buy me some time.'

'Oh, damn.'

'And maybe like, another hundred bucks cos I also got a fine jumping a fucking turnstile the other day,' Belle huffs, then continues, 'Anyway, I don't need you to come in and play Superman. I'll make my own money how I've always done.'

'Wait, are you going to go and . . . ?'

'What, is there a problem?'

'What about us?'

'What about us?'

'I mean, are we not together?'

'What the fuck? So that means I can't go and . . . '

'Strip? No. Of course not.'

'I don't strip, I dance.'

'Oh, for fuck sake.'

'Listen, I don't know who you think you are, coming outta nowhere, trying to control me. You don't own me.'

'You're right. I don't own you, Belle . . . but I don't mean nothing to you?' Michael asks almost pleadingly. The restaurant falls into a synchronised silence; the conversations, the waiters, the music playing in the background, all held on the same note as if a fermata hovered above them.

'Man, fuck you, and your guilt-trippin' ass. Your broke ass was cryin' over five hundred dollars the other day, and you think you can help me?'

Belle stands up, knocking her chair backwards on to the floor – the people around them gasp as she runs out of the door.

'Belle!' Michael desperately calls her name, but she is out of the door before he can even finish. He leaves $50 on the table and chases after her.

He catches a glimpse of her shiny burgundy-red coat, with

its hood up, heading down the steps into the subway. He heads down the flight of stairs in one giant leap.

'Belle,' he shouts, as he watches her enter through the turnstiles. He rummages through his pockets for a ticket, then just runs and jumps over the turnstile.

'Belle!'

He sees her standing at the end of the train platform and paces over to her.

'Belle,' he says, quieter, softer. He places his hands on her shoulders and looks into her eyes, empty.

$1,230

'I don't understand, Belle, why won't you let me help you?'

'You wouldn't understand, Michael. You don't come from where I come from. You don't know what I've been through.'

'But that doesn't mean I can't help.'

Belle scoffs and walks past him towards the other end of the platform, as the beaming light of the train emerges from the hollow darkness of the tunnel. Michael takes rapid steps to catch up with her, and stands in front, blocking her path. He tries to speak but the roar of the train, and its screeching as it slows, is too loud for him to edge out a word. Belle and Michael stand in front of each other, eyes sinking in each other's depths. The train doors open and the passengers exit, floating by them as though they are ghosts, and Belle and Michael are the only living things in this world. The train leaves, and silence follows.

'I just want to make everything okay for you ... ' Michael says, voice quivering.

'But you can't, you didn't come here for me. I am NOT your responsibility,' Belle sighs, 'and I won't allow myself to be your burden neither.'

'I can fix things ...'

'You can't! You think it ends here, at just the money? There's too much. And I can't let you in, I won't. I've been fixing all this shit by myself, one way or another, for years, and I'll fix this by myself too ...'

'You don't always have to be strong ...'

'I got no choice but to be. My mother had to be, and her mother before her. My daughter will have to be too. Shit ain't gon' change. All these years, if there's one thing I've learned, it's to rely on no one, especially not no man. People always disappoint you in the end, and I won't give you the chance. I should have never even let it get this far in the first place.'

Belle walks past Michael, this time pushing past him resentfully. Her steps echo along the tunnel. Michael's heavy steps follow. The roar of another train appearing consumes them both.

'What the fuck do you mean?' Michael shouts, and grabs Belle by her shoulder, turning her around.

'I mean this shit should have never happened. Us. Whatever it is that's going on here. I let it go too far, and I'm done.'

'I can't believe this,' Michael mumbles bitterly as the doors open and the passengers exit the train. 'Well, if you're really done,' he continues, 'then you'll get on this train, and you'll never see me again.'

The train doors remain tauntingly open, as if for longer than usual. Michael closes his eyes as Belle walks back past him, maybe even says a prayer to a god he doesn't believe in.

He turns around to look for Belle and she is gone. He sees her on the carriage as the train pulls away. It moves in slow motion; one carriage passes, then the next, then the next, until the whole trains roars and disappears into the everlasting darkness.

Michael makes his way back to the apartment in Brooklyn. He stops at an ATM and checks his balance: $1,200. He withdraws everything and stuffs the money into his side pocket, still clutching it in his hand. *Maybe I should just throw it all away or burn the money and be done with all of this now. Fuck it, because I have had enough. There for everyone else, but not for myself. This is always how my life unfolds, unravels. Yet nobody sees it, nobody knows what it's like to bear this weight, this suffering. Nobody ever believes me, believes my sadness. I am alone in this. And I never let anyone know the true extent of how I feel, because it is so deep that I am frightened of what I will do to myself if it ever gets close enough to the surface. And in the meantime, what do I do? I watch, and watch, as if I were prey, as people come and exploit and eradicate, bit by bit, any semblance of joy, of peace, that I may have to hold on to.*

I had to fight through all kinds of madness just to be here, I can't walk down the street without being reminded about some pain I have felt; this kid stabbed over there, this person shot, this person in prison, this person raped, and over an ocean away, I have another family, whom I barely know, but love so deeply, greater than my heart could ever reach, and it is only more suffering. I know no peace, here, there or anywhere; there is not a single place in my life I know peace; no matter how much I try to cultivate a space for myself and my being, eventually, when I let someone in, they destroy it, not all at once, well maybe some-times, but usually bit by bit, and it hurts me so much to have to live this way. Am I better off alone? Maybe? For a little while, but for a whole life? I don't know. Then maybe I am better off not being here, but again, this is the battle, the battle that I have been fighting my whole life and I don't know how much longer I can keep fighting. So, I'll take off my gloves, and lay down my arms ... I am no longer fighting.

Michael stumbles into the apartment, the stench of alcohol oozing like bad perfume. Bottle in hand, lying on his bed, staring up at the ceiling, he only begins to realise that he is crying when he feels a cold stream trickle down the side of his face from the corner of his eye. Belle. This is a decision he must make, the inevitable choice, but it is his. He sees her face every time he closes his eyes; her visage haunts him like a spectre, a recurring dream. He cannot keep his eyes open, but he does not want to close them. He does not want to see her face; he wants to feel her; her skin, her touch, her breath. This insurmountable pain as though something inside him is dying. It is. It already has. And he must bury it. The stream of tears is now a deluge down his face. He lies on the bed, motionless. Belle. Belle. Belle. Her name echoes in his head until he falls asleep.

'Who's there?'

'It's me.'

'I said who is it?'

'It's me, open up!'

'Michael!' Belle stands in front of the door, her sweet face an expression of surprise.

'Why are you here?' she says as he walks past her into the living room and takes off his coat.

'I had to see you.' She closes her front door and takes heavy steps towards him, her face looking down at the ground.

'Please, don't go ...'

'We've already had this conversation, Michael.'

'Please, Belle. It doesn't have to end this way. You can't expect to me to be okay with this. Imagine you were in my shoes.'

'Well, that's something you're gonna have to come to terms with. This is me, okay? I'm not going to change.'

'Change? I'm not asking you to change. My life changed when I met you. You made me forget. You made the pain go away. I've never felt about anyone the way I feel about you. And I know I never, ever will again. But—'

'But what?' Belle erupts. 'What happens after? Are we gonna get married? Are you going to stay? Here? For me? Or go back to London? You didn't come here for me, Michael, you came here for you. This was never going to work.'

'It's not over. I know you need the money, but it'll be okay, we'll sort something out.'

'Aargh,' she groans, raising her hands to her head, 'why won't you listen?!'

'Look.' He reaches into his side pocket. 'One, two, three, four, five ... just ... here.' He holds it out to her. 'A thousand dollars.'

Her mouth hangs wide open.

'Take it.' He gives the money to her. 'And here's an extra hundred, for that fine.'

Belle weeps. She sits on the sofa with her head in her palms.

He looks at her and wishes he could collect her tears and turn them into diamonds, then give them all back to her. To see her happy through all the pain she has lived through would be worth more than all the riches in the world. Michael places his arms around her. 'It's okay,' he says, stroking the baby hairs on her forehead, 'it'll be okay.' She looks at him, her eyes a watery grave. He kisses her on her forehead.

'And Belle, I have been in love – it was with you.'

They sit, entwined in each other's being, breathing in the same air, synchronised hearts beating. Everything is silent, even the city streets have been quietened as if they too could feel what is felt in this room. Belle wipes her tears and stands up.

'I'm still going to go.'

'What?' Michael erupts.

'I can't take your money. I can't do it.' She holds out the money in front of him.

'What do you mean?' He gets up and grips her by the shoulders. 'Belle! Why are you doing this?' She stares right through him, her eyes a vacant room.

'Because I have to, Michael. I can't take your money.'

'Don't worry about the money, it doesn't matter!'

'It does! I can't take it. I can't,' she continues, repeating herself, holding the money out in front of her. He paces up and down the living room in a panic.

'Belle,' he calls her name, pleading. She remains silent and shakes her head from side to side. Michael sits down on the floor, with his hands on his head. On his knees, he crawls to her. 'Belle, please.' He wraps his arms around her, resting his head on her navel below her bosom, holding her, breathing her in, for a moment he knows is the last.

'Take your money,' she says, turning and facing him as he heads for the door.

'Please, keep it. It's for you. I meant everything I said.' Michael opens the door and turns to look back at her. She lowers her hand. Her face is a blues song – a poem. He walks towards her and kisses her on the lips, feeling every tingling sensation for the last time.

'Goodbye, Belle.' He walks out and closes the door.

$100

'AAARGH!' Michael screams into the darkness.

'There's only two things that could make a man sit outside in the cold and dark screaming,' a man's voice, hoarse and croaky, emerges from the shadows, 'money or women.' The man breaks into raucous laughter.

'How about both?' Michael replies, and looks over to see a man, with a pushcart, sit down next to him on the bench in the eerie park. The man's clothes are worn and shabby, dark brown from accumulated dirt, wrapped in layers and layers. His hair stands upright on his head, as if he is a cartoon caricature of someone who has been electrocuted. The man stretches and makes himself comfortable, somehow finding respite on this cold hard bench.

'So, you not gon' say?'

'Say what?'

'Say whatever's got you sat out here in the dark hollering.'

'Well, I'm not the only one sat in the dark.'

The man chuckles heartily.

'I'd rather not say. I'm trying to forget.'

'It hurt that bad, huh?'

'I would rather eat a rubber tyre.' Michael lets out a deep sigh and the cold air forms a mist before his face.

'It can't be that bad; even I don't wanna do that and I'm hungry all the time.'

'I'm tired. I'm just so tired. I want to lie down and fall asleep, for a long time, and hopefully never wake up.'

'The unexamined life is not worth living.'

'Huh?'

'You have to ask yourself why? Why did this happen? Ask yourself what is the meaning behind your suffering?'

'There is none. We're born, we die, and in-between we suffer. That's life, it happens.'

'Suffering must be given a voice, a platform from which to speak, it is then that suffering becomes art and, in turn, becomes truth.'

'I would prefer a life without suffering.'

'Show me a man who has not suffered, and I'll show you a man who has not lived.'

'To live is to suffer. Nietzsche. I get it. I've read a little bit, seems you have too. But beyond your cute little Tumblr quotes and witty sayings, the world is fucked up. Somewhere in the world right now, there's war, there are refugees, a child will die because they are starved, or someone out there is just lonely, miserable, depressed, suicidal. I mean, are you telling me that you would rather be out here on the streets than somewhere warm?'

'Ha! You think I still wouldn't be suffering if I had a roof over my head?! Suffering is our shared language, our common bond. One of the two things that remind us, all of us, that we are acutely and intensely alive. That we are all the same. The other is love.' The man laughs hysterically and continues, 'But suffering is also the thing we all deny and act like we're not going through it.

'We are beings towards death, driving full speed to our demise.'

'Okay, you're really not helping now.'

The man explodes with laughter.

'There's actually something wrong with you,' Michael adds, scoffing.

'What, you thought I would be the homeless bum who gives you some profound epiphany and meaning to your life? You thought I'd give you hope? How romantic. The only reason you're sat in this place – heck, the only reason you're talking to me – is because right now, you're a little closer to knowing what it feels like to be like me, to know what it feels like to not exist.'

'I want to not exist.'

'What?'

'I want to die.'

'You don't want to die. You just want the hopelessness to end.'

The wind howls furiously. The dark void surrounding consumes them as if it is alive.

'It will end. It will end.' After a long, drawn-out silence, the man laughs again, loud and full bellied, until the laughter turns into coughing and spluttering.

'What's your name?' the man asks.

'Why? You won't ever see me again.'

'You're right about that.'

Frustrated and furious, Michael gets up to leave, having taken all he can of this man.

'Ay, man, you got a dollar?' the man asks. 'A man's gotta eat.' He looks up at Michael from the bench. Michael looks back down at the man.

'How about a hundred?' Michael reaches into his pocket and holds out the note in front of him.

'My man! It's my lucky day.' The man reaches forward and grabs the money with his callused fingertips, both hands in fingerless gloves. The man's face opens into a smile, revealing teeth that are yellow and stained. He holds out his fist, Michael reaches forward, and they dap. The man folds back into a ball on the bench.

Michael's sitting at the desk, in his room in the apartment, putting into an envelope the letter he has written to Mother for the last time. Tomorrow he will send it to her. He deletes everything of himself on the internet, all his social media, even though he had stopped posting long ago. He checks his emails for the last time. Jalil. He opens the email.

Hey bro,

I've tried calling you for a while, your phone's off? Anyway, sad news, man. Baba passed away. But, with God's grace he got to witness my union before his return.

And I am pleased to show you me and my beautiful wife. I can't wait until you guys meet. Love you, bro, looking forward to hearing from you.

Jalil

PS You were right.

Michael opens the attached picture. Jalil and his wife – rings on their third fingers. The girl isn't Aminah. Jalil is wearing a smart, fitted James Bond-style black suit, and she wears a sleek dress, off-white, fitted to her slender body. She is the kind of beauty that inspires poems. They look so good together, as if somehow this is how it is all meant to be. It angers Michael; eyes glowing green in his reflection questioning why life seems to go the right way for everyone else apart from him. He slams his fist on to the table and starts to shake uncontrollably. He crawls into the bed shivering. He cries himself into a rageful, sorrowful sleep.

Michael feels peace, an odd kind of peace, the view of a sunset during a war. He sees the faces of the people who he has deeply loved and cared for. He sees Mother. Father. He sees Jalil. He sees Belle, her face eternally engraved in his memory. An act such as this is prepared in the quiet of the heart. The war is finally over. The war has been won.

Deep in the middle of the night, Michael will wake. Resolved, he'll put on his shoes, coat, hat, gloves, and head to the car he rented, gas tank full in preparation, for this, his final trip. He'll drive the long silent stretching roads into the darkness to Harriman; to the woods and the wilderness, to the looming cliffs, the tall trees, the deep, sweeping waters, that it may all take him; that none may hear him, that none may see him. That his body may never be found.

I held on as long as I could, I'm sorry.

These hands simply grew tired of holding, this heart, tired of beating, these lungs, tired of breathing. This world was too unforgiving to me, but I was more unforgiving to myself; I hated myself more than anyone had ever loved me. But maybe, in the beyond, there is a joy greater than my sadness, a joy greater than all the pain that I have known. Life is a tender unravelling, an outpouring of self into the world. And I have no more of me left to give. So, this is it, the final hour, the last mile. The road was long, but finally, here am I.

Chapter 32

Temple of Our Lord Church, Central London; 2.11 p.m.

I walked in and the service had begun. The church was full to the brim. People stood, shoulder to shoulder, along the walls on the side, at the back and even outside trying to enter. I found a space at the back wall, near the shelf of Bibles, trying to blend in. Outside I could hear the traffic building up.

'We shall find today's reading,' Pastor Baptiste spoke softly and solemnly, 'in Psalm 23, verses one to six. We shall begin reading in the name of the Father, and of the Son, and of the Holy Ghost.'

The LORD is my shepherd; I shall not want.
He maketh me to lie down in green pastures: he
*   leadeth me beside the still waters.*
He restoreth my soul: he leadeth me in the paths of
*   righteousness for his name's sake.*
Yea, though I walk through the valley of the shadow

of death, I will fear no evil: for thou art with
me; thy rod and thy staff they comfort me.
Thou preparest a table before me in the presence of
mine enemies: thou anointest my head with oil;
my cup runneth over.
Surely goodness and mercy shall follow me all the
days of my life: and I will dwell in the house of
the LORD for ever.

Amen.

'Amen,' the congregation repeated in unison.

Pastor Baptiste looked to the room full of people. After several moments of silence, he began to speak.

'Family, brothers and sisters, friends, we have all gathered here today, with our hearts heavy, our hearts broken and filled with pain.

'Today, with all the sadness in our hearts, we have come to remember, and to lay to rest, a young man whose life was tragically cut short. A young man who had an impact on many of our lives, and the fact that this room is so full today is a testament to that. A young man who was a son to his mother, a brother to his siblings, a friend to his friends, a student to his teachers, a basketball player to his coach and teammates, and so much more. He was a young man trying to find his way in the world, cut short, at the tender age of fifteen years old.

'It is in these moments that we are compelled to question the meaning of life, and whether life has any meaning at all; moments when tragedy hits us so unexpectedly, and so suddenly. But it is also in these moments that we come together, as a church, as a family, as a community, and find meaning in each other, supporting each other through it all. For no matter what life may bring at you, remember you are never, ever alone.'

'Amen,' the congregation said, in unison.

'Today, we remember the life of Duwayne Harvey Brown.'

There were sniffs and weeping spreading across the room.

'The casket will be opened, so that you may pass to pay your final respects. After which, we shall make our way to the cemetery, so Duwayne may be laid forever in peace.'

A funeral bearer, dressed in uniform black, grey and white, walked towards the casket and slowly lifted it open. A wailing scream ripped through the air; Duwayne's mother, sitting in the front row, fell on to the floor waving her arms. She was surrounded by other women trying to console her. People walked up to the casket bowing their heads, paying their respects. I joined the line leading to the casket. I had still not yet seen him, but I watched the reaction of others as they looked down. I was next in the line. I approached the top corner of the finely carved and skilfully polished mahogany casket. I could see the top of Duwayne's head; his jet-black hair appeared freshly cut, and neatly brushed, as if he had just stepped out of the barbershop. I took two steps closer. His arms were laid beside his body. His skin glowed, accentuating his features. I looked at his face, his nose, his eyes, his mouth and how they all rested. I saw flashes of him in the classroom, sat at the back, flashes of him on the bridge with his hood up, flashes of him and the words he said to me, to come to watch his basketball cup final, and here I was watching him. Oh, how would we treat the people in our lives if we knew which conversation would be the last? Would we act differently?

Appreciate every moment? Tell them we love them?

My lips trembled, my face struggling to hold itself together. Tears fell from my eyes on to the floor. I felt someone reach up and place their hand on my arm whispering, 'It's okay, man. It'll be okay.' I heard his words, but any faith I had in such words had lost its wings. I made my way out, passing Mr Black. We nodded at each other; that nod was a hug, an embrace. In the car park, I looked up at the bright blue sky, cursing life, cursing this futility and the endless pain we are forced to endure.

'Sir?' I heard a young voice call from the distance. Whilst their footsteps approached, I took the chance to wipe my face of tears before turning around.

'Sir.'

'Alex.'

We both looked at each other with benign resignation. I hugged him. He crumbled under a heavy guilt. I patted him on the back, offering some words of reassurance.

'I feel like it's my fault,' Alex said.

'Why? No. It's not your fault. You should never ever think that.'

'I wish we didn't have that fight. I should have tried to help him more ... I was jealous.'

'Jealous?'

'He was the popular one. Everyone liked him. I did all the hard work, I did everything right, but no one ever noticed me.'

'It's perfectly normal to feel regret, but don't hold yourself responsible. We all could have done something, but we only did what we could at the time.'

'Sir, they stabbed him ... twelve times. Whoever did it still hasn't been caught. People know who did it, but they don't want to snitch.'

This reminded me just how distant I had been from work lately; how distant I had been from myself.

'It's not fair, sir, it's not fair.' Alex started crying, his face a broken image of the bright, happy boy I'd always known him to be. Alex all the As: Anger, Anguish and Acrimony.

'Where are his crew? All the guys he hung around with? All of them that used to come meet him at the school gates. I don't know. They didn't come, they don't care. It was just us – some of his school friends who'd known him from primary, and his family and family friends . . . ' Alex paused. 'Are you going to come to the burial, sir?' he then asked, eyes watering, looking up at me.

'I can't, Alex. I'm sorry. I have to go.'

I did not bother putting up any decorations in my class this year. The children noticed my silence and irritability. I was less and less myself, and thus began my slow disappearance into memory.

I sat on my desk staring at the clock in my classroom after the last day of school term. The students had long left during the day. The staff had gone to start their afternoon drinks. I had slowly started to clear my desk. All that remained to take with me was the small box that I had packed up, which made it look less like I was leaving for good, and more like I was taking work home over the holidays, as per usual. I watched the sun set, and the sky turn into a tumultuous darkness. I waited until the corridors were quiet before getting my things to leave.

'Mr Kabongo,' I heard, as the door opened, 'have you got a moment?' Mrs Sundermeyer said, as she popped her head through the door and walked in. I was surprised to see her, but in many ways not so surprised.

'Of course,' I replied. She walked in and stood directly in front of me, on the other side of the desk.

'Did you manage to watch the basketball cup final?' she asked.

'No. I couldn't,' I answered, without saying why, yet she understood.

'We lost, unfortunately.'

She paused and smiled a firm smile with her lips.

'Well, I just came to wish you all the best on your next journey.' Her voice changed into something solemn.

'Thank you.'

'I, er, hope you are not discouraged, and that you take the time to find whatever you need. You've made an incredible impact on the lives of so many young people, and I don't think this is the last time.'

'Thank you. But I think it is.'

Mrs Sundermeyer took a seat on the table in front of me, her demeanour relaxing slightly.

'You know, Mr Kabongo . . . Michael, if I may,' she paused, 'I know it may seem like all I care about is work, work, work. But I don't. About eighteen years ago, I was diagnosed with cancer. I was recently married and had given birth to a little girl. I was on my way to something of an ideal life, and then my world was turned upside down. My friends and family, my partner, everyone was incredibly supportive, telling me to be strong, to keep fighting, and that I would beat it.

'I didn't want to. I had thrown in the towel before the fight had even begun. But no matter how much I had resigned myself to lose to this monster, something in me kept going. And I overcame it. I don't know how. I don't know why. But I remember not wanting to overcome it, and it really taught me a lesson: no matter how many times we say we want something, it doesn't necessarily make it true. Sometimes, we should listen more to what the silence says than that little voice in our heads.' Mrs Sundermeyer got up from the table and walked to leave the room.

'You can't save everyone, Michael. Life just isn't designed like that. You have to find the one or two people in your life who you truly care about, who you truly love, and give to them all of your heart; sometimes that person is yourself. Everything else will work itself out.'

As she left, she turned around one last time, and offered me a look of compassion and acceptance, something outside of the realm I was used to seeing her in. It brought the distance a little closer than before, but it was a distance too wide, brought closer too late.

I shut down my computer, tucked my chair under the desk, picked up the box and left my classroom, switching off the light on the way out. The corridors were dimly lit and lugubrious as I walked through them. I reached the front gate and was met by rainfall. I looked back at this tall-standing building, a symposium of memories slipping into the past, never to be lived again. I turned and walked away.

Chapter 33

Peckriver Estate, London; 5.27 p.m.

I had spent most of the day sat by the window, drinking cups of tea, staring into the outside world from the quiet peace of my bedroom; watching as the day turned to night, watching as the trees swayed from the wind, watching how the clouds passed, and the birds sang, and the people went on and on. I thought how this would all go on without me; on and on, another day shall pass, on and on, another sun will set, on and on, winds will blow, on and on, the world goes on and on. This was my peace, the reconciliation of my absence.

I decided to go for a walk. I walked along the busy high street, filled with revellers and merry drinkers on their night out, past the tube station they poured out of, past one high-street shop and another, and another, past the market, past the tattooed man handing out leaflets, past another holding up an illegible sign, past the traffic lights at the junction in the road, past the construction works abandoned for the night, past the bridge where I saw the same group of boys and a ghost floating among them, past the dark, murky canal, the lugubrious water a living thing of its own, past the expensive houses on the one side, and the council estates on the other, past the homeless people who slept in tents in-between, past a memory, past a memory, past a memory, past a memory, past a memory, past a memory.

I walked back to the tall tower block I had spent most of my life in, the only place I had ever learned to call home – the place that had now become no home at all.

Back in my room, all that remained was to pack. It is one thing to leave to go on holiday or for a trip when you know you will be back, but what does it mean to pack knowing you will never return? What do you take with you? Favourite shoes and clothes? I had spent the last few weeks slowly donating my belongings to charity. Along with them, I had donated my most prized belongings: my books. I had removed myself of any physical attachment to my material possessions; the only thing that remained was the emotional attachment, which, too, in time, would go. I took my backpack and stuffed it with the most basic supplies I would need, until I would not need them any more. Spare change of clothes and underwear, toiletries, and my favourite book I have travelled with, no matter the reason, no matter the distance, near or far: *Two Thousand Seasons*. As each moment passed, I felt an anxious anticipation. A longing dread rose and fell like a wave from deep within me.

I sat on top of the now packed backpack, hand on chin, in the comforting darkness. I was alone in the flat. I had not seen Mami for a few days, perhaps all of the week; she was spending more time with Pastor Baptiste. I had reluctantly accepted their wish to be together as long as it did not require my involvement. I was decidedly avoiding her, coming back later than I usually would, leaving first thing in the morning the next day. Mami did not know I was leaving. I concluded that it would be better for the both of us if I did not see her before and if nothing between us was said. However, I decided to write her a note:

Mami,

I'm going away. Do not worry. Do not look for me.
Everything will make sense in a while.
With love,
Your son, Michael

That night, sleep evaded me. I lay down on my bed, staring at the ceiling, letting each painful, burdened memory flow by like a stream cutting through jagged rocks. I had not seen Sandra since the email. I thought about calling her, maybe at a stretch going to see her one last time, but this was not the mountain I was meant to climb. Jalil – I thought about him a lot, in a special way, and about Baba. I thought about how often we sabotage our own potential for happiness in pursuit of something that is fleeting. Perhaps we think we are undeserving, perhaps misery is just the more familiar feeling, and like most things, we stick to what we know.

I picked up my phone in the dark to check for any messages and missed calls. There were none. I put the phone back down, feeling more resolved in my decision. Tomorrow morning I will fly to the United States of America, first to San Francisco and then I will travel around as free as I choose. Why America? For no reason but romance, poetry;

the only land I know that calls itself free. And I want to live free. But what does that mean? To live a wild and exciting life? Maybe, sometimes, yes, even. Or to live free of burden, or expectation, to carry no weight, and to bear no arms; to live authentically as myself, no matter how flawed that may be; to do, or not do, as I please. Oh, America. It is a place I had grown up watching, a place I had always wanted to get lost in. I had dreams as a child of being an aimless wanderer, living the life of freedom I could only imagine; a life where I answered only to myself. For in the end, I am all I have; and I am all that I can be. Dying, then, by my choice, is the most total freedom. Dying. Death. The more I said it, the more comfortable I became with it, and the more I realised that it was a decision I had made long ago. It had sprouted deep within my barren heart like a beautiful wildflower in the desert.

An act such as this is always prepared in the quiet of the heart.

I had booked my tickets a long time ago and arranged everything else I would need in the quietest, least suspicious manner. I am going to take my life savings – the summation of my life's value in this world. And live through a place I'm going to for the first time. A place where I have no memory, no association, no connection, where I know no soul, spending the money as I see fit, until it runs out, and then, after this, I will take my own life. I will leave the world as I came into it, by the wondrous beauty of nature. I want to disappear into the world quietly, unseen, unknown. I want to go with the kind of peace that I am seeking; a death that walks quietly into the night.

Chapter 34

Mami walks through Dalston market. The bright colours of the fruit and veg bowls contrast against the grey, brooding sky above. Bodies pass by her, to the left and to the right, as if she is walking through a forest of trees. The cacophony of market traders boom in the background like a familiar symphony orchestra: 'come an' 'ave a look please' and 'poun' a bowl, poun' a bowl', in G major, the most popular pieces. Mami carries a bag of makemba, frozen pondu, makayabu and kwanga, which she will prepare later in the evening. She places them all in her shopping trolley; her hands tremble far too often now for her to carry the bags in-between her fingers the way she used to.

Mami finishes her shopping and makes her way to the overground station, Dalston Kingsland. The next train will arrive in four minutes. She struggles with the weight of her shopping trolley down the steps. A multitude of people rush past her, until a young Black boy in grey tracksuit bottoms and a hooded jumper approaches her and says, 'Aunty, can I help you?' Mami smiles at him. His familiar face brings a sadness to her heart. He

carries Mami's shopping trolley to the bottom of the steps and
waits with it until she arrives. Mami thanks him profusely, 'God
bless you, dear. God bless you.' The young Black boy skips back
up, taking two or three steps at a time, feet light like a gazelle.

Mami arrives home, unloads the shopping and starts
cooking right away whilst listening to Congolese gospel; *Tata
Nzambe, sali sa biso, Tata Nzambe, sali sa biso, na ba mpasi
oyo, toko monoka*. She still makes the same portion of food,
enough for many mouths, yet she eats alone. She sits down
to watch her favourite evening soap operas, cursing at the
television at the young man who is cheating on his wife to
be with her best friend, a familiar storyline. The night comes
slowly and quietly. Mami first falls asleep on the sofa, head
leaning back, mouth wide open and snoring from the fatigue
of having to survive another long week. She wakes in the
middle of the night and goes to her bedroom where she will
have another restless night, tossing and turning. The sleep-
lessness brings back the terrors she thought she had escaped;
in the darkness she hears the screams of strangers, the sounds
of the crack of bones on pavements, and the tanks rolling
over them, of bullets ricocheting, empty shells laying on the
road like fallen leaves, or pebbles on the beach, shining like
the gifts that we keep, of babies crying to the background of
violent winds, violent rains, violence, trees swaying against a
blazing sky, it passes by until it all falls down, down, down,
into the immutable silence.

Mami wakes up, bones heavy as bricks. She pulls the curtains open, letting the light break through. She has been falling
asleep more and more during the day, some days not getting
out of bed at all. No matter how bright it is outside, the lifeless

gloom in the flat remains the same; and has been the same, ever since Michael left. Mami tries not to think of him. She's placed every framed photo of him in the flat face down, preparing her heart for the news she knows she will not be able to take. Don't worry. He's a young man, he needs time to figure things out. It'll be fine. Others tell her this, but Mami remains unconvinced; her gut stirs and stirs, knowing it is something more, something deeper. She's received his letters; she keeps them in a drawer beside her bed. The last letter read:

Mami,

This is the last letter I will send you.

I'm writing to say I'm sorry. I'm sorry for all the pain that I have caused you. For not seeing sooner how much you had to sacrifice for me, just so that I could have at least the little bit that I had. I did not see your struggle. I did not think about how it must have felt, night after night, to worry about so many things, and then to add me on top of it.

I never ever intended to cause you pain. I just need you to know this. I was simply looking for a way to get some quiet, some peace. And it hurts me that even now, I am hurting you, but there's nothing else I can do. What's done cannot be undone. But I will forever be grateful to you for everything; I hope I did not disappoint you. I hope you can still find space for me in your heart. And that one day, we'll meet again.

With love,

Your son,

Michael

But all of this only accentuates her pain, only makes her stomach feel as though it is swimming in acid. This is a dizzying test of her faith, as though she was placed on top of a tower and forced to jump by someone who told her, if she believed enough, she could grow wings along the way down. She keeps holding on.

The only thing Mami hasn't touched is Michael's room, not since she was last in there and found the note he left for her. She has made of his room a shrine, preserving every memory into something ancient and sacred.

Mami goes into the kitchen and makes the breakfast she should have eaten hours ago; the food she has not been eating lately; though people compliment her, saying she's lost weight, not knowing it has been because of the stress and strain she's been going through. She returns to the living room, switching on the television to watch the monotone dullness of the faces on the screen. She zones out, letting the droning noise of the television transport her into a place void of any feeling; a place vacant of all she is, a barren wasteland of the imagination – the safe place of nothingness.

The buzzer rings once from downstairs; someone trying to get into the building.

Mami ignores it. The buzzer rings again, for the second time, but cuts halfway through. After a few moments, there is a knock on the door. Mami takes a while to respond, as the knocking persists. She shuffles across the floor, each step heavier than the last.

'Who is it?' Mami asks.

'It's Detective Peterson and Inspector Lawson, from the Metropolitan Police. Can we speak to Mrs Kabongo?' Mami watches through the eyehole as the police officers – the man, Peterson, dressed smart and boring, and the woman, Lawson, beside him, in her uniform – wait patiently on the other side.

'I am Mrs Kabongo,' Mami says, as she opens the door.

'Mrs Kabongo, would we be able to speak to you inside?' Detective Peterson says.

Mami does not move.

'Please, Mrs Kabongo. It would be best if we went inside,' the woman says, her face layered with empathy. Mami trusts her, she trusts her face, more than the man's, there is something honest about her, a visible pain showing that this is something more meaningful to her than just a job. Mami moves aside, and lets them in. They sit in the living room, TV muted in the background. Detective Peterson and Inspector Lawson on the adjacent sofa.

'Mrs Kabongo, thank you for welcoming us into your home.' Inspector Lawson speaks with mild apprehension. 'I'm afraid we have some news to bring to you.'

Mami sits up. She reaches for the remote and switches off the TV. She can hear her own heart beating, pounding as if there is a bass drum echoing in the middle of the room. She looks over at Detective Peterson and Inspector Lawson, trying to read their faces, hoping she can anticipate the news and maybe feel less shock.

'The body of Pastor Baptiste was found hanging in his home. It appears to be a suicide; he has taken his own life. There was no note, or any indicator. Nothing he left behind.'

Mami does not move. Her eyes do not blink, her hands do not tremble, her lips do not quiver, her body does not shake.

The shock she feels renders her to an immovable stillness, a consuming paralysis.

'We are so very sorry to bring you such tragic news. We worked as fast as we could to establish next of kin, relatives and close friends. And so, we reached you only as fast as time could allow. We know that the Pastor was dearly loved by his church community, and that this must come as a total shock to you. Do you have anyone who you can call to come and stay with you? Friend or family?' Mami thinks of Michael. 'We just don't think it is best for you to be left alone.'

'No, it's okay.' Mami stands up, gesturing them to also stand, and shows them to the door.

'It is fine. I will be okay,' Mami says, interrupting Inspector Lawson as she speaks.

'If you ever need to talk, or if you just have any questions,' Inspector Lawson stops at the door, reaches into the inside of her uniform jacket and places her card in Mami's hands, 'you can reach me directly here.'

Mami sits back on the sofa, staring into empty space, into the nothing that is in front of her. The silence consumes her like a plague. She tries to think of the last time she saw Pastor Baptiste, but her mind is too frazzled to recollect any memory. She just remembers the distance, how she had slowly started to pull away from him, but only because she was pulling away from herself. He should have been at Friday prayer, and so should she, but there they both were, dying a different kind of death. Mami labouredly stands up from the sofa. She shuffles across the floor to her bedroom, wailing, tears dripping along the way.

*

Morning comes. Mami sleeps through it. The night was heavy on her; she spent it crying the well of her spirit dry. Mami had switched off her phone as soon as she got the news, so that no one could reach her. She could already feel the intrusive questions that would be asked: did you not know? Couldn't you tell something was wrong? How could you let this happen?

Questions she has already asked herself a thousand times over, as if she was somehow responsible.

Mami wakes up in the darkness of her room. She struggles to tell whether her eyes are open or closed. As she lies there, she sees Pastor Baptiste's face, again and again and again, floating in the darkness beside her. The memories she has of him wade in: long walks in the park during sunset, holding hands; drinking milkshakes; meals at quiet, dimly lit restaurants; the morning breakfasts; the brisk cold air she formerly only felt on her way to work – all of the ways in which others did not know him, and everything that was to be. She hears his voice, she feels his touch; it comes close, closer, until, in an instance, it disappears.

Mami pulls the Bible from the drawer beside her, and clutches it to her chest, seeking comfort, but it does not come. Her faith is the thinning air and she is struggling to breathe. For her the world has become a wasteland from which nothing can emerge. She rips the pages and throws the Bible across the room and begins to wail. She curses, blasphemes into the dark, screaming, 'What kind of God?! *What kind of God?*'

The morning passes. Mami lifts herself out of the bed. She drags her feet across the corridor, to the toilet and then goes into the living room, where she will sit for most of the day. Later, there is a knock on the door. Mami wonders if it is people from the church. They have come, in their swarms, to see her. Rather than waiting or asking her questions on the phone, they have decided to bring their questions to her face, feigning their sorrow as if they too could feel what she feels right now. Another knock echoes from the door; it repeats.

Mami feels a frustration grow within her, an explosive chemical reaction between her tragedy and sorrow. She screams, 'Leave me alone!' but her voice is a feeble gust of wind, unheard. She groans and lets out a sigh of exasperation. The sound of the knocking on the door transforms itself into the headache she feels pounding against her forehead. The knocks continue. Mami places her hands on her knees and pushes up against herself to stand. She ties her kintambala around her head, closes her homely cardigan, and takes reluctant, lead-heavy steps towards the door.

'Okay. I'm coming. I'm coming,' Mami says as she approaches the door. She opens it.

There is a man stood in front of her, who appears as though a ghost; a man whose face has changed but remains ever the same.

'Michael!' Mami gasps, her eyes widen at the sight of him. She breaks down into tears, holding her face in her hands.

'I'm home,' Michael says, as he hugs Mami and holds her in his arms tenderly.

She sobs whilst standing enveloped in his presence. 'Michael, Michael,' she repeats again, again, again, as if it could not be true.

And this is life's journey, though we understand it not. We move, in our stillness, from solitude, from loneliness, and longing. We move, from fear, from the times we forget ourselves, because there is no one to tell us who we are. We move, from sinking, from drowning, from trapped beneath, from trapped within, to the moment you realise this is not how it has to be; there is always another way.

Always. We move, from this, to love and being loved, to dying in the night, and waking in the morn, to realising you are of minute insignificance in the vastness of the universe, and never forgetting how important you truly are; you are everything within it, and everything within it is you. To finding joy in the sorrow, beauty in the despair; the strength of our hearts letting go and the softness of our hands holding on. This unheard melody; oh, quiet yearning, gentle sorrow, art in our mind's eye, dreams of our future. The flutter of the butterfly in flight, the stutter of nervous lips proclaiming joy. This is the redemption, reconciliation and revival. The revelation that you are not driftwood, you are the ocean. The caterpillar realising it does not need to change to be beautiful; self-acceptance is the true transformation; the makeover, the glow-up is the you who you have always been. The new beginning that comes with the end, from day to night, darkness to light. And back again. This is the bird's nest, angel feathers, the moon, the poet and the poem, the dance and the song, the prayer, the hymn. This is radical hope; that we believe better will come, no matter the situation. And above all, it is love, that spark of bright light, that dazzling flame, ephemeral or eternal, may it find us, may it be us, the will that carries us forward, the bond that brings us back, from beyond this lonely feeling, to healing; the selfless act of breathing.

Acknowledgements

I did not believe it possible to write such a story, nor that it would ever be published, but I would like firstly to thank my agent, Maria Cardona, at Pontas Agency, for really believing in me and this story – and trusting my vision, even if you did not see it yourself, Maria. Every writer, every artist, every human, needs someone to advocate for them to bring their ideas and passions to the fullest, and what you did was extraordinary. Sharmaine Lovegrove, and the team at Dialogue Books/ Little, Brown, thank you for your tireless work, your dedication and your passion for stories that represent the fullness of our human experience. I feel privileged to be able to contribute to that.

To all the special people that I have met over the many years, who have somehow contributed to the unravelling of this story. To my loved ones, who I hold space for in my heart, as they hold space for me in theirs. Thank you, truly, for loving me, beyond ways which you could ever possibly know.

And lastly, to the readers, thank you for supporting me on this inconceivable journey. I pray that my words are enough for you as you are enough for this world. Love, always.

Bringing a book from manuscript to what you are reading is a team effort.

Dialogue Books would like to thank everyone at Little, Brown who helped to publish *The Selfless Act of Breathing* in the UK.

Editorial
Sharmaine Lovegrove
David Bamford
Nithya Rae
Amy Baxter

Audio
Louise Harvey

Contracts
Anniina Vuori

Sales
Ben Goddard
Hannah Methuen
Caitriona Row

Design
Charlotte Stroomer
Jo Taylor

Production
Narges Nojoumi

Publicity
Millie Seaward

Marketing
Celeste Ward-Best

Copy Editor
Alison Tulett

Proof Reader
Lydia Cooper